KT-365-307

Jennifer E. Smith

FIELD NOTES ON

Love

MACMILLAN

First published in the US 2019 by Delacorte Press,
an imprint of Random House Children's Books

This edition published in the UK 2019 by Macmillan Children's Books
an imprint of Pan Macmillan
20 New Wharf Road, London N1 9RR
Associated companies throughout the world
www.panmacmillan.com

ISBN 978-1-5098-3171-5

Copyright © Jennifer E. Smith 2019

The right of Jennifer E. Smith to be identified as the
author of this work has been asserted by her
in accordance with the Copyright, Designs and Patents Act 1988.

All rights reserved. No part of this publication may be reproduced,
stored in a retrieval system, or transmitted, in any form or by any means
(electronic, mechanical, photocopying, recording or otherwise),
without the prior written permission of the publisher.

Pan Macmillan does not have any control over, or any responsibility for,
any author or third-party websites referred to in or on this book.

1 3 5 7 9 8 6 4 2

A CIP catalogue record for this book is available from
the British Library.

Interior design by Trish Parcell
Printed and bound by CPI Group (UK) Ltd, Croydon CR0 4YY

This book is sold subject to the condition that it shall not,
by way of trade or otherwise, be lent, resold, hired out,
or otherwise circulated without the publisher's prior consent
in any form of binding or cover other than that in which
it is published and without a similar condition including this
condition being imposed on the subsequent purchaser.

FIELD
NOTES
ON
Love

Bromley Libraries

30128 80403 979 3

ALSO BY JENNIFER E. SMITH

Windfall

For Jack,
who has many adventures ahead of him

Prologue

Mae wakes, as she does each morning, to the sound of a train.

Even before she opens her eyes, she can feel the low rumble of it straight through to her toes, but it's the whistle that finally tears at the thin gauze of sleep. She turns over to peer through the blinds. Just beyond their backyard, a long chain of silver cars is streaking past.

Two weeks from now, she'll be standing in the middle of Penn Station, waiting for a train not so different from this one. The minute she steps on board, she'll no longer be a fixed point on the map, the way she's been her whole life.

On the other side of the ocean, a boy named Hugo is holding the tickets that will carry them both across the country. He's thinking of that old maths problem, the one where two different trains leave from two different stations traveling at two different speeds.

The point was always to figure out where they'd meet.

But nobody ever explained what would happen once they did.

They both sit very still, three thousand miles between them. Hugo is staring at the word printed neatly across the bottom of the tickets: *California*. Mae is watching out her window as the train disappears. If you saw them, you might think they were waiting for something. But what they actually are—what they've each always been—is ready.

Hugo

The shock of it takes a few minutes to absorb. During that time, Hugo sits with his head bent, his fingers laced behind his neck, trying to process the fact that Margaret Campbell—his girlfriend of nearly three years—is breaking up with him.

"You know I'll always love you," she says, then adds, "in a way."

Hugo winces at this. But Margaret seems determined to forge ahead.

"The thing is," she says, and he lifts his head, interested to find out what—precisely—it is, this thing that's apparently happening. She gazes back at him with something like sympathy. "You can't stay with someone only out of inertia, right?"

It's clear the correct answer here is "Right." But Hugo

can't bring himself to say it. He just continues to stare at her, wishing his brain weren't quite so muddled.

"I know you must feel the same way," she continues. "Things have been off between us for ages now. It's obvious that it's not working—"

"Is it?" Hugo asks, and Margaret gives him a weary look. But he's not trying to be cheeky. It's just that none of this seems particularly obvious to him, and his face prickles with warmth as he wonders how he managed to get it all so wrong.

"Hugo. Come on. It's been hard enough when we're right across the road from each other. We must be barking mad to think we can do this when I'm all the way in California and you're—"

She stops abruptly, and they both blink at each other.

"Here," he says eventually, his voice flat.

Margaret sighs. "See, that's just it. Maybe if you'd stop acting like getting a scholarship to a perfectly good uni is the worst thing that's ever happened to anyone in the history of—"

"I'm not."

"You are."

"I'm—"

"Hugo," she says, interrupting him. "You've been in terrible form all summer. I'm not the only one who's noticed. I realize this isn't what you wanted, but at some point you just have to . . . well, get on with it, I suppose."

He scratches at his knee, unable to look at her. She's right, and they both know it, but the fact of this makes him want to crawl under the bed to avoid the rest of the conversation.

"Listen, I get it," she says, playing with the end of her blond ponytail. "If things were different, this wouldn't have been your first choice."

This is only half true. Hugo certainly wouldn't have minded trying for Oxford or Cambridge or St. Andrews, all of which would've been options had his A levels been the only consideration. But the University of Surrey is highly regarded too. It's more that he never had a choice in the matter, that his path was set out for him long ago, and something about that has always made him feel like an animal at the zoo, penned in and pacing and a bit claustrophobic.

"But if things were different," Margaret continues, "you wouldn't have been offered the scholarship at all."

She says this as if it were nothing, an incidental detail, and not the very thing Hugo has been torturing himself over for years now. Because he didn't get a scholarship to the University of Surrey for being a brilliant essayist (which he is) or a maths genius (which he's not). He didn't get it for his skills as a pianist (though he's decent) or his ability on the football pitch (he's completely rubbish). It's not the result of any particular skill or talent or accomplishment.

No, Hugo got the scholarship—as did his five siblings— simply for being born.

The minute they arrived in the world—one after another, Hugo bringing up the rear—they were showered with gifts. The local market gave them a year's supply of formula. The pharmacy sent a truckload of free nappies. The mayor came to visit with keys to the city: six of them, one for each of England's fifth-ever set of sextuplets, affectionately dubbed "the Surrey Six." And a wealthy donor presented their exhausted and deeply overwhelmed parents with scholarships to the local university for each of their half-dozen newborns.

The man—an eccentric billionaire who made his fortune through a chain of upscale coffee shops—had got his start at the University of Surrey, and was elated at the thought of the publicity that would one day be generated by having the sextuplets there. When he died a few years ago, he left the scholarship in the hands of the university council, and they've been equally enthusiastic, making all sorts of plans for their arrival.

It's only Hugo who isn't thrilled. He knows he's a complete monster for being anything less than grateful. It's just that he hates the thought of accepting something so big simply because of the unlikely circumstances of his birth. Especially when his whole life has been about that.

"Look, I don't want you to get the wrong idea," Margaret is saying. "About us. About why we're—"

"Not an *us* anymore?"

She flinches. "I know I've been hard on you, but I don't want you to think this is happening just because you've been moping all summer. Or because of the distance. It's more that—well, I suppose it feels like it's time, doesn't it?"

Hugo scrubs at his eyes, still trying to absorb all this, and when he looks up again, Margaret's face has softened.

She moves over to sit beside him on the bed, and he automatically leans into her, their shoulders pressed together. They're both quiet for a moment, and he tries to focus his thoughts, which are zipping around in his head. Somewhere inside him, buried so deep he's never thought to examine it, is the knowledge that she's right about them, and his heart sinks because he's somehow the last to know everything, even his own feelings.

"What about the trip?" he asks, and she looks almost relieved, as though she's been given permission to move on to the business end of things. *Three years*, Hugo thinks. Three whole years, and here they are, working out their future like a long-married couple debating the fine points of a divorce. Margaret picks at a loose thread on her jumper, which is gray with little foxes on it. Hugo realizes it's the same one she wore on their third date, when they'd gone to the cinema and kissed for the first time during a fight scene.

It's only now occurring to him that maybe that was a sign.

"I think you should still go," she says, and he looks up in surprise. The whole thing had been her idea. Margaret thought a train trip would be a romantic way to see America, where she'd be spending the next four years. She was the one who found the promotion online and booked the tickets, surprising Hugo for his birthday a few months back. They were meant to go from New York to California, with a few stops in between. And then Hugo would drop her off at Stanford before returning to Surrey, the place where he'd lived his whole life and was apparently never leaving.

"Why me?" he asks, staring at her. "Why not you?"

"Well, you're the one staying behind. So I figured it might be nice for you to . . ." She pauses when she notices his expression, and her pale skin flushes a deep pink. "Sorry. I'm mucking this up, aren't I?"

"No," he says, thinking of the plans they'd been making all summer, the photos of the train, sleek and silver, moving west across America. "It's just—how could I go without you?"

"You're a bit hopeless sometimes, it's true," she says with a smile, "but I think you could probably manage to get there in one piece."

She reaches for her bag, which is slumped on the floor near his desk, and hands him a blue folder with the name of a travel company embossed across the front. When he takes it, their fingers brush, and suddenly his head is swimming with doubts. But then she leans forward to kiss him on the cheek before standing up, and something about the gesture—the sheer friendliness of it—reminds him of why this is happening and steadies him again.

"I hope you'll still come to see me," she says. "When you get to California."

"Sure," he answers without really thinking about it, and the trip starts to rearrange itself in his head: instead of sitting beside Margaret, the two of them talking softly as the train rattles through the night, it's only him now, inching his way across a strange country alone.

Alone, he thinks, closing his eyes.

Hugo can scarcely imagine what that feels like. He shares a bedroom with Alfie and a bathroom with George and Oscar too. At the kitchen table, he's wedged between Poppy and Isla, and when they watch TV, he's somehow always the last to dive for a sofa, which means he usually ends up on the floor with a cushion. On rare holidays, they all pile into a cottage in Devon that belongs to a friend of Mum's, and the farthest he's ever been from home—the only place he's really been at all—was Paris for a school trip, which meant all his brothers and sisters were there, too, making the weekend brighter and funnier but also more crowded, the six of them laughing and tripping along the cobblestone streets, a built-in team, a six-piece band, an entire unit of their own.

Alone, he thinks again, and his chest feels light.

He stands up to fold Margaret into a hug, his throat thick. For a long time, they hold each other, neither quite ready to let go. Then, finally, he kisses her check and says, "I love you." She leans back to look at him and he cracks a grin. "In a way."

"Too soon," she says, but she's laughing too.

When she's gone, he sits back down on his bed. There's a dull pounding in his ears, but otherwise he feels oddly numb. An hour ago he had a girlfriend, and now he doesn't. It's as simple and as complicated as that.

He flips open the blue folder. There's a note inside that says *Happy Birthday, Hugo!* in Margaret's neat handwriting. He moves it aside to look at the itinerary, thinking back on all their conversations about this trip. She teased him about his long legs, promising to book an aisle seat on the flight from London, his first one ever, and he rolled his eyes when she talked about going for tea at the Plaza. "We live in England," he'd said. "We're already drowning in tea."

There were nights in Chicago and Denver, and also in San Francisco, where they'd planned to stay a couple of days before Margaret needed to head down to Stanford. It's all a bit harder to picture now, and he shuffles through the pages, trying to imagine how different the trip will be.

This is when it dawns on him that every single sheet of paper has Margaret's name on it. He looks a little closer. The train tickets, the hotels, even the general booking from the company—all of it has *Margaret Campbell* printed across the top.

He glances down to the bottom of the confirmation from their hotel in Denver to see the words spelled out in bold letters: ***nonrefundable and nontransferable.***

Hugo almost laughs.

Happy birthday to me, he thinks, and his heart falls as he realizes what this means. But just as he reaches for his mobile to call the tour company—to see if there might be any exceptions at all—the door to his room flies open and Alfie sticks his head in.

Among the six of them, there are two sets of identical twins: his sisters, Poppy and Isla, and then Hugo and Alfie, who are carbon copies of each other, right down to the flecks of green in their eyes. They have matching dimples and ears that stick out a bit, the same brown skin and black hair. At the moment, Hugo's is longer than Alfie's, which is cropped close to his head, but otherwise they're almost impossible to tell apart. Except for their personalities.

"Hey, mate," Alfie says, uncharacteristically reserved. He steps into the room and shuts the door. But instead of flopping onto his bed, he just stands there, scratching the back of his neck. "So, uh . . ."

"You ran into Margaret," Hugo says with a sigh.

Alfie looks relieved. "Yeah. We did."

"We?"

He opens the door to reveal the others out in the hall. All four of them. They file in a little sheepishly. "Sorry," George mumbles, sinking onto the bed and giving Hugo an awkward pat on the back. George looks deeply solemn, but then he always looks solemn, as if being born first instilled in him a certain seriousness of character. "This is rubbish, isn't it?"

"I can't believe it," says Isla, spinning the desk chair around and sitting backward in it, her chin resting on her forearms, her dark eyes fierce and protective. "How could she do that?"

Hugo gives them a smile, but he can feel it wobble with effort. "It's okay," he says. "I'm fine. Really."

Poppy is still standing near the door, absently twisting the ends of her box braids. She fixes him with a skeptical look, as if she can see straight through him. Which she usually can. "Hugo."

"Really," he says again. "It'll be fine."

There's a long silence, in which Hugo stares at his

hands to avoid watching the rest of them exchange glances. Finally, Alfie shrugs. "I never liked her much anyway," he says, which makes Hugo laugh in spite of himself, because they all loved Margaret. If anything, they thought she was out of his league.

But still, one by one, they join in.

"Yeah," says Oscar, who has been hovering on Alfie's side of the room, never one for drama. He generally tends to prefer the world of his video games to the real one, but now he runs a hand over his twists, cracking a grin. "She was the worst."

"A real monster," Isla agrees, trying to keep a straight face.

"Remember that time she spilled her drink on you, Pop?" asks George, and for a moment, Poppy hesitates. Of all of them, she's the closest with Margaret, and Hugo can see that she's torn. But in the end, she nods.

"I still haven't forgiven her for that," she says gamely. "And now I never will."

They carry on like that for a bit, and Hugo does his best to smile, but he's still thinking about everything that happened and about the itinerary in his hands, and it isn't until Alfie chimes in that the idea occurs to him and a plan begins to form.

"Don't worry, mate," Alfie says merrily, reaching out to give Hugo's shoulder a little pat. "There are other Margaret Campbells out there."

Mae

Mae claps a hand over her eyes as she presses Play, but the moment the film begins, she can't help peeking through her fingers. There's the familiar swell of music, then the black screen with the words *mae day productions* scrawled across it, and then—

She punches at the keyboard of her computer, and the window disappears.

Clearly, this is ridiculous. She's probably watched the film a thousand times, and she's not even sure that's an exaggeration. Just a couple of months ago, she'd been practically gleeful about it, filled with a fizzy lightness when she imagined all the praise that would be coming her way. Most of all, she was certain the members of the admissions committee at the University of Southern California School of Cinematic Arts would see its brilliance. How could they not?

All her life, people have been telling Mae she has talent. She was nine when she made her first short (a stop-motion film about a muffin named Steve who falls in love with a bagel named Bruno), ten when she started hanging around the high school's A.V. club in the afternoons (too overzealous to realize that her mockumentary about the older kids wouldn't get a warm reception), and eleven when she got her first real camera—a beautiful Canon DSLR with a 35-millimeter lens and 1.8 f-stop—for her birthday (after threatening to hock all her possessions to pay for one).

So far, she's gotten by on passion and determination and an unwillingness to take no for an answer, drafting friends as actors, talking her way into shooting locations, and watching YouTube tutorials for new tricks. Now she was supposed to graduate into the big leagues, finally getting a real education at the best filmmaking school in the world, which is the only thing she's ever really wanted.

It just never occurred to her they might not want her back.

She sets her jaw and faces down the screen again. She hasn't been able to bring herself to watch since the letter came, the one informing her that she'd been accepted to the university—just not to the film program. But she knows it's time. If she's ever going to have a shot at transferring, she'll have to make another audition film. And if she's going to do that, she'll have to figure out what went wrong with the first one. She doesn't mind learning from her mistakes; in fact, she's desperate to. She just hates the idea that what once seemed so shiny and impressive will now inevitably look different to her: a bruising collection of flaws and mistakes that will surely hurt even more than the rejection.

Still, she grits her teeth and presses Play. But as the first image appears—a time-lapse shot of clouds on one of those perfect spring days in the Hudson Valley, the sky so blue it almost looks like a special effect—there's a knock at the door.

Mae half turns, pushing her glasses up on her nose. "Yeah?"

"Want to come down and help me with dinner?" Dad asks, poking his head in. "Not with anything important, obviously, since none of us are quite over the Great Mashed Potato Incident of Last Tuesday. But you can always do something menial, like grating cheese, or . . ." He pauses, noticing her computer, where the screen is still frozen on the clouds. "Ooh," he says, walking over. "I love this part."

"It's not . . ." Mae says, quickly shutting the laptop. "I'm not . . ."

But it's too late. He's already sitting down on the edge of her bed, leaning forward with his elbows on his knees, ready to watch. Right then, with the late-day sun coming through the window, the resemblance between them is clear. They're both short, with matching freckles and light brown hair and fair skin. Even their reading glasses have the same prescription.

When Mae was born, her dads did a coin toss to decide whose last name she would get. They'd already agreed to keep the bigger question—which one of them was her biological father—a mystery. But as she got older, it started to become pretty obvious whose swimmers had won the race. Her other dad—Pop—is tall and broad-shouldered and athletic, with jet-black hair and deep blue eyes, about as different from Mae as can be. "Well," he always says when she trips over her own feet or struggles to reach a high shelf, "at least I won the damn coin toss."

Dad claps his hands. "Come on," he says a little too cheerfully. He's still wearing his signature tweed blazer, though all he had today was a faculty meeting. "Let's roll tape."

Mae shakes her head. "I think I need to do this alone."

"Right," he says. "Sure. But just to make a counterargument—"

"Here we go."

"—you've been trying to do it on your own all summer, and clearly that hasn't worked. So maybe it would help if you had some moral support."

She considers this for a moment, then swivels back around and opens the laptop again. The clouds, almost imperceptibly, start to shift into shapes: a rabbit and a guitar and a wave. Mae leans forward and stops the video again. "Nope. Sorry. Can't do it."

"Why not?"

"Because," she says, "I love it. Or at least I *did*."

"Okay, let's say it's horrible."

"What?"

"Maybe," he says, "it's the worst thing anyone's ever made. Maybe it's a colossal failure of a piece of art. A

16

disaster on every imaginable level."

She blinks at him. "Is this supposed to be a pep talk?"

"Just stick with me," he says. "I'm getting there."

"Okay, so . . . maybe it sucks. If it didn't, I would've been one of the four percent of people accepted to the program. But I wasn't, and now I don't know if I can stand to watch it again through their eyes."

"Aha," he says. "That's just it. Do you know how often my students scoff at the paintings I show them in class? *Professor Weber, you do realize that's just a red square, right? I could do that in my sleep.* But the thing is, those kids are being jackasses."

Mae laughs. "Are you trying to say that the admissions people at USC are jackasses too?"

"He's trying to say that art is subjective," says Pop, who has appeared in the doorway, still wearing his suit and tie from the gallery. "Just because they didn't love your film doesn't mean it's not great. And just because they had a different opinion about it doesn't mean you have to change yours."

"Actually," Dad says with a grin, "I was gonna say the thing about jackasses. But his was better."

Pop shakes his head, but he's still looking at Mae. "You were really proud of that film," he says with a smile. "I guess I don't see why that has to be any different now."

She glances back at her computer. "Garrett's always saying——"

They both let out strangled groans.

"*Garrett,*" Dad says, rolling his eyes so hard that Mae

worries they might get stuck like that. She knows he's mostly teasing; they act the same with any boy she brings home. But Garrett's flashy red car and swanky Park Avenue address haven't helped matters.

Pop pushes off the doorframe and walks over to sit beside Dad on the bed, their shoulders touching. "Hasn't he gone back to the city yet?"

Mae had met Garrett at the start of summer, when they were the only two people at an arthouse screening of *Cinema Paradiso*. She'd seen it a million times, of course; it was her grandmother's favorite. And though it was a bit sappy for Mae's taste, Nana was in the hospital at the time, and something about sitting in the darkened theater and watching the flickering screen felt almost reverential, the closest thing she had to a prayer.

Afterward, she discovered Garrett waiting for her in the lobby, as if they'd planned to meet there. With his square jaw and blond hair, he looked like he should be anywhere else on a Saturday night: at a party or a baseball game or possibly even a movie premiere. Instead he was holding a half-empty bucket of popcorn in the crook of one arm, and he lifted his eyebrows expectantly. "So? What did you think?"

Caught off guard, Mae studied him for a moment, then shrugged. "Brilliant, if overly sentimental."

"Right," Garrett said, looking thoughtful, "except the sentimentality is intentional. Which is why I think it works."

"Even well-intentioned nostalgia can be saccharine."

"Only if it's manipulative," he argued, "which it's not in this case."

Mae squinted at him. "What are you, a film critic or something?"

"Aspiring," he said matter-of-factly. "What are you, an expert in Italian cinema?"

"Aspiring," she said with a grin.

Later, after several cups of coffee, they still hadn't come to an agreement about the film, but they *had* managed to get into a heated argument about their favorite directors—Wes Anderson for her, Danny Boyle for him—and at least ten other film-related topics. Mae was in the middle of a rant about the lack of female directors when he leaned over to kiss her. Surprised, she pulled away, made a final point about how the statistics are even worse when it comes to women of color, and then kissed him right back.

It was never something that was meant to last, and that suited Mae just fine. Garrett lived in the city and was just at his family's sprawling farmhouse for a couple of months before heading off to Paris, where he planned to study French cinema at the Sorbonne.

"*In French*," he said that first night, and she knew then that he was all wrong for her. But his smile was dazzling and his hair was tousled just right and his taste in films was so ridiculously nostalgic that she was already looking forward to spending the next six weeks arguing with him. Which is pretty much what they did.

"You just like him because he's cute," Dad says. "But he has the personality of a croissant."

Mae tilts her head to one side. "Do croissants have bad personalities?"

"I don't know. I was just trying to think of something needlessly fancy."

"How can a piece of dough be—"

"You know what I mean," Dad says, rolling his eyes. "So what did he say?"

"The croissant?"

"No, Garrett."

"He says it's impossible to make a great piece of art if you haven't really lived."

Dad snorts. "And I suppose *he's* really lived?"

"Well, he's been all over the place. And he grew up in the city. Plus, he's going to the Sorbonne next year."

"Trust me," Dad says, "there are as many idiots there as everywhere else in the world."

"Look, he's not totally wrong," Pop says more gently. "If there's one thing I've learned after twelve years at the gallery, it's that sometimes art isn't a matter of skill or technique. Sometimes it *is* about experience. So maybe you've got some more living to do. But that's the case with everyone, whether you've grown up in a big city or a small town, whether you're going to school in Paris or not."

Mae nods. "I know that. It's just . . ."

"It's hard," Pop says with a shrug. "It is. But the hurt and rejection and disappointment? It'll help you grow as an artist. And it'll all be worth it when you finally get it right. You know that as well as I do." He nods in the direction of her computer and gives her a small smile. "So what do you say? One more screening for old times' sake?"

This time Mae relents, opening her computer before she can chicken out again. When she first showed them the film last fall, they were eating popcorn and joking around and bursting into spontaneous applause at some of the shots. But now the three of them watch in silence, and when it's over, nobody says anything for what feels like a very long time.

Finally, Mae turns to where they're both sitting on her bed, and they raise their eyebrows, waiting for her to speak first.

"The good news," she says, "is that I don't know what I'd do differently."

"And the bad news?" Dad asks.

She shrugs. "I don't know what I'd do differently."

"You will," Pop says like it's a promise, and for a second, Mae can almost picture him as he once was, a struggling painter whose first show sold only two pieces, both of them to a young art professor who happened to be walking by, and who—as he always likes to say—was lured in by the brilliant yellows and greens but stuck around for Pop's baby blues.

"And in the meantime," Dad says, "I guess you'll just have to do some more living. Which works out pretty nicely with this whole going-off-to-college thing."

"I guess so," Mae says, trying not to think about the course booklet on her desk, all the film classes she'll be missing out on because of the math and science requirements, the hours she'll have to spend writing essays on World War II and Shakespearean sonnets and behavioral psychology, when she could be learning how to be a better filmmaker.

"But before all that," Pop says, "maybe you could set the table? If we don't eat soon, your nana is going to have my head."

Dad laughs. "Unless you're still not over the Silverware Drawer Debacle of early June . . ."

"You're the worst," Mae says, but she doesn't mind. Not really. In fact, she feels lighter already. The film is behind her now. And everything else is still ahead.

Hugo

The travel company is impressively unhelpful.

"All bookings are nonrefundable—"

"Yes, and nontransferable," Hugo says for the third time. "I was just hoping you might make an exception. See, my girlfriend booked the tickets, but we've split up now, and I'd still quite like to go, but—"

"Is your name Margaret Campbell?" asks the customer service representative in a flat, bored voice.

Hugo sighs. "No."

"Well then," she says, and that's that.

Alfie and George are the only two at home that afternoon. Hugo explains his new plan to them, expecting a bit of support, but they both stare at him, gobsmacked.

"You're a nutter," Alfie says. "A complete nutter."

George rubs the back of his neck, where his hair is cut

into a fade. He still looks incredulous. "Even if someone was mad enough to actually agree to this, why would you want to spend a week with a total stranger?"

"Yeah, you're always on about what a chore it is to share a room with *me*," Alfie says. "Now you don't mind being stuck in a train compartment for days on end with some random girl?"

"It would still be better than sharing a room with you," George points out, and Alfie throws a rugby ball at his head.

"I'm a delight," he says.

Hugo ignores them. He knows how it sounds, this makeshift plan of his. There's only one real reason to do it: he wants a week on his own before starting uni in the company of his five siblings. Having to share that time with a stranger isn't particularly appealing. But given the circumstances, Hugo doesn't see a way around it.

"I still want to go," he tells his brothers. "And this is the only way."

In the end, they agree to help him write the post, and the three of them huddle around his laptop, cracking up as they spend the afternoon crafting the world's strangest wanted ad. Though he had to reel Alfie in a bit—"I don't think it hurts to be open-minded about the sleeping arrangements"—even Hugo has to admit the final result isn't bad:

Hello there!

First of all, I realise this is a bit odd, but here we go. As a result of a breakup (that was not my idea, unfortunately), I've found myself with a consolation prize: a spare ticket for a weeklong train journey from New York City to San Francisco. The catch is that I can't change my ex's name on the reservation, so I'm sending this out into the universe in case there happens to be another Margaret Campbell who might be interested in rescuing my holiday and getting one of her own in exchange.

I know what you're thinking, but I swear I'm not a nutter. I'm a fairly normal eighteen-year-old bloke from England, and I think most people would say I'm a nice guy (references available upon request).

The train leaves from Penn Station in New York City on August 13 and arrives in San Francisco on August 19, and if you'd prefer not to sit with me, I'll do my best to sort something with the travel company. Honestly, I just need someone by the name of Margaret Campbell to get us on board, and then the rest is up to you. There are a few nights in sleeper cars with bunk beds, which we may not be able to help, but there are also hotels booked along the way in New York, Chicago, Denver, and San Francisco, which you're welcome to have to yourself. I'm happy to find somewhere else to stay. All that I ask is that you stick with me long enough to get us both on the train at each stop. We can sort the rest of the details later.

So if your name is Margaret Campbell and you're

interested in a bit of an adventure, please email me at
HugoIsNotANutter@gmail.com with the answers to these
three questions, and if there's more than one entry, I'll pick
the grand-prize winner once I've read them:

What's your biggest dream?

What's your biggest fear?

What's the most important thing you'd bring with you
on the train?

Good luck, Margaret Campbells of the world—I'm
counting on you!

Cheers,

Hugo W.

They're just about finished when they hear Mum calling
them down for dinner. Out the bedroom window, a fog has
settled over the garden, the edges laced with gold as the
sun sets. Hugo presses his laptop shut, but Alfie reaches
out and opens it again.

"You didn't post it."

Hugo's eyes flick back to the glowing screen. "I'll do it
after dinner."

"This isn't a homework assignment," George teases him.
"You don't have to proof it a thousand times."

"I know. I—"

Alfie frowns. "He's pulling a Hugo."

"I'm not . . . pulling a Hugo. I just need to think it
through a bit more."

George nods sagely. "That's the very definition of
pulling a Hugo."

"Listen," Alfie says, standing up, "you should know I think this idea is completely mad. . . ."

Hugo waits for him to continue. "And?"

"And nothing. That's it. I think this idea is completely mad." Alfie grins as he walks to the door. "Which is exactly why you should do it."

When his brothers are gone, Hugo takes one last look at the post, letting his finger hover over the button that would send it out into the world. But he can't bring himself to press it. What if nobody writes back? Or what if they do? What if he accidentally picks a serial killer? Or, worse, someone who talks a lot? What if *his* Margaret sees it? Or what if his parents find out?

Earlier, after they all scattered for the afternoon, Isla sent a message to their group chat asking who should break the news about Margaret to Mum and Dad. *Assuming Hugo doesn't want to*, she added, which was a fairly safe assumption. He'd been with Margaret long enough that she became a regular fixture around the Wilkinson house, and Hugo can't imagine telling his parents, who adore her. In fact, they like her so much he half suspects they'll be cross with him for letting the breakup happen at all.

Anyone but Alfie, he'd written back, half joking, and it had been Isla and George—the two most reliable ones— who did the job in the end. But now, when Hugo walks into the kitchen and is greeted by the smell of chicken curry—his favorite—and a sympathetic look from Mum, he wonders if he should've picked Alfie after all. If anyone could've figured out how to make this whole thing seem like a laugh, it would've been him, and then maybe they could've skipped straight over this part.

"How are you doing, darling?" Mum asks, standing on her tiptoes to give him a kiss on the cheek. She's almost a foot shorter than any of her children, a diminutive woman with pale skin and flyaway hair who might seem a bit scatty if you didn't notice the determination around the edges of her mouth. When his parents found out they were having sextuplets, she was the one who decided they needed to get creative, and from the moment the children were born, she started blogging about their lives. This eventually turned into a book on parenting, and then another, until there was a whole series about them. And though Hugo has always found the books entirely mortifying, they've also made it possible to keep a family of eight going on more than just his dad's teacher salary.

But to Hugo's alarm, his mum—who is usually in constant motion, sweeping through their lives like someone in fast-forward—is now looking at him with watery eyes and an intense stare. It occurs to him that she might try to have a talk about the breakup right here in the middle of the busy kitchen, so he gives her shoulder an awkward pat and sidesteps away as quickly as he can.

"I'm fine, Mum. Really."

She looks like she wants to say more, but the oven dings, so she just gives him one last look of concern before hurrying over to take out a loaf of garlic bread, another of Hugo's favorites.

When his dad walks in, he's wearing his Tottenham

Hotspur shirt, which makes Hugo laugh, because Margaret is a huge Arsenal fan, and he knows this is for him. To his relief, Dad just winks at him as he grabs a stack of plates from the cupboard and begins to set the table.

When everything is ready, Hugo slides into his usual seat between his sisters. Isla gives him a friendly shoulder bump, and Poppy makes a funny face at him.

"So," Dad says, running a hand over the top of his shiny black head. Hugo can't remember what his father looked like before he was bald; it's as much a part of him as his smile, which makes his whole face brighten and his dimples come out so that he seems like a kid again, like he could easily be just another Wilkinson brother. On the first day of primary school, Hugo watched all the other children fall under the spell of that smile like bowling pins dropping one by one, and it gave him such a burst of pride that he'd run up to hug his dad at the end of the day, the word pounding fiercely through his head: *mine*.

"Give me the headlines," Dad says now, as he does every night, and Hugo is quick to lower his eyes. But he doesn't have to worry. Alfie chimes in about his rugby match, and Poppy has a story about her summer job at the cinema; Oscar made some progress on the football app he's been coding, and Isla went to the park with her boyfriend, Rakesh. George, whose obsession with *The Great British Baking Show* led to a job at the local bakery, spent the day learning how to make a lemon meringue pie, and the biggest news is that he brought one home for dessert.

"You didn't drop a penny in there again, did you?"

Poppy asks, and George gives her a withering look.

"One time," he says under his breath.

"As it turns out," Poppy says, "that's all it takes . . ."

Afterward, everyone automatically turns to Hugo. Then, just as quickly, they look away again, making a forced and not-altogether-believable effort to pretend it isn't his turn, so that he's spared reliving the newsiest thing of all.

"Actually, I've got something too," he says, and they all turn to him in surprise. "Despite, uh, recent developments, I've decided I'm still going on holiday to America."

To their credit, nobody asks for any particulars on the recent developments. Dad simply raises his eyebrows. Mum presses her lips together and sits forward in the chair. Alfie says, "Well done you!" and reaches across the table for a fist bump. Then, sensing the mood, he slowly pulls his arm back again.

"Margaret wanted me to have the tickets," Hugo continues, deciding to leave out the part about how they might be worthless to him. "And I'd like to go."

"With who?" Mum asks in a way that seems maybe a little too calm.

Hugo avoids looking at any of his siblings. "By myself."

"That's a big trip to do on your own," Dad says, keeping his face neutral. "You've never even gone to London by yourself, much less to another country."

"I'm eighteen now," Hugo points out. "And if we didn't—if we weren't—well, I could just as easily be going off to uni a lot farther away. I don't see how this is any different."

"Honestly, it's different because you can't make it half a mile without losing your keys or your wallet," Mum says, sounding both apologetic and exasperated. "I love you, Hugo, and you're brilliant in a lot of ways, but you've also got your head in the clouds more often than not."

Hugo opens his mouth to protest, but he knows she's not wrong. When he was little, she used to call him Paddington because he was always getting lost from the rest of the group.

"I'm close to pinning a note to your jumper," she'd say, her face still white with worry after finding him under a clothes rack at Marks & Spencer's or in a completely different aisle at the local Tesco. *"Please look after this bear."*

There's a banner at the top of her blog, an illustration of the six of them lined up from oldest to youngest, a fairly ridiculous distinction, considering all that separates them is eight minutes. In it, they're marching one by one toward the right side of the page. First George, who is carrying a fishing rod and strolling in that jaunty way of his. Then Alfie, a football tucked under his arm and a hint of a grin on his face. Poppy—always in motion—is skipping after them, and Oscar is whistling as he makes his way leisurely across the screen. Behind him, Isla's head is bent over a book. And then, last of all, there's Hugo, forever falling behind, perpetually trying to catch up with his brothers and sisters.

He's always hated that image.

"Darling," his mum is saying, her voice gentler now.

"It's okay to sleepwalk your way around here. But I'd worry too much about you being on your own in a place like New York or San Francisco. The truth is, you're just not . . ."

"Responsible," Poppy offers.

"Ready," suggests Oscar.

"Sensible," says Isla, winking at him.

"Good-looking," Alfie says. "Sorry, what were we talking about?"

Mum ignores them. "Can you not take one of this lot with you?"

"That's not the point," Hugo says, feeling the heat rise in his cheeks. He doesn't know how to explain about the extra ticket without giving away his plan to find another Margaret Campbell. The rest of them know this, of course. They're in on it too. But what they don't know is this: even if he *could* bring anyone he wanted, he still wouldn't be all that keen to choose one of them. Because this isn't about his siblings. For once, it's about Hugo.

"The point is to escape for a bit," he says, sounding a little desperate. "To see what it's like to be on my own. Especially since . . ."

"You'll all be at uni together," Dad finishes, and Hugo looks up at him gratefully. He's spent the whole summer trying not to say this out loud. He's not the only one who could've been accepted elsewhere, but he was always the one with the highest marks, and because of that, the others have given him a pass for being so miserable about their lack of options. But what he hasn't said—what he's barely even let himself think—is that it's about them too.

"It's not that I'm not happy about it," he says weakly, looking from Alfie to Oscar to George, who are sitting three in a row across the table, watching him with unreadable expressions. "You know how much I . . . well, you guys are my . . ." He turns to Poppy, whose mouth is twisted as she waits to hear what he has to say. On his other side, Isla is looking at her plate. "We've always been a team."

"And now you wish you could be transferred?" George asks. His voice is intentionally light, but Hugo can hear the stiffness in it. When they were little, Dad used to joke that George was like a sheepdog, always looking out for the rest of them, trying to keep the pack together. To him, the scholarship isn't a duty; it's a stroke of good luck. A chance to keep moving through the world as they always have: as a unit.

Hugo shakes his head. "Not at all. It's just . . . I can't be the only one who's wondered what it would be like to . . ." He doesn't finish the thought, though he knows they understand what he's saying. They always do. But if they agree with him—if they're even the slightest bit sympathetic—none of them shows it. They all watch him impassively, the looks on their faces ranging from hurt to miffed to annoyed.

Hugo swallows hard, feeling like he's flailing. But then he thinks of what Alfie said earlier, about pulling a Hugo, and fights his way forward.

"The thing is, I can't imagine being anywhere without you all," he says, which is true, the truest thing he can think to say. "But that's why it feels like I have to try it.

33

Even if it's only for a week."

They're all quiet for a moment, even Alfie, until—finally—Dad nods. "Then you have to go," he says simply, and at the other end of the table, Mum lets out a sigh.

"Just don't lose your passport," she says. "All things being equal, we'd prefer to get you back at the end."

Mae

At breakfast Nana is telling a story about a boy she dated when she was eighteen.

"His father was a prince," she says as she ladles some sugar into her coffee, "and his mother was a debutante. He was *very* handsome, and he took me to the most fabulous parties all over New York City. Once, we danced until five in the morning. Then he kissed me on a street corner just as it started to rain. It was unbelievably romantic."

"Mom," Pop says, looking at her over his newspaper. "You didn't date a prince."

She winks at Mae. "I didn't say I did. I said his *father* was a prince. He decided to get out of the family business."

"Sounds like a swell guy, Mary," Dad says with a completely straight face, and Nana throws a balled-up napkin in his direction. He catches it and throws it right back.

"Enough, you two," Pop says with a weary look. Ever since his mother came to live with them this spring, meals—at least on the days when she's been up to joining them—have turned into sparring sessions, with Nana and Dad trading good-natured jabs across the table. They're so eerily well matched that one day, while they went back and forth about the merits of green tea, Pop leaned over to Mae and whispered, "I think I married my mother."

Mae finishes her cereal and rinses the bowl in the sink. "Well," she says, her voice light as she turns around again, "I'm off."

"What about the gallery?" Pop asks with a frown. She's been working there a few days a week, packing boxes and answering the phone and talking to the more casual customers who come up from the city and act like they're on the brink of buying a painting, before they move on to the antique shop next door and go through the same routine with an old lamp.

"Yeah, I was hoping I could come in later." Mae does her best not to meet any of their eyes. "It's just that Garrett is leaving this afternoon, so . . ."

To her surprise, they all look thrilled.

"Well, why didn't you say so," Dad says with a grin. "Please. Go. We certainly wouldn't want to keep him. Not even a minute longer than—"

"Give him our best," Pop says, ever the diplomat.

"I think it's lovely," Nana says with the same dreamy look she gets when they watch old movies together. "A dramatic send-off."

"I'm not sure how dramatic it will be," Mae tells her. "We always knew we were going our separate ways."

"That doesn't make it any less romantic," she says, beaming. She's wearing a blue silk robe, and she looks tiny inside it, lost in the folds of fabric. All the chemo she went through this spring—a course so intensive she was in the hospital for over a month—seems to have shrunk her. But it worked, and now, whenever someone remarks on how much weight she's lost, Nana only grins. "Must've been a whole lot of cancer in there."

It rattles Mae sometimes to hear her joke about it; she knows how close they were to losing her. When Mae was little, some of the kids at school used to ask whether she missed having a mother, and she was always quick to bite their heads off: "I have two dads," she'd say, eyes blazing. "And I bet they're both better than yours."

But that was only half the truth. The other half was that she had Nana.

Every Sunday, they'd drive down to have brunch in her sunny brownstone on the Upper West Side. The place was cluttered with a lifetime of knickknacks, but whenever Mae asked about anything in particular, Nana's answers were always short on details. "I've lived a big life on a small island," she'd say. "You can't expect me to remember every piece of flotsam and jetsam."

It wasn't the things you'd expect that made her so important to Mae. Her dads were perfectly capable of helping her pick out clothes or teaching her about the birds and the bees. It was more about drinking tea on

Nana's window seat and watching old black-and-white movies together and listening to stories about her past. It didn't matter that they were sometimes hard to believe. ("There's no way she had cocktails with JFK," Pop would say, exasperated.) That wasn't the point. The point was that she was there at all.

It was like having an extra sun in their orbit, an inexhaustible source of warmth and energy. They were a constellation of their own, Mae and Pop and Dad, but knowing Nana was there on the edges made their little universe feel complete.

Now Nana's eyes are bright as she peers at Mae over a mug of coffee. "Go enjoy your date. If there's one thing I know, it's that a girl your age should be out having adventures."

"But not *too* many adventures," Dad chimes in as Mae grabs her bag and heads for the door. She gives them a wave over her shoulder.

"I'll be back later."

"But not *too* much later," he calls out behind her.

Outside, she cuts through the neighbor's yard and then winds her way through a few side streets until she reaches the edge of town. She can see Garrett waiting outside the cheese shop, busy with his phone. When he looks up, with his messy hair and thousand-watt smile, she feels a tug of regret that this will all be over soon. It's not like the way her best friend, Priyanka, described it when her boyfriend, Alex, left for Duke last week: like their souls were being ripped apart. Mae's summer with Garrett has been a mixture of arguing and making out, all of it passionate, but none of it having very much to do with souls.

"Hey," he says, giving her a kiss as they begin to walk. "How'd it go?"

"What?"

"The film. I thought you were gonna watch it."

"Oh," she says flatly. "Yeah. It didn't help."

"Really? Still no idea what went wrong?"

"Nope. And the *not knowing* is basically killing me."

Garrett stops and turns to her. "What if I watch?"

"No way," Mae says, continuing past him. "Not a chance."

"But I'm a film critic."

She rolls her eyes. "Having a Twitter account doesn't make you a film critic."

"Fine, but I will be someday," he says, jogging to catch up to her. "So I can give you an honest opinion. And you already trust my taste, so—"

Now it's Mae's turn to come to a stop. "I don't, actually. You have terrible taste. Everything you like is overwrought and pretentious. Plus, all your favorite directors are men, which really sucks."

"That's not my fault," he says, but there's a spark in his eyes because he loves a good debate. They both do. "It's the industry's. Besides, it could be a good thing that we have different tastes." He pauses. "Obviously, the admissions board did."

She glares at him, and he holds up both hands.

"All I'm saying is that you need answers, and I have opinions."

They're nearly at the river now, picking their way down the hill toward the maple tree where they've spent the better half of the summer bickering about movies and kissing until their lips were swollen. When they get to the bottom, Garrett drops down in their usual spot, but Mae remains standing. She fishes her phone out of her back pocket and pulls up the video file.

"Here," she says, holding it out to him.

"Really?" he says as he takes it. To Mae, it feels like handing over a tiny piece of herself.

Be gentle, she wants to say, but she doesn't, because she's tougher than that.

The film is eighteen minutes long, and Mae can't bear to sit there while he watches, so she walks along the edge of the muddy river until it's time to circle back again. Garrett's head is still bent over the phone, but he looks up when she sits beside him, his expression hard to read.

"Well?" she asks, sounding much too casual.

"Technically speaking," he says, "I think it's brilliant."

Mae frowns at him. "Meaning?"

"You're an awesome filmmaker," he says, his face serious. "I don't know how you managed some of those camera angles. And that transition near the end? You're really, really talented, and this is really, really impressive."

She can feel the next word coming as surely as if he'd already spoken it. "But?"

"You want me to be honest?"

"I do," Mae says, her mouth dry.

Garrett's forehead creases. "Well, it's just . . . it's kind of impersonal."

"Impersonal?" she repeats, caught off guard. She'd been prepared for a thousand other criticisms. But *impersonal* definitely wasn't one of them.

Of all the films she's ever made, this one is closest to her own life. Someone else did the acting—a girl from school who'd been the star of every play and was eager to use it for her audition reel—but the rest of it was Mae, her story laid out for anyone who wanted to see.

"It's about a girl with two dads who lives in the Hudson Valley," she says to Garrett, an edge to her voice. "What could be more personal than that?"

"I know it's *about* you," he says. "That's really obvious. The problem is that it doesn't *feel* like you."

"Well," she says stiffly, "maybe you don't actually know me."

Garrett looks surprised. "Maybe I don't. But that's not really my fault, is it?"

Mae almost wants to laugh, but it gets stuck in her throat. Nobody has ever accused her of being mysterious before. In fact, she's never had a problem speaking her mind. When she was eight, she showed up at a town hall held by her congressman and gave an impassioned speech in defense of gay marriage. When it was finally legalized in the state of New York, she sent him a postcard that read *No thanks to you*. Once, she broke up a fight between two boys on the street and ended up with a black eye of her own. And every so often, she likes to wander into the comments section of her favorite film channel and write impassioned rebuttals to all the idiots who feel threatened by female remakes of their childhood favorites.

She is not exactly a wallflower.

Garrett squints at her, trying to figure out his next move. "Come on, Mae. We both know you're not the best at—"

"What?" she demands.

He hesitates, then shrugs. "Letting people in."

"That's not true."

"See?" he says. "If you can't even allow yourself to be introspective in this conversation, how are you ever gonna do it in your films?"

There's a hint of arrogance in his face as he says this, and for a second, Mae can see what her dads have been talking about all summer. But then his expression softens again, and he reaches for her hand, and she steels herself for whatever he's going to say next, which is probably that she really shouldn't be steeling herself against anything at all.

"You're obviously super talented. But the difference between a good film and a great one has nothing to do with jump cuts and cool techniques. It's about showing people who you are."

Mae opens her mouth to argue with this, but he hurries on.

"We both know you have a lot to say," he tells her, offering a smile even as she untangles her hand from his. "You just have to get out of your own way and actually say it."

"I did," she says.

Garrett shakes his head. "You didn't. Not yet."

"But—"

He holds up a hand. "Just think about it for a while before telling me I'm wrong, okay? The point of criticism is to help you get better, and that's all I'm trying to do."

"Fine," Mae says with some amount of effort. "Then . . . thanks. I guess."

"You're welcome," he says magnanimously. He glances down at her phone, which he's still holding. "Oh, and Priyanka texted while I was watching. I tried to swipe it away and accidentally opened the link she sent."

Mae's head is still swimming with thoughts about the film, but she reaches for the phone and stares blankly at the screen, which is open to an unfamiliar social media platform.

"Apparently some kid is looking for a Margaret Campbell to go on a train with him," Garrett says, leaning forward to look. "Crazy, right? That's so close to your name."

"It *is* my name," she mutters, already skimming the message.

He shrugs. "I'm sure it's just some creepy fifty-year-old trying to meet someone."

Mae bristles at this, though she's not sure why. He may be right. But there's something about the tone of the message that makes her believe it.

"I wonder who'll go," he says. "It would be such a weird thing to do."

"Would it?" she asks, looking up.

"To go off with a complete stranger?" he says, looking

at her incredulously. "Yeah. Besides, the trains here are the worst. Eurail is really the way to do it. I think I'm gonna start with Amsterdam next month."

"Cool," Mae says, but she's hardly listening. She's too busy reading the post again. *So if your name is Margaret Campbell and you're interested in a bit of an adventure . . .*

Garrett watches her for a moment, and something in his face shifts. "You're not actually thinking about this," he says, and though it started out as a question, it lands flat-footed and certain, a statement meant to convey how ridiculous that would be. "A week on a train with some random dude?"

"You're not jealous, are you?" Mae teases, but the expression on his face tells her that she's right. She inches forward so that their knees are touching and gives him a serious look. "I thought we decided—"

"We did," he says quickly. "But now that I'm leaving, I just . . ."

"I know," she says, though she doesn't. Not really. She thinks again of the way Priyanka had felt about Alex's departure, the hours of crying and the constant texts flying between them, the two of them desperate to bridge the sudden distance. Mae feels none of that with Garrett, and his words bob to the surface again: *We both know you're not the best at letting people in.*

She feels a prickle of something unfamiliar, something a little like doubt.

"I guess you're right," he says, but he's looking at her as if hoping she might disagree with him. "I'm leaving for

Paris next week, and you'll be in California, and it's not like we were ever . . ." He fumbles for the right word, unable to find it, while the options scroll through Mae's head: *long-term, compatible, serious, in love.*

She closes her eyes for a second, trying to muster up something bigger than what she's feeling now, which is a mild sadness at the thought of saying goodbye. But when she peeks around it, there's nothing more.

"It was a really great summer," she says, taking his hand.

He nods. "I guess now it's time for the next thing."

They look at each other for a moment, and then Garrett's eyes brighten a little.

"We still have a few hours, though," he says with a grin, and when he leans in, Mae kisses him back automatically. But her mind is miles away, already busy thinking about the next thing.

Hugo

Hugo knows he can't pick this girl. He can't. He only just broke up with his girlfriend, and he'll be sharing a small space with whomever he chooses, and there's simply no need to make it more complicated than it already is. He knows this. He does.

But that doesn't stop him from watching her video for a third time.

"Here it is," says a voice behind the camera as the shot pans out to reveal a long row of boxy storefronts on a quiet street. "This is where I've lived my whole life."

The way she says that last part, the intensity behind the words—that's what stopped him cold the first time he watched.

She answers his questions as she walks around the town, but it's not an ordinary video. It's like a little movie, the shots changing swiftly from one frame to the next. At the end, she turns the camera to reveal a round white face with a dusting of freckles across her nose. Her brown hair is pulled back into a ponytail, and her eyes are a bright blue behind her glasses.

"My name is Mae Campbell," she says with a little smile. "And as you can probably tell, I'm in desperate need of an adventure."

There's a soft knock at the door, and Hugo is quick to minimize the video on his screen. A moment later, his dad steps inside with an armful of laundry.

"I heard there was a sock emergency," he says, tossing the laundry onto Alfie's bed.

"I think we're well past emergency." Hugo spins around in his chair. "He's been wearing the same manky old pair since Thursday."

"Why doesn't he just borrow some of yours?"

"Mine aren't as lucky, apparently."

"Ah," Dad says, sitting down beside the pile on Alfie's bed. There's a ghost of a beard along his jawline, and he runs a hand over it, looking at Hugo with a serious expression. "You know, I wanted to talk to you. I was thinking more about what you said at dinner the other night. The truth is, I was an only child, and all I ever wanted was—"

"—a big family," Hugo finishes.

Dad laughs. "I suppose it's possible I might've told this story before."

"A few times," Hugo says, but he doesn't really mind. Dad's father died when he was little, and his mum worked three jobs to keep them afloat. At night, with only the TV for company, he would play a game with himself, imagining a house full of brothers and sisters.

"We had eight plates, for some reason," Dad says, taking off his glasses and rubbing his eyes. "I suppose you had to buy them as a set. I used to wedge them onto our tiny table and pretend we were about to have a big dinner together. Which was obviously a bit pathetic. But it's the reason I like to set the table now."

"You never told me that part before," Hugo says, and Dad smiles at him. It seems impossible that a man with six kids could have a smile specific to each one, but he does.

And this one is Hugo's.

"It still feels like a gift to have a person for each plate," he says, reaching out to place his hand over Hugo's lighter one. "And you should know I'm going to miss setting yours while you're away."

Hugo nods, slightly overcome by this. "Now I'm feeling a bit guilty that we're *all* leaving next month," he says, his voice thick with emotion. "Six plates in one go."

"That's different. You'll be right up the road. I'll keep them handy for weekends." Hugo's face must shift, because Dad gives his shoulder a little pat as he stands to leave. "Everyone grows up dreaming of something different, Hugo. And that's okay. It's what makes life so interesting."

Alfie comes crashing through the door then, dropping his rugby kit and falling onto his bed in the manner of a dying man.

Dad shakes his head, but he looks amused as he points to the scattered laundry. "Clean socks for you."

"Cheers." Alfie sits up and peels off his old ones, which are damp with sweat. "Might be time to retire these."

"Please don't let us get in your way," Dad says, winking at Hugo, then closing the door behind him.

Once they're alone, Alfie motions at Hugo's laptop. "So what's new in the world of crackpots and freeloaders?"

"They're not—"

"How do you know one of these girls isn't planning to steal your identity or something?"

"I don't," Hugo says with a shrug.

Alfie frowns. "What're you gonna do if Mum and Dad find out?"

"They already said I could go."

"Right, but not with a stranger. Hard to imagine they'll be too keen on that."

Hugo ignores this, returning to the in-box they set up yesterday. He sifts through the emails that have come in so far, way more than he would've expected at all, let alone in twenty-four hours. When he gets to the most recent one—Mae Campbell from Hudson, New York—he pauses for a second, trying and failing not to be so delighted at the thought of her video. He's saved by a new email coming in. At the dinging sound, Alfie vaults off his bed and throws himself onto Hugo's, still in his sweaty clothes.

"What've we got?"

Hugo opens it to find a message from Margaret P. Campbell of Naples, Florida, who is eighty-four years old.

In the picture she included, she's on a roller coaster, her halo of stark-white hair whipped back by the wind. She's smiling a huge, gold-capped smile.

"This is definitely the one," Hugo says, only half joking.

"Only you," Alfie says, "would invite an eighty-four-year-old woman on holiday with you."

"It's not a holiday," Hugo says. "It's a business arrangement. They get a ticket, and I get a train ride. Besides, she doesn't look like the type to nick my wallet. Or my identity."

Alfie wrinkles his nose. "What kind of snacks do you reckon she'll bring? Prunes?"

"Stop being such an ageist," Hugo says, shoving his brother until he tips off the bed and onto the floor with a yelp. Alfie remains sprawled there like that, staring at the ceiling, while Hugo reads the rest of Margaret P. Campbell's email:

> When I was a girl, I took the train from Florida to South
> Carolina with my father, and ever since then, I've wanted
> to see the rest of the country by rail. But there was
> school and then a job and kids and family, and then
> my husband died, and my own health was poor, and it
> seemed like I must be too old for such a thing. But then
> my granddaughter sent me your letter, and even though I
> know she probably meant it as a joke, I can't stop thinking
> about it. Because why not, right? And maybe more
> importantly, why not now?

Why indeed, Hugo thinks.

Alfie's voice drifts up from the floor, where he's lying on his back, staring at the crack in the ceiling that they long ago decided was shaped like a whale. "Did you mean what you said the other night?" he asks. "About wanting some space next year?"

Hugo is quiet for a long time. "Yes," he says eventually.

"I didn't know," Alfie says, propping himself up on his elbows.

"You don't ever feel that way?" Hugo asks, twisting in the chair to face him.

Alfie considers this. "I suppose I'd prefer to have my own room, but otherwise I like having you all around. Most of the time."

"I do too," Hugo says. "It's not that. It's just . . . we never got a choice, did we? This is the time when most people move away from home and leave their families and start something new. But we've always known we're going to Surrey together. We never really had any other options."

"Right, because it's free."

"Not really. You know there are strings attached."

"If the problem," Alfie says, his eyes gleaming, "is that you're worried about looking like shite next to me at the photo shoot, I'm sure you can stand next to Oscar instead."

Hugo rolls his eyes. "Did you even read that schedule they sent? They've got us doing seven interviews the first weekend. Is that really how you want to start uni?"

"You mean with a live stream of us moving into the halls of residence?" Alfie says with a grin. "I quite like the idea, actually. Gives me a chance to show off how much I can lift."

"Well, I'd rather not be a spectacle, if it's all the same."

"It's not all the same," Alfie says, more serious now. "It's part of the deal. You know that."

"It's like we're circus animals."

"Circus animals who get to go to uni for free."

"I know," Hugo says with a sigh. "And I realize how lucky that makes us. But haven't you ever thought about what you'd do if things were different?"

"Sure," Alfie says. "I'd be starting fly half for England."

"Seriously."

"Seriously? I don't know. What about you?"

The question needles at something in Hugo. "I don't know either," he admits. "Which is why I need to take this trip."

"To figure out what's next?"

"No, the opposite," Hugo says. "Because I already *know* what's next."

"And you want to see what it's like to be on your own," Alfie says, then grins. "Well, I can tell you this much: I won't miss your snoring."

Hugo tosses a pen at him, but Alfie dodges it. They're both silent for a moment, and Hugo gives his chair a spin. When it stops again, he looks down at his brother.

"Do you think they hate me?"

"A bit," Alfie says, picking at a patch of mud on his knee. "So do I, for the record."

Hugo rubs his eyes, deflated. "I'm sorry. I really am.

But you do realize it's not actually about—"

"I know," Alfie says. "And they do too. It'll be fine. We'll get over it eventually."

"Even George?"

"Well," he says, "maybe not George."

"Brilliant," Hugo says with a groan.

"Oh, hey!" Alfie scrambles to his feet, walking over to open his sock drawer. He pulls out a small package wrapped in newspaper. "I think I was supposed to wait on this, but . . . sod it."

Hugo takes the package and unwraps it carefully. Inside is a brown leather passport case. He looks up at Alfie in surprise, his chest flooding with warmth again.

"Mum wanted to get you neon orange so you wouldn't lose it, but then Dad pointed out that would make it easier for someone else to find it, too, and then Poppy picked out this horrid red one that you'd have been embarrassed to carry around, and then George suggested camo—camo! like you're going off to war!—and Oscar wanted to get you a flask instead, which would've been cool but sort of beside the point, and then I found this one, and Isla suggested getting your initials put on"—Hugo opens the flap to see a small *HTW* pressed into the soft leather—"and it seemed like we were in business. Do you like it?"

Hugo runs his fingers across the smooth surface. "I love it," he says, and there's enough emotion in his voice that they both know what he really means, which is this: *I love all of you.*

Mae

Exactly one week after receiving the email from Hugo W. telling her how much he enjoyed her video but explaining that he hadn't chosen her for the train trip, Mae gets another message with the subject line "Funny story."

Dear Mae,

I feel a bit sheepish writing to you again, but it turns out my travel companion needs to have bunion surgery next week, which means I've found myself in need of a Margaret Campbell who might still be up for an adventure (and who doesn't have bunions). I know it's poor form to ask this of you now, when the trip is only a week away

and I already passed you over once. But I sincerely
loved your video, so I hope you'll consider it.

Cheers,

Hugo

Here we go, she thinks, jangly with excitement. Though
this, of course, is immediately followed by a list of all the
reasons this probably isn't the best idea: it's impulsive and
impractical and possibly unsafe; she has no interest in being
anyone's second choice; her dads would never let her travel
cross-country with a stranger; and mostly—mostly—what
kind of person would actually do this sort of thing?

But then she thinks of what Pop said about how she
has more living to do, and what Garrett said about making
great art, and the way this town has always felt like a pair
of jeans that's a size too small, and she realizes she's exactly
that kind of person.

She leans back in her desk chair and sees a small blue car
parked in the driveway. Confused, she hurries downstairs
and out the front door, bounding over to where Priyanka
is sitting in the driver's seat, the engine idling. Her long
dark hair is pulled into a low ponytail, and she's wearing
the Cornell sweatshirt that her parents gave her when she
found out she got in. She looks up in surprise when Mae
appears at the window.

"I thought we were meeting in town," Mae says, and
Priyanka adjusts her grip on the wheel.

"We are."

Mae frowns. "Then why are you picking me up?"

"I'm not," Priyanka says, looking a little sheepish. "I just wanted to do this one last time."

"Do what?"

"I don't know. Drive from my house to your house. Wait in your driveway because you're always late. I mean, how many times have we done this?"

"I'm not *always* late," Mae says with mock indignation. "But yeah. A lot."

"And this is the last time."

"It's not the last time ever. We'll be back at Thanksgiving."

"I know," Priyanka says. "But still."

"Well, as long as you're here, you may as well give me a ride." Mae grins as she climbs into the car. "Lucky for you, that means you'll have to drop me off, too, so you don't have to say a tearful goodbye to my driveway just yet."

Priyanka rolls her eyes. "How can you be so entirely unemotional about all this?"

"I'm sad to be saying goodbye to you," Mae tells her. "But I'm pretty sure I'll survive without seeing my garage door for a few months."

At the pizza place, they sit at their usual table. Just after they order, Priyanka's phone buzzes, and even before she checks to see who it is, her whole face lights up.

"Alex?" Mae asks, taking a sip from her straw.

Priyanka nods, still smiling. Her boyfriend left last week for a pre-orientation camping trip and hasn't had much cell service. "Only a couple more days till he's out of the woods."

"I can't believe you guys are actually attempting to do this."

"What?"

"Stay together."

Priyanka looks up from her phone with a puzzled expression. "Why wouldn't we?"

"Because you're going to be in two different states for the next four years."

"Yeah, but I love him," she says, as if it's just that simple. "And he loves me."

Mae sips her soda loudly while Priyanka finishes her conversation with Alex. It's not until the waiter brings their pizza—half veggie, half pepperoni—that she sets the phone down and they watch the steam rise off the cheese.

"Love is like this pizza," Mae says, sweeping her hand over the table. "It's warm and gooey and delicious, but it doesn't last."

Priyanka laughs. "Are we talking about Garrett now?"

"I wasn't in love with Garrett," she says. "That was just fun."

"Did he know that?"

Mae takes a defiant bite of her slice, which is still too hot. She winces and downs half a glass of water in one go. Priyanka shakes her head.

"If you weren't so careful—"

"I'm not *careful*," Mae says, practically spitting the word.

Priyanka looks like she wants to laugh, but she manages to bite it back. "I don't mean in life," she says more gently. "I mean with your heart."

Mae—who was all set to argue—is stopped short by this.

"You're the least guarded person I know," Priyanka continues, pressing forward. "To a fault, sometimes. But when it really counts, you play it safe. The minute any guy starts to fall for you, there's a Mae-shaped hole in the wall."

"That's not true."

"It is," Priyanka insists, gesturing at the pizza. "You're afraid of the warm, gooey parts. You think I'm nuts for trying to stay together with Alex, but I'd rather take a chance and end up with someone I love than protect myself and end up—"

Mae scowls. "Why are we even talking about this?"

"Because," Priyanka says, more softly now, "sometimes I think you're more interested in making movies than living your life. Not everything is supposed to be material. It's like you go out into the world with a camera and leave your heart behind on a shelf. But if you don't ever truly risk anything—"

"I do," Mae says quickly, trying not to show how stung she is. "In fact, I was going to tell you—"

"No," Priyanka says, "I do *not* mean that kind of risk."

"What? You don't even know what I was going to say—"

"Mae," she says, already exasperated. "Only you would hear that and take away that you should sign up to be murdered by some guy on a train."

"You're overreacting."

"I sent that post as a joke, not a suggestion. Honestly, tell me you're not actually thinking of going."

"I'm not actually thinking of going."

"Really?"

"No, not really," she says with a grin. "Come on. It would be amazing."

Priyanka shakes her head. "I literally *just* watched this show where a girl gets stalked by someone on a train, and—"

"You watch too much TV."

"Well, you watch too many movies."

Mae laughs. "So what happened in the show?"

"It was all a big mix-up," Priyanka says, picking up a slice of pizza. "The guy turned out to be great and they fell in love and lived happily ever after."

"Really?"

"*No*," she says. "She got murdered. What do you think?"

After lunch, Priyanka drives Mae home, steering her car into that familiar circle at the top of the driveway. For a moment, they just sit there staring at the blank face of the garage.

"Okay, you're right," Mae says, tipping her head back against the seat. "Now I'm kind of sad."

Priyanka laughs. "See?"

"We'll talk all the time, right?"

"Definitely."

"Promise you'll call me more than you call Alex?"

"Only if you promise you won't get on that train."

"Let's just agree to play it all by ear," Mae says cheerfully. As she starts to unbuckle her seat belt, Priyanka puts a hand on her elbow.

"Listen," she says, her brown eyes searching Mae's. "I don't want you going off to college thinking that love is like a pizza."

"Would it be better if I thought it was like a calzone?"

Priyanka ignores this. "Love is . . . I don't know. Something bigger than that. It's like the sun."

"In that you can get burnt by it?"

"No," she says wearily, but already her eyes have that starry quality they get whenever she's thinking of Alex. "In that it makes everything brighter and happier. And it warms you from the inside out."

"So does pizza," Mae says, and this time Priyanka swats at her.

"You know what I'm saying. Just promise me you'll be open to the possibilities."

Without quite meaning to, Mae finds herself thinking of the video she sent to Hugo W., and how easy it had been to answer his questions. She takes a deep breath and nods. "I promise."

Priyanka seems satisfied by this. She reaches for the door handle and gets out of the car, and Mae does the same. They hurry around the front to give each other a hug.

"I love you like a pizza," Priyanka whispers in her ear, and Mae laughs.

"Safe travels."

Priyanka steps back and gives her a long look. "You too," she says finally.

Up until that moment, Mae wasn't completely sure. But right then, she realizes they both know exactly what she's going to do.

Afterward, she walks around the side of the house and finds Nana out on the porch, her favorite spot to nap these days. Her eyes flicker open as Mae jogs up the old wooden steps.

"And then there were two," Nana says with a melodramatic sigh. "I can't believe Priyanka busted out of here before us."

Mae laughs. "Won't be long now."

"Five days," she says. "But who's counting?"

They tried to persuade Nana to stay permanently, arguing that the country would be more relaxing for her. But she made it clear she has no interest in relaxing, and now that she's got a clean bill of health, she insists on moving back to her own apartment in the city.

"You know what I *will* miss about living here?"

"Giving my dads a hard time?"

Nana laughs. "No."

"The burnt coffee?"

"No."

"What, then?"

"You," she says, and Mae smiles.

Out on the street, a red car that looks just like Garrett's comes spinning around the corner, and for a second, Mae thinks maybe it's him. But of course he's already gone.

As if she can see right into Mae's head, Nana says, "You doing okay with everything?"

This strikes Mae as funny, coming from someone who recently went through four straight weeks of induction chemotherapy for acute myeloid leukemia. But she doesn't say so. "Yeah," she says instead. "I'm doing fine."

"You know, the only way to get over a broken heart is to find someone new."

"This isn't a broken heart, Nana. Honestly, I'm not even sure it's bruised." She thinks about what Priyanka said, imagining her heart packed carefully away, a tiny fence around it. Then she glances sideways at her grandmother. "Have you ever been on a train trip? Not the train to the city, but something longer."

Nana is quiet, but her eyes have a faraway look. "I was only a little older than you," she says with a wisp of a smile. "Maybe nineteen or twenty. A friend and I took a train to New Orleans for Mardi Gras. She had some family down there, so we went on a lark. That first morning, I met a boy in uniform, and he bought me a cup of tea. My friend barely saw me for the rest of the trip."

Mae sits forward. "So what happened?"

"What do you mean what happened? We talked. We flirted. We kissed."

"You did?"

"Of course we did," Nana says impatiently. "We were in love."

"People don't fall in love that quickly," Mae says, thinking this sounds suspiciously like one of the old romantic movies her grandmother loves so much.

But Nana is adamant. "They can. And we did. We spent the whole weekend together, dancing and eating and listening to jazz. We were practically giddy. Couldn't keep our hands off each other and couldn't stop—"

Mae hurries her along, eager to move past this description. "And then what?"

"Then we said goodbye."

"But if you were in love . . . ?"

"He was on leave from an army base in Texas. I had a life in New York City. It wasn't meant to be." She shrugs. "Love isn't magic. It doesn't transcend time and space. It doesn't fix anything. It's just love."

"But—"

"I was in love many times before I met your grandfather," she says. "Some of them lasted a long time; some of them didn't. The trick is not to worry about it. If you spend too much time thinking about when it will disappear, you'll miss the whole thing."

"So what happened to him?" Mae asks, suddenly impatient.

"He was killed in Vietnam. But we kept writing postcards until the day he died."

Mae is quiet, trying to decide if this is memory or imagination. It sounds like it could be true, but so do most of the stories her grandmother has told them over the years. Nana, too, is silent for a while, thinking about her soldier, perhaps, or lost in the movies that take place in her head. After a moment, she sets her mug on the table between them and turns to Mae. "So," she says, "tell me more about this train ride."

"What train ride?"

"The one you're deciding whether or not to take."

Mae looks at Nana in surprise. And then the story comes spilling out: the twinge she felt when she saw that post, and the video she sent zipping across the ocean; the way she felt when she watched her film again, like she was stuck, like she couldn't figure out how to peer around the edges of her own life, and how it smarted when Garrett said the word *impersonal*; the message from Hugo W. and the questions he asked, which are still sliding around in her head like pinballs, even days later. When she's done, Nana simply nods.

"Your fathers will never go for it," she says, and Mae's shoulders slump, because she knows this too. But then, to her surprise, Nana winks at her. "Which isn't a reason not to do it."

Mae tries to hide her smile, but she can't. "Yeah?"

"Yeah," says Nana, leaning forward. "You said your new roommate is from Brooklyn, right?"

Which is how, later that night, Mae comes to be sitting across from her dads at the diner—which is appropriately shaped like an old train car—and telling them that she and her future roommate, Piper, have hatched a plan to take a train to California together.

"A train?" Dad asks, lowering his BLT with a look of horror. "You do know it's faster to fly?"

"I do," she says. "Yes. But apparently she was gonna go

with her mom, and then something came up, and she had already bought the tickets, so she needs a travel buddy."

"You're going to be living together in a shoebox for the next nine months," Pop says. "Are you sure you want to start it all a week early?"

"She's bound to find out about the snoring eventually," Dad says, and Mae gives him a withering look. "But what if she's terrible?"

"What if she's great?" Mae shrugs. "Either way, it would be an experience. You're the ones who told me I've got some more living to do."

"We meant college," Dad says. "Not riding the rails like a hobo. Will you be on the train the whole time? Like, you'll sleep there and everything?" He glances sideways at Pop. "My back hurts just thinking about it."

"They booked some sort of package where you get a few nights in hotels, too, so we'll be able to see some cities along the way." She shifts uncomfortably, dropping her eyes to her grilled cheese. She's never lied to them about something this big. But she needs to do this, and she knows they'll never go for it otherwise. "It'll be fun."

"You sure you want to leave home a week early?" Pop asks, and she can practically feel the disappointment radiating off him.

Mae's eyes drift to the window. The sun is low in the sky, so that everything is golden, like it's already a memory, and the old buildings with their peeling paint make the town seem charming rather than stifling, cozy instead of just plain small.

"Yes," she says quietly, turning back to her dads. Their arms are twined now, and she knows they're holding hands underneath the table, which only makes her heart hurt more. "That doesn't mean I'm not going to miss you guys like crazy. But Nana will be back in the city by then, and we've got to say goodbye at some point anyway, and honestly, it just feels like this is one of those times where the right answer is yes."

Her dads exchange a look.

"You'll stick together the whole time?" Pop asks. "Day and night? You'll look out for each other?"

Mae swallows hard. "Yes."

"And if she turns out to be either a terrible person or a terrible influence," Dad says, "you'll use your good judgment?"

"Yes," Mae says, hiding a smile.

"And you'll check in with us three times a day?" Pop asks.

"Four," Dad says. "No, five."

"Yes, of course."

Pop gives her a long look. "And you'll stop obsessing over your film?"

She hesitates. "No promises."

"How about thinking of starting a new one?"

"Definitely."

"Then, I suppose," he says with a satisfied nod, "that the right answer is yes."

Hugo

Hugo stands in the middle of Penn Station, which is not only the very worst rail station he's ever been in but also quite possibly the very worst place, full stop. It's dark and gray and dingy, filled with too many people and too much noise.

A police dog stops to sniff his rucksack, and when Hugo reaches to pet it, the officer snaps at him. "Watch it," he says, and Hugo shrinks back, keenly aware that he's in America now, and for all the warnings his mum gave him about keeping track of his belongings, it's the ones his dad has given him over the years—about the extra layer of caution required to exist in the world when you're half black—that are running through his head in this crowded station.

It doesn't seem like the most auspicious beginning to the trip.

There's still no sign of Mae. Hugo leans his rucksack against the wall, careful to keep it close. It would be just like him to have it stolen even before he gets on the train. So far, he's managed not to get lost or mugged or anything worse. It's been only twenty-four hours, but it still feels like something of a victory.

Without either of the Margaret Campbells, he couldn't get into the hotel that had been booked for them last night. Instead he found a grimy chain on the edge of Times Square, where he could hear people arguing through the paper-thin walls. It didn't matter, though. Hugo couldn't remember the last time he'd had a room to himself, and he was too excited to sleep.

He woke early, jet lagged and ready to follow the itinerary Margaret had mapped out for them. But without her, he realized, he could do whatever he wanted, and that thought sparked a strange sort of joy in him. He was alone in a foreign country, no parents or siblings or girlfriend; in fact, there wasn't a single soul who knew where he was at this exact moment.

He was completely and entirely free.

Instead of the Met, he went to the High Line. Instead of the fancy restaurant Margaret had booked, he ate a hot dog from one of those little carts with the umbrellas. Later he went for a pint at an old alehouse in the West Village but was promptly declined.

"Does it count if I'm English?" he asked hopefully.

"Does this look like England to you?" asked the scowling bartender, and that was the thing: it didn't. It was all wonderfully, amazingly, heart-thuddingly new. And he loved it. All of it. Even the pigeons.

Now a text pops up from his mum: *You still in one piece?*

Hugo sighs. As if she can hear this, another one appears: *I'm only asking. No tattoos or anything?*

Hugo: No tattoos. But I did get my nose pierced last night.
Mum: Hugo!
Hugo: I'm just winding you up. Stop worrying.
Mum: You'll take a picture of the ocean for me, won't you?
Hugo: Too late. I'm about to head west.
Mum: I meant the Pacific. I've always wanted to see it.

The gate for their train is announced, and the crowd around him begins to swirl again. Hugo squints up at the giant board, an alphabet soup of times and destinations.

Hugo: Mum, I've got to go. Train is here. Love you.
Mum: Love you too.
Hugo: And don't worry, I've got my passport.
Mum: I wasn't going to say a word.

He shoves his mobile back into his pocket and looks around for Mae, trying to call up the image from the video, but he doesn't see her anywhere. It's now ten past three, which means she's officially late. The train is due to leave in exactly thirteen minutes, and he stands on his tiptoes and scans the station again. He's so busy looking around that it takes him a second to realize she's suddenly there, standing a few feet away from him.

He blinks at her, startled. She's wearing a black cotton dress with a jean jacket, her hair pulled back into a messy ponytail. Her red trainers are scuffed and worn, and on her back there's a green rucksack that looks about as tall as she is.

"Hugo," she says, though it's not exactly a question.

After she wrote back to his second email, he sent her a photo of himself so that she'd know he wasn't some weirdo from the internet. (Although maybe he was now? It was hard to be sure.) For a while, he'd avoided giving his surname, because he wasn't that keen on her stumbling across the many articles about his family, not to mention his mum's blog, a treasure trove of embarrassing anecdotes. He wanted to start this trip as Hugo Wilkinson, not as one of the Surrey Six.

But as their volley of messages continued, she pressed him on this, and he didn't blame her. If one of his sisters was mad enough to go on a trip with a stranger she'd met on the internet, he'd want her to find out every scrap of information she could. Still, he'd been bracing himself for the kind of thunderstruck reaction he always gets when people discover he's a sextuplet. But from Mae, there was nothing. To his relief, her next reply was just a request for the full itinerary.

Even so, he knows she must've done her homework on him. So it surprises him, at first, the way she's staring, like she's trying to decide whether or not it's him. But then he realizes it's not that at all. It's more like she's measuring something about him, and he stands up a little straighter as he waits for her verdict.

Finally, she takes a few steps toward him. "Hi."

He smiles reflexively, still slightly flustered by the directness of her gaze. She's a good foot shorter than him, but there's a certainty that makes her seem anything but small.

"Hi," he says.

"I'm Mae." She reaches out to shake his hand. It's an oddly formal gesture, but it sets a definite tone: they are partners in this. "Sorry I'm late."

"No, it's fine. I'm just so glad you made it."

"Me too," she says, and there's laughter in her eyes. "Guess it's lucky I don't have any bunions."

"I guess so," he says, feeling his cheeks flush, still a little guilty about rejecting and then inviting her. "So did you drive down or take the . . ."

He makes a gesture toward the giant board hanging in the middle of the station, and she looks amused.

"My parents drove me."

"Oh," Hugo says, looking around. "Are they . . . ?"

"No, they had to take my grandmother to her apartment. It's sort of a long story. But we already said our goodbyes and everything."

"Right, since you're . . ."

"Going straight to school at the end of this, yeah. I'm a light packer," she adds when she sees him glance at her bag; then she cracks a grin. "Just kidding. We shipped the rest."

Above them, a final boarding announcement for the

Lake Shore Limited comes over the loudspeakers, and Hugo hooks his thumbs beneath the straps of his rucksack.

"Well," he says with a smile, "I suppose this is it."

She smiles back, but there's something steely about it, and he can almost see it then, the way this means something to her too. It isn't simply a lark or a freebie or an adventure. It's something bigger. And from nowhere, the thought pops into his head: *This is going to be okay.*

Another announcement comes over the speakers, more urgent this time, and it stirs him to action. "Ready?" he murmurs as he adjusts his pack, but when he looks up again, she's several steps away, moving through the crowds toward the platform.

"Ready," she says over her shoulder, but he can barely hear her.

She's already on her way.

Mae

The minute they step onto the train, Mae feels it like a bubble in her chest: a sense of exhilaration so light and airy that she suspects she could float all the way to California.

It doesn't matter that she lied to her dads. Or that her grandmother can't keep a secret. It doesn't even matter that her strategy of regarding Hugo as nothing more than a human train ticket has already been complicated by the very fact of him standing beside her.

She'd looked him up, of course. She wasn't an idiot.

But whatever she'd been expecting, it wasn't what she found: a disarmingly good-looking Brit who was biracial and extremely tall and apparently somewhat famous for being a sextuplet, of all things. As she sifted through the articles and blog posts and family photos, Mae was surprised—and a little alarmed—by how excited she was to meet him, even though she already knew what this was. She needed a ticket. And he needed a girl named Margaret Campbell. That's all.

But now, here he is, no longer pixilated or imaginary, no longer just an email address and a crazy idea. Instead, he's a person with an adorable accent and a kind smile, who has to bend a little to get through the door of the train as he climbs aboard.

An attendant named Ludovic leads them down a narrow hallway toward their compartment. "We only have a couple of dinner seatings still available, so I suggest you make a reservation now." He checks his notebook. "Six-thirty or nine?"

Hugo and Mae exchange a look.

"Six-thirty is great," Mae says to Ludovic, who marks the time down.

When they reach their compartment, they all three form a knot around the door. Mae's first instinct is to laugh. Beneath the large window, two blue-cushioned seats face each other, so close it's hard to imagine how their legs will fit in the space between. Around them are various shelves and compartments and hooks, but that's about it. The whole thing is no bigger than a coat closet.

Beside her, Hugo is frowning. "I don't get it."

"What?" Ludovic asks.

"Where are the beds?"

"The seats fold down," he says, reaching up to a slanted board above the window and tugging on the silver handle. It falls open to reveal the top bunk, which is maybe ten inches from the ceiling and comes with what looks like a cross between a net and a seat belt.

"What's this?" Mae asks, pointing to the straps.

"I think it's so you don't fall out," Hugo says. She must look stricken by this, because he's quick to add, "Don't worry. I'll take the top."

She peers up at him incredulously, the long legs and lanky torso, the way his dark hair is nearly brushing the ceiling.

"I'll manage," he says good-naturedly. "I'm half pretzel."

"Well," says Ludovic, "I hope the other half is sardine."

And then, without another word, he turns and walks back down the hall, leaving them at the door of their tiny room.

"A bit cozy, isn't it?" Hugo says, and then his face flashes with panic. "I only meant cozy like small, not like—"

"It's okay," Mae says, charmed by his earnestness. "As long as you're not a serial killer, we'll be totally fine."

"I'm not," he says. "I swear. Though I suppose that's what a serial killer would say too."

She smiles at him. "I guess I'll just have to trust you," she says, stepping inside and dropping into one of the seats. They're still stopped beneath Penn Station, so the enormous window beside her is mostly dark, and she can see Hugo's reflection in the doorway. "You can sit, too, you know."

"I was just thinking that I hadn't thought to ask if *you're* a serial killer," he says, but he's already taking the seat opposite her. His legs are so long that their knees brush against each other, and Mae feels it like a bolt of electricity.

"I wouldn't say *serial*," she says, and he looks slightly startled. "Just kidding. The only thing I've ever killed is a spider."

He grins at her. "Whenever I find one, I take it outside in a cup."

"You do not," she says, but even as she does, she's thinking that it's probably true. How odd it is to have known someone for all of twenty minutes and still feel so sure of this.

"What if I were to kill it and then its friends and family came back for revenge?" he says very seriously. "I can't take that sort of risk."

She laughs. Beneath them the train stirs, a low rumble that vibrates up through their feet. Their eyes meet, and there's a hint of a smile in Hugo's, an excitement that matches her own.

"Last chance," she says, and he looks confused.

"For what?"

"Second thoughts."

"None for me," he says. "You?"

"Nope. Let's do this."

There's a hiss and a squeal, and then the blackness out the window becomes blurrier as they lurch away from the platform, moving deeper into the system of tunnels that wind their way beneath the city. It's a strange, disjointed feeling, to be surrounded by nothing, hurtling through a darkness so deep that all they can see is their own ghostly reflections. But then, all at once, the light comes slicing in, and they blink as the train emerges into the sun-drenched afternoon.

Mae's phone buzzes, and when she digs it out of her pocket, she sees that there's a message from Priyanka: *Are you on the train yet? How's it going so far? Does he seem shady? Are you okay? If you're okay, give me a sign . . . like maybe an O and a K.*

Smiling, she types the two letters, and another message pops up: *Good. Phew. Call me later. I want to hear everything.*

"You know, if you need to ring anyone . . ." Hugo says, nodding at the phone. "I did promise you'd have your own space, so I'm happy to nip over to the café."

"No," Mae says quickly. "It's fine. Just my best friend checking to make sure I haven't been murdered yet."

He laughs. "Fair enough."

Out the window, flashes of graffiti brighten the dull grays of the city. When Mae turns back to Hugo, he's pulling out a book, and it occurs to her that maybe he only asked if she wanted space because *he* does. After all, it's not like this is some vacation they're taking together. He was supposed to be here with his girlfriend, and Mae has only come along to do what she's already done: stand in line at the station and show her driver's license and present the ticket with another Margaret Campbell's name on it.

Now that part is over, and maybe that's all it was supposed to be.

She stands so suddenly that Hugo looks at her with alarm. "Actually, I think maybe I will go make a call."

"Oh." He blinks at her. "I was just—"

"In case you need a little space—"

"No," he says, flipping the book around so she can see that it's a collection of facts about the United States. "I was just going to—"

"It's okay, I should probably try to do a little work anyway."

"Work?"

"Yeah, I mean . . . not *work* work. Just film stuff."

"Oh, brilliant."

"Thanks. I might . . ." Hugo's green-brown eyes follow her as she spins in the small space, reaching for her camera and then her computer too. "It's only a couple of hours till dinner, so I'll probably just hang out in the café, as long as you don't mind—"

He shrugs. "I don't mind at all."

She pauses for a second, and they stare at each other. Her bag is already dangling from her shoulder, and her phone is buzzing in her pocket again.

"You sure?" she says at the exact same time he does.

They both laugh.

"Yeah," Mae says. "It'll be good to do some brainstorming on my own."

"And I live in a house with seven other people, so I can probably cope with some time to myself," he says, sitting back and opening his book. But just before she walks out, he looks up again. "Hey, be sure to tell her about the spiders, yeah?"

Mae pauses. "What?"

"Your friend. Don't forget to tell her I wouldn't even harm a spider."

"I will," she says with a smile.

Outside the compartment, she begins to work her way down the length of the train, feeling like a pinball as she's jostled from side to side. The halls are lined with rooms, some small like theirs, others much bigger, with private bathrooms and sinks and seats lined up to form couches. She can see the people inside leafing through books and examining maps and staring at their phones, their socked feet propped up on the seats, and she thinks of Hugo alone in their compartment, his legs stretched out in the empty space where she's meant to be.

When she reaches the café, she buys a cup of coffee and sits at one of the picnic-style tables. There's an old man reading a newspaper behind her and an Amish couple eating a packed lunch nearby, but otherwise it's empty.

Just as she's about to call Priyanka, she notices a new text.

Nana: Well? Have you fallen in love yet?

Mae: No!

Nana: Tell him he has lovely eyes. That works every time.

Mae: There's no way I'm doing that. How does it feel to be home?

Nana: Wonderful, but your dads won't leave. I told them I'm fine and they should go, but it was like swatting a couple of puppies on the nose. Now I think they're staying the night.

Mae: Roommates for life!

Nana: So it would seem.

Mae: I'll check in again tomorrow.

Nana: Sounds good. But don't forget what I said.

Mae: What?

Nana: Tell him he has lovely eyes. Trust me on this one.

Mae: What if he doesn't?

Nana: Does he?

Mae: That's really not the point.

Still, when she puts the phone down, Mae finds herself thinking about Hugo's eyes, the peculiar mix of brown and green, and the way they were shining when he first saw her. To distract herself, she tries calling Priyanka, but she must be in class now because it goes straight to voice mail. Instead Mae opens her computer and stares at a blank white page for a while, hoping an idea for a new film might magically appear. But when that doesn't work, she grabs her book—a technical guide to filmmaking that's required reading for film majors, which she's not, but that she wants to read in case she manages to transfer early—and passes the time that way.

Later, as the sun dips lower in the sky, getting tangled in the tops of the trees, the train begins to slow for the first time. Mae looks up from her book, spotting landmarks that are familiar from her many trips to the city: the bend in the river where the geese always gather, the old boathouse with crumbling blue paint, the church with the narrow steeple. Just beyond it, she can see the very top of a redbrick building, the one next door to her dad's gallery, and the rows of telephone poles that run along their street.

She has no right to be homesick. Not yet. But she feels a tug of emotion at the sight of it all, and even though nobody is home right now—the three people she cares about most are still in the city—the proximity to the old yellow house makes her heart ache.

A few people spill out of the train doors when it comes to a stop, and others start to climb on, hefting their suitcases aboard with the help of attendants. Mae looks out the other window at the Hudson, which has turned flat and gray, mirroring the sky.

It occurs to her that she's never taken the train beyond this point before, not in the direction they're going. She has no idea how much longer they'll hug the river, at what point the houses will give way to farms, what the landscape will look like as they move deeper into the western part of the state. And she realizes she's excited to find out.

The train begins to move again, and she leans her forehead against the window, taking one last look at the town, the word *home* pounding in her ears like a heartbeat as it disappears from view.

Hugo

Hugo, alone. He leans forward until his nose touches the window, and watches the river slip by. All afternoon it's continued to change, shifting from blue to gray to brown. Sometimes it reminds him of the river Wey back home, where he and Alfie and Poppy and George and Oscar and Isla used to play the stick game when they were little or else paddle around in their wellies, coming home speckled with mud. The thought tugs at him, a hook to the heart, but then he blinks again and the river is something entirely new: wide and white-tipped and glittering beneath a sun too bright even for the England of his memories.

He supposes all rivers must look somewhat alike.

Their compartment is quiet, tucked in a corner toward the end of the train, so there aren't too many people walking by. At one end of the car, there are two small bathrooms and a shower that Hugo hasn't brought himself to peek at yet. A pile of luggage is sloped on the racks near the metal doors. But that's about it.

At first he'd been delighted to have it all to himself, this little corner of the train, and he'd settled inside all that silence and space like it was a woolly blanket. There was something so peaceful about it: nobody telling him to take his feet off the seat or asking him for help with their homework or nattering on while he tried to read.

But soon the quiet starts to feel loud, and he's unable to shake the feeling that something is missing. Maybe it's that Margaret was supposed to be here, the two of them wedged together on a single seat, the hours flying by as fast as the telephone poles. Or maybe he's just not used to being alone; maybe that's something you need to practice, like playing football or the violin.

He picks up the phone and sends a text to the group.

Hugo: Hi from New York.

Poppy: Hi from the kitchen.

Alfie: Hi from the loo.

Isla: Gross.

Oscar: Hurry up. I need to get in there.

George: How's the train?

Alfie: How's the girl?

Hugo: Nice.

Poppy: The train or the girl?

Hugo: Both.

George: Do you miss us yet?

Hugo: At least two or three of you.

There's a knock at the door, and then Ludovic pops his head in.

Hugo pulls his socked feet off the opposite seat. "Hello," he says so brightly that the attendant looks a little startled.

"Hello," Ludovic says, examining his notepad. "So we'll need two sets of sheets in here, yes? What time do you want me to make up the beds?"

"Uh," Hugo says, wishing he'd thought to ask Mae before she left. "I'm not sure. What time do you reckon?"

"A lot of people have requested nine," Ludovic says with a shrug, "but a lot of people are also very old. How about ten?"

"Sure," he says, but once Ludovic is gone, Hugo glances at his watch and realizes that ten o'clock is still hours away. He yawns and presses his cheek to the window, still knackered from all the travel and excitement and jet lag. The rumble of the train is enough to make his eyes flutter shut, and he wakes later to an announcement about dinner.

"All passengers for the six-thirty dinner seating, please make your way to the dining car. That's six-thirty, folks."

Hugo stands and examines what he's wearing: worn jeans and a fraying yellow shirt and a thin pair of flip-flops. He wonders if he looks smart enough, suddenly picturing the scene with all the tuxes in *Titanic*, which is probably not the best image to call to mind. But it's not as if he has anything much nicer to wear, so he pulls a jumper on over

84

his shirt and heads off, swaying as he makes his way down toward the dining car.

When he reaches it, there's a backlog of people waiting to be seated, and so he stands in the metal section that joins two of the cars, the plates sliding beneath his feet like the base of a Tilt-A-Whirl. He looks around for Mae and spots her at the other end—past all the waiters and white tablecloths and other diners, the bread baskets and silverware and menus—waiting in the same spot, and she gives him a smile.

They've spent only twenty minutes together. Maybe thirty.

But still, there's already something familiar about her, standing there in the doorway with a book in her arms, and Hugo can't help wondering if maybe the thing he was missing earlier was her.

Mae

For the past few hours, Mae had watched a steady tide of people drifting into the café, ordering hot dogs and cookies and chips, trying not to spill their cans of beer as they tottered out again. Each time the door opened, she found herself looking up as if waiting for something, though she wasn't sure what.

It isn't until this very moment that she realizes maybe it was Hugo.

The waiter motions her over, and she picks her way through this strangest and narrowest of restaurants, giving Hugo a nod as they meet in the aisle.

"Hi," she says, and he grins at her.

"Hi."

They're seated at a table with an elderly white couple who are already poring over their menus. Hugo slides into the booth first, and Mae joins him, careful to leave a few inches of space between.

"Hello there," the woman says with a faint Southern drawl. "I'm Ida. And this is my husband, Roy."

Mae starts to introduce herself at the exact same moment that Hugo says his name. They exchange a glance, both a little flummoxed, but Ida just smiles at them.

"Where are you two from?"

Hugo says, "England," and Mae says, "Just up the road," the words once again crossing between them. Part of her wants to laugh and part of her wants to crawl under the table. It's like dancing with someone you don't know very well, and she feels like she should apologize for stepping on his toes.

"You two are either very much in sync," Roy says, "or very much out of sync."

"England and New York?" says Ida. "That's quite the long-distance relationship."

"Oh no," Mae says quickly. "We're not—"

"You know, Roy was in the navy when we first met, so we had to write letters between visits. But I suppose the world is a lot smaller now."

"Not *too* small," Hugo says with a smile. "Still takes a bit of time to cross it by train."

Their waiter appears, and Roy is ready for him. "I'll have a burger and an apple pie. I know what you're gonna say—you'll be back to take dessert orders later. But last time, they ran out of pie. So I'm not taking any chances. In fact, we should get slices all around."

The waiter seems to realize it's pointless to object.

Once they've all placed their orders, Hugo sits back in the booth. "So you're old pros at this train business, then?"

"Oh yeah," Roy says. "Ever since I retired, we've been going pretty much every summer. Right, hon? Different route each time. It's a great way to see the country."

"Is this your first trip?" Ida asks, and both Hugo and Mae nod. "You'll love it. Trains can be very romantic, you know."

Hugo—who has just taken a bite of a roll—starts to cough, and Mae tries not to laugh. "We're actually not—"

But Ida is already off again, talking about the various trips they've taken: the one where they stopped off at the Grand Canyon and the one where the train broke down outside Baltimore. At some point, Roy picks up the thread, and then Ida tags in again, and they go back and forth like that through the salad course and straight into dinner.

"We did one in Canada once too," Ida says when they're all done eating. She glances down at her empty plate. "The summer after our son died."

Mae lowers her glass, her throat suddenly tight. Across the table, Ida's eyes are watery, and they all go quiet for a moment, searching for the right thing to say. Then Roy reaches out and puts a big hand over his wife's smaller one.

"Remember the dinners on that trip?" he asks in a gruff voice. "We ate like royalty."

The wrinkles on Ida's face rearrange themselves as she breaks into a smile. "We really did," she says, looking at him so fondly that Mae almost feels like she and Hugo are intruding.

It's fully dark outside now, the night punctuated only by the glowing windows of farmhouses and the occasional town, and Mae can't help thinking about all the miles Ida and Roy have crossed, all the sights they must've seen.

The waiter arrives with apple pie for everyone, and Hugo closes his eyes after taking a bite. "I have to admit I was expecting the food to be rubbish, but this is brilliant."

Roy grins at him. "You know what they say."

"What?" Hugo asks, his face blank.

"Oh, uh . . . as American as apple pie."

Hugo frowns. "What is?"

"Well, anything American, I guess," Roy says a little less certainly. "But especially apple pie."

"Huh," Hugo says, stabbing at his pie. "I hadn't heard that one."

"How long have you been over here, sweetie?" asks Ida, and to Mae's amusement, Hugo looks at his watch.

"Just about thirty hours now."

Across the table, Ida and Roy both stare at him.

"Oh," says Roy. "So you two met across the pond, then?"

Mae looks at Hugo. And Hugo looks at Mae. He lifts an eyebrow, and she can see the hint of a smile at the corners of his mouth.

"No, actually," she says, her eyes still on him. She can feel a laugh rising in her throat because suddenly it all seems so ridiculous, the unusual circumstances of their meeting, and the very fact that they're here together right now, racing through the dark on a train in the middle of nowhere. "We met a few hours ago."

Hugo looks at his watch again. "Five, to be exact."

"Would've been five and a half," Mae says, "but I was a little late."

"So you two . . . just met?" Ida says, her brow furrowed like this is a puzzle she can't quite work out. "But I thought you were—"

"Nope," says Hugo.

"But it seemed like you were—"

"Not even a little bit," says Mae. "We're both just along for the ride."

Roy shakes his head. "Well. So then how *did* you meet?"

"Honestly, Roy," Hugo says, sitting back with a smile, "it's a bit of a long story."

"And kind of a weird one," Mae adds.

"Right?" says Hugo, shifting in the booth to face her. "I swear I've never done anything like this before."

"What? Spend a week on a train with a total stranger?" Mae laughs. "Me neither. Do you think that makes us equally crazy or equally awesome?"

"I'd prefer awesome," he says. "Though popular opinion back home was leaning towards crazy."

"I didn't even tell my parents. Well, I told them about the trip. But they think I'm with my soon-to-be roommate. If they knew it was some random guy, they'd kill me." She stops to think about this. "Actually, no. They'd probably kill *you*."

"Good to know," he says. "Hey, totally unrelated, but . . . how big is your dad?"

Mae laughs. "I have two of them."

"Even better," he says with a grin. "They can kill me twice."

"Did you tell your parents?"

"They're under the impression I'm traveling alone. But I did tell my siblings. Just in case you were planning on murdering me."

"And I told my grandmother. Just in case you turned out to be a serial killer. Which we've already established you're not."

Hugo laughs and then glances over at Ida and Roy, whom they've more or less forgotten. The older couple are staring back across the table, their mouths open and their faces a picture of confusion.

"Well," Hugo says, and when he turns back to Mae, his eyes are dancing. "Now Ida and Roy know too. Which makes it all feel rather official, doesn't it?"

Mae nods and lifts a forkful of apple pie. "Cheers."

"To what?" Hugo asks, lifting his own.

"To being awesome."

"And promising not to kill each other."

"To really long train rides."

"And partners in crime who are not actually criminals."

"To being young," Ida chimes in, "and adventurous."

"And to apple pie," Roy says, raising his fork too.

Hugo laughs as he and Mae clink forks. "I'll toast to that."

Hugo

As they're leaving, Mae doubles back and bends to say something to Ida. Hugo watches curiously from the doorway as the old woman's face splits into a grin. When Mae joins him again, she's smiling too.

"What was that about?"

"I asked if I could interview her."

He laughs, surprised. "What for?"

"Honestly? I'm not totally sure yet. But there's something interesting about her, isn't there?"

Back in their compartment, Mae switches on the yellow light above the seats, then reaches for the black bag she tucked on a small shelf. She unzips it and pulls out her camera with a dreamy look. Hugo sits down across from her, watching as she tinkers with the lens.

"You're really making a film about Ida?" he asks, incredulous.

"So it would seem."

"But . . . why?"

She looks up at him, her blue eyes glinting. "Do you ever have one of those ideas where you don't quite know what it is yet, but you have this feeling that something will come of it? That's what it was like talking to Ida tonight."

She holds the camera up and points it at him, closing one eye.

"Cheese?" Hugo says, and she laughs.

"This is the fun part," she tells him, lowering the camera again. "Ever since—well, I've been waiting for a spark for a while now. I didn't know if it would ever happen again."

"I don't suppose they grow on trees, do they?" he says, and when she looks up at him, he scratches his chin and adds, "Ideas, I mean."

"No, they definitely don't grow on trees. But it was never a problem for me before."

"Before what?"

"Before I got rejected from film school." She says it fast, like she's ripping off a bandage, but the next part—the next part comes out a whole lot softer. "For a film I was really proud of."

Hugo isn't sure what to say to this. He fumbles around for a question or a word of encouragement, but the silence stretches between them. Finally, he says, "What was it about?" which turns out to be the exact wrong question. To his surprise, her face immediately clouds over, and she unzips the case, carefully tucking the camera back inside.

"It doesn't matter anymore," she says. "Clearly, it didn't work."

"But do you have any idea why—"

"It's fine," she says abruptly. "I still got into USC—just not the film program. So my plan is to put in for a transfer. That's why I need to make another film."

"When do you need it by?"

She twists her mouth up to one side. "Well, technically, you can't apply till the end of sophomore year. But I figure it wouldn't hurt to try before then, especially if I can make something good enough. Something too good for them to ignore."

"Something like . . . Ida describing each of their four hundred and eighty-two meals on a train?"

This makes her smile. "Sometimes the best ideas come from the most unlikely sources."

"Maybe you should be interviewing Roy, then," he jokes.

Later, Ludovic arrives to make up their beds, and then they take turns standing in the hall so the other can change. Mae goes first, and when she returns to find Hugo in a gray T-shirt and pajama pants with rubber duckies on them, she can't help smiling.

But it's his turn to laugh a few minutes later, when he sees that hers are so similar. "Are those clouds or cotton balls?"

She looks indignant. "They're sheep."

"Right," he says as he climbs up to the top bunk, barely managing to wedge himself into the coffinlike space. "Is that so you can count them if you have trouble sleeping?"

"Something like that," she says, switching off the light.

For a while, they both lie there quietly in the dark. Every now and then, there are noises in the hall as other passengers make their way to the tiny loo. But Hugo can see how you might get used to sleeping like this; there's something oddly soothing about the gentle rocking of the train. He does his best to keep his eyes from fluttering shut, thinking of all the things Alfie has compared his snoring to over the years: a buzz saw, a trumpet, an elephant, even—ironically—a train. The idea is to wait for Mae to doze off first so he won't embarrass himself, but he can still hear her shifting around below.

He tries to turn on his side, but there's not quite enough space. For some reason, he keeps thinking about the way Mae walked back over to Ida earlier, so full of purpose, and he's surprised by how badly he wants to find out what will come of the interview.

"Is that why you're here?" he asks, the words loud in the dark. Beneath him, he hears Mae stir in her own makeshift bed. "To make a film?"

"Maybe," she says. "That's part of it, anyway."

Hugo stays very still, waiting for her to say more, and when she doesn't, he asks, "What's the other part?"

There's a long pause, and then: "Do you ever feel like you need to shake things up? Or just step outside your life for a minute?"

"Yes," he says, his heart thudding with recognition.

"I wanted it so badly: to get in to that film program. You

have no idea. The worst part wasn't even being rejected—it was the shock of it." She laughs, but there's no humor in it. "I thought I was a shoo-in."

"Did you?" Hugo asks, unable to imagine being so sure about anything.

"Yup," she says. "Want to know why?"

"Why?"

"Because I'm good. Maybe that's a weird thing to say. But it's just a fact. And I want the chance to get better."

"You will," he says, though he has no idea really. He's never loved anything the way Mae loves making films, and he wishes he knew what it feels like to have that kind of passion for something. For anything.

Her voice rises up to him again. "What about you? Why are *you* here?"

"Because my girlfriend broke up with me," he says with a wan smile.

"Right. But most people wouldn't have come after something like that. Much less go through all the effort of finding a girl with the same name to take the ticket. I mean, what if I were a total psycho?"

He laughs. "The jury's still out."

"Really—why did you come?"

Hugo hesitates. Even in the cramped bunk, there's something so pleasant about the motion of the train and the sound of her voice, and he's reluctant to spoil it with talk of his knotty feelings about his future and his family and everything else. But he can sense her waiting below him, the silence lengthening.

"It's a long story," he says eventually, and he can almost feel her peering up at him through the dark.

"The good ones usually are."

Mae

They talk late into the night. There's something about the darkness that makes it easy, and when she checks the time and realizes it's after two, it occurs to Mae that she's already shared more with Hugo—whom she's known for less than a day—than she ever did with Garrett.

She can't help feeling as if she's stepped out of her life as quickly and thoughtlessly as you might a pair of jeans; it seems impossible that she could be sharing a room with a boy she met less than twelve hours ago.

"It's not that I don't want to go to uni at all," he's saying, and she hears a dull thump as he knocks a fist gently against the ceiling of the train. "I'm not a bloody idiot. And I quite like studying, actually. I just don't particularly want to go to that one."

"So why are you going?"

"Because I've got a scholarship," he says in a voice so miserable that it sounds like he's telling her he has some sort of disease.

She can't help laughing. "What am I missing here?"

"I didn't get it because I'm clever," he says. "Even though I am."

"Okay," Mae says, amused. "So, what? Was it a safety school or something?"

"No."

"Sports scholarship?"

He snorts. "Definitely not."

"Let me guess," she says. "You have a hidden talent. You can play the piano with your toes. Or juggle knives. Or wait . . . are you in a marching band?"

"We don't really have those at home."

"Then, what?"

"It's because of my family," he says. "I'm a sextuplet."

Mae lies perfectly still for a few seconds, not sure how to play this. Because she already knows, obviously. It's basically the only thing that comes up when you google the name *Hugo Wilkinson*. And there's no possible way he hasn't guessed that she knows.

"Wow," she says, testing the waters.

"Yeah," he says, giving nothing away.

"That's . . . amazing. Do you guys look alike?"

"A bit," he says, which isn't exactly true. Mae has seen dozens of photos online, and they look a *lot* alike. All six of the Wilkinson siblings are striking on their own—with their huge smiles and matching dimples—but as a group, there's something almost dazzling about them. It's easy to see why they're minor celebrities in England.

Mae searches for an appropriate follow-up question. "How many brothers and sisters?"

"Five," Hugo says, like she's asked him what color the sky is. "We're sextuplets. That means six."

"I know. I meant how many of each."

He laughs. "Oh. Sorry. Three brothers and two sisters."

"Can you remember all their names?" she teases, and he laughs.

"Let's see. George, Oscar, Poppy, Alfie, and . . . um . . . uh . . ."

This goes on for so long that Mae finally rolls her eyes. "Isla," she says, and he leans down so his head is hanging over the side of the bed.

"I knew it."

"Well, what do you expect? I had to make sure you were legit."

"Fair enough," he says, returning to his bunk. "I looked you up too."

"Yeah, me and every other Margaret Campbell in the world."

"What I'm curious about," he says, "is how you managed to get yourself arrested for trespassing last spring."

Mae's mouth falls open. "You found that?"

"Oh, I found it all right," Hugo says cheerfully. "Well done, you."

"It was film related," she says, and he laughs.

"Sounds to me like it was cow related too."

She groans. "I swear that farmer is never around. And if the fence hadn't broken, it would've been fine. But then we had to try to round them all up again, and the police showed up, and it was a whole thing."

"The lengths we go to for art," he jokes, and even after they've both stopped laughing, Mae can't seem to get rid of her smile.

She's not sure what it is, this electricity that's buzzing through her right now. Maybe it's Hugo, or maybe not. Maybe it's leaving her parents, or being on her own, or the fact that she's on her way to college—so many changes all at once. Or maybe it's the train and the exhilaration that comes from being swept across the country like a tumbleweed. But here in the dark, talking so easily as they rumble through the night, the music of Hugo's accent filling the tiny cabin, she's struck by the unexpected joy of it all.

After a few minutes, she clears her throat, not sure if he's fallen asleep yet. "So that college . . ." she says, and for a long time, there's no answer.

"Right," he says eventually. "The University of Surrey."

"They gave all six of you a scholarship?"

"Not exactly. It was some rich guy who went there."

"Seriously?" she says, surprised. "He just handed you a whole bunch of money?"

"Well, he died a few years ago, so technically he handed it to the university. And we had to get the grades first. But otherwise, yeah. He thought it would be good publicity for them. Which it will. Basically, we get a free education and they get to parade us around campus."

"I've heard of worse deals," Mae says.

Hugo sighs. "I know. That's just it. What kind of prat would have the nerve to be ungrateful for something like that?"

"A prat who wants something different?"

"Did I mention it's also in my hometown?"

"Oof," she says. "Really?"

"And I'm the only one who seems to mind it. I love my brothers and sisters. I do. They're my best mates, and it's strange to imagine being without them—like losing an arm. Or five."

"That's a lot of arms."

"And it's not as if I didn't know this would be happening. It's been the plan since we were born. Literally. I thought I was fine with it, but then I started hearing about classmates who are off to new places, and Margaret . . ." He trails off. "She's going to Stanford. And she'll be meeting all these new people and doing all these exciting things while I'm stuck at home, about a mile from our secondary school, surrounded by all my siblings, like nothing has changed at all."

"Have you ever thought about not going?"

"And do what?" he asks. "We can't afford anywhere else."

"What about loans?"

"I can't—" He pauses, frustrated. "I can't just abandon them. That's not how it works with us. We're a unit."

"But it won't be that way forever," Mae says.

He's quiet for a moment. "Do you have brothers or sisters?"

"No," Mae says, shaking her head, though he can't see her. "It's just me."

"Then you can't understand. It's not that easy."

Maybe not, she thinks. But they've always been a unit too—she and Dad and Pop and Nana—and she'd left them behind because it was time to go. And because she has dreams that are too big to fit back home. She suspects Hugo's problem isn't that he can't bear to leave. It's that he hasn't figured out where he wants to go.

"Most things are easier than you think," she says. "It's deciding to do them that's hard."

"I suppose," he says with a sigh. "Though we can't all be intrepid filmmakers who run headlong into a field of cows. Or whatever dreams we're chasing after."

She smiles at this. "Well, why not?"

"For starters, I don't even know what my dreams *are*. All I know is that I feel . . . restless. And I'd love to do something different, you know? Something new."

A few seconds pass, and Mae looks up at the bottom of his bed. "Hugo?"

"Yes?"

"Who ever told you that doesn't count as a dream?"

Hugo

Hugo wakes not from the motion of the train but from the absence of it. He blinks at the ceiling, which is alarmingly close to his face. Below, there's the scratching of a pen on paper, and it takes him a moment to place himself.

He nudges open the curtain beside the bed, wincing as the light comes streaming in the window. Outside there's a sign that says *Toledo*. Beside it, the man from across the hall, bleary eyed beneath the brim of a cowboy hat, is smoking a cigarette. It's early still, not quite six, and the sky is glowing and shimmery. Hugo flops onto his back again.

"Mae?"

"Morning."

He traces a finger over a squiggly line that someone has drawn on the ceiling, which doesn't seem to lead anywhere in particular. Maybe it's a map. Maybe it's their route. Or maybe it's just a line. "Where's Toledo?"

"Ohio," she says.

"What happened to Pennsylvania?"

"It's still there. We just slept through it."

There's a pause, filled once again by the scrape of a pen, and he asks, "What are you writing?"

"Just some notes," she says.

Hugo shimmies over to the edge of the bed. His legs get tangled in the harness as he tries to get down, and he nearly tumbles sideways but manages to right himself before dropping to the floor. Mae, who is sitting on the lower bunk with a notebook balanced on her knees, looks up at him. She's already dressed in black jeans and a gray T-shirt with the *Ghostbusters* logo on it, her feet bare. He notices that her toes are painted the same color purple as her glasses.

"I didn't think anyone used pen and paper anymore," he says, and she smiles as if he's paid her a compliment. He leans an arm on the top bunk and takes a peek at the page. It's a bit awkward, hovering over her like this, but there's not really room to be anywhere else. "Wow. Your handwriting is truly terrible."

"It's not *that* bad."

"You know those blue lines aren't just suggestions, right? You're supposed to write in between them."

She gives him a look of mock outrage, then tucks her legs in so that there's room for him to sit on the other end of the bed. "I'm working up some questions for my interview with Ida."

"Want to practice on me? I do a mean American accent."

"I'm sure you do," she says. "But you're no Ida."

"Fair enough. What sorts of things are you going to ask?"

"Questions about her life. Her hopes. Her fears."

"Well," he says, leaning back against the window, "we know Roy's fear is that they'll run out of apple pie."

Outside, there's the muffled sound of Ludovic yelling "All aboard!" and then heavy footsteps as people climb back onto the train. The curtain is still drawn across their compartment's doorway, but they can hear their neighbor return to his room, and the train jerks forward once, then twice, before starting to pull away from the station.

Hugo nods at her notebook. "So what's the plan?"

"I think," Mae says, looking up at him through her glasses, "I might be making a documentary."

"About Ida."

"Sort of. I mean, you saw the way she was with Roy last night. Think about how many other people are on this train right now, how many other love stories. That's what I want the film to be about."

"Love and trains?"

"Love and trains," she agrees, and then she tips her head to one side, studying him. "Hey, if you had to describe love in one word, what would it be?"

Hugo blinks at her, his heart quickening for no particular reason. "I have no idea."

"It could be anything. Like, say . . . pizza."

"Pizza?" he asks, surprised. "Why pizza?"

"That's . . . not important," she says. "It could be something else too. Anything."

"Wait, do *you* think love is like a pizza?" he asks with a grin, and she looks at him impatiently.

"This isn't about me."

"How do you reckon love is like——"

"Hugo."

"Okay, okay. I'd need to think about it more. Especially if I'm going to come up with something better than pizza."

"You have to say it quick. The first thing that pops into your head."

Hugo's first thought, for some reason, is of their conversation last night, how easy it had been to talk to her in the darkness. But that's not a word, and they're not in love, so he turns his mind to Margaret instead, flipping through the pages of their years together, trying to find something that might sum it all up. But his mind goes entirely blank.

"This isn't really my style," he says with a frown. "I prefer to think things through."

"You're no fun."

"You know what might help?"

"What?"

"Pizza," he says, and when she rolls her eyes, he laughs. "Only joking. I meant coffee."

They decide to skip the more formal breakfast in the dining car. Instead they buy a box of doughnuts in the lounge car and then find an open table to themselves. Behind them, a couple of the assistant conductors are sorting through tickets, and there's an old man playing solitaire with a deck of Chicago Cubs cards. Otherwise it's mostly quiet at this hour.

"So why love?" Hugo asks as he opens the box of doughnuts.

"It might be a little too early for big philosophical questions," Mae says, raising her cup of coffee.

"No, it's just . . . I understand the train part, obviously. But why love stories?"

"Because," she says, her eyes flashing, "what could be more personal than that?" Hugo is still trying to figure this one out when she goes on. "Also, I've never had a chance like this before. All my films have been really small because my life has been really small. I think that was part of the problem. I mean, I once made a short about a squirrel that got stuck in our heating vents, and honestly, that squirrel was only a marginally worse actor than the drama club kids I usually put in my films. Most of them were set at the grocery store or the high school or the gas station, because there was really nowhere else. And now here I am on a train full of all these different people from all these different places, and they must have a million stories to tell."

He considers this a moment. "So you're taking field notes."

"I mean, it's not super scientific or anything, but . . . yeah." She licks some powdered sugar off her finger. "I guess I am."

"Field notes on love," Hugo says, glancing out the window, where the world is moving by too fast.

Mae nods. "And trains."

"Do you remember that video you did for me?" he asks, turning back to face her, and she raises her eyebrows. "Sorry. Not for me. For this trip."

"Yeah . . ."

"Well, it didn't feel small to me at all. In fact, the moment I saw it, I knew—"

She cracks a smile. "That you wanted to invite an eighty-four-year-old instead?"

He shakes his head, eager to be understood. "No. I knew there was something interesting about you. Something that made me want to meet you. And all that happened in just a couple of minutes. It was short. But you managed to say so much."

"You asked good questions."

"Maybe. But your answers—they meant something." He feels his face grow warm. "Or maybe they didn't. I don't know. But it certainly felt that way."

Out the window, there's a blur of houses and trees and highways. For a while, Mae stares at the telephone lines as they zip past. Finally she turns back to him with an unreadable expression. "You're right."

"About what?"

"Those questions, my answers . . . they did mean something. They meant a lot, actually." She smiles at him, and it's the kind of smile that feels like a beginning— though the beginning of what, he isn't entirely sure. "I think we should see if it might be the same for anyone else."

Mae

They start with Ida, who tears up at the very first question.

"My biggest dream?" she says. "I know this will sound awfully old-fashioned to you, but my dream was always to marry Roy. We met when we were twelve. He bought me an ice cream and was the only boy who didn't laugh when I spilled it on my dress. It sounds small. But there was such kindness in that. I knew right then. I've always known."

Mae tries to imagine what it would be like to be that sure of someone. She's spent the last six years watching Priyanka and Alex write love notes and hold hands and make impossible promises, and to Mae it's always felt like witnessing some unfamiliar custom. But listening to Ida now is like fast-forwarding to the end of this particular movie. And to Mae's surprise, it doesn't seem like such a bad one.

At the bar, Ashwin—the head dining attendant, who agreed to let them use one of the tables—is restocking cans of soda. But Mae can tell by the way his head is tilted in their direction that he's listening too. Same with Roy, who insisted on waiting a couple of tables away. "For privacy," he said, but his ears have gone bright red at Ida's answer.

Hugo is sitting next to Mae in the booth. She put him in charge of the external microphone and warned him not to talk. But they're one question in, and already he can't help himself. "That's so lovely," he says to Ida, and Mae leans back from the camera to give him a sharp look. He holds up his hands. "Sorry, sorry."

"It's okay. We can edit you out."

"If only it were always that easy to get rid of me," he jokes.

"And what's your biggest fear?" Mae asks Ida, who looks completely at ease in front of the camera. Even more than that, she looks happy. Mae gets the impression that for as much talking as she does, there aren't always many listeners.

"Oh," she says. "I don't . . . um . . . well, I don't really like snakes, but that's probably not exactly what you're looking for, is it?"

Mae gives her a reassuring smile. "We're just looking for honesty."

"Honesty. Well." Ida turns to the window. "I suppose my biggest fear is never seeing my son again. You don't know what happiness is—what it really means—until it's taken away from you. Then you realize the world will never be as bright as it was."

Across the room, Roy puts his head in his hands. Mae leans away from the camera and stares at his broad back, stricken. Then she takes a deep breath and returns to the shot.

Ida dabs at her eyes. "But my greatest hope is just the opposite," she says. "That somehow I'll see him again one day."

Hugo reaches across the table and takes her hand, and the gesture is so thoughtful, so sweet, that Mae can't bring herself to scold him for ruining her shot. The truth is, she wants to do the same. But instead she just says, "I'm sure you will."

"I hope so," Ida says, then lets out a laugh as Mae pans in closer. "Probably won't have to wait too long either. Right, Roy?"

Roy half turns; his eyes are rimmed with red, but he's grinning. "I don't know, hon. Every year we say it'll be our last train ride. But we're still rolling along somehow."

"We sure are," she says, and they smile at each other from across the tables.

Mae glances down at her notebook. Those first two questions had been Hugo's, pulled straight from the email that had started all of this. But these last two—these are Mae's.

"What do you love most about the world?"

Ida smiles. "I love that every generation thinks they've invented it. They think they're the first ones to fall in love and get their hearts broken, to feel loss and passion and pain.

And in a way, they are. We've been there before, of course. But for young people, that doesn't matter. Everything is new. Which I love, because it means everything is always beginning again. It's hopeful, I think. At least to me."

When Mae leans back from the camera, she sees that Hugo's eyes are shiny, and she's surprised by how much she wants to ask him the same question. But she doesn't. Instead she turns back to Ida. "Last one," she says. "If you had to describe love in one word, what would it be?"

Ida blinks at her. "Oh. Well. I guess I'd probably say *peace*."

The word snags at something inside Mae, small and thorny as a burr. *Peace*. To her, it seems like an awful lot to ask of love. But still she finds herself jotting it down in the margin of her notebook, eager to capture it.

"That's a fair bit better than pizza, anyway," Hugo says, but Mae ignores this, switching off the camera and turning back to Ida.

"Thank you," she says. "That was beautiful. All of it."

"Thank *you*," Ida says as she reaches for her purse. "Now I'm going to go freshen up before lunch. You can keep Roy, though, if you want."

Roy twists around in his seat. "I'm all yours," he says. "And I was barely listening, so it doesn't count as cheating or anything."

This interview is shorter. Roy insists on opening with a joke ("Why was the train engine humming? Because it didn't know the words!"), then spends most of the rest of the time talking about fishing, which—incidentally—is the word he'd choose to describe love.

"But if Ida asks," he says with a wink, "tell her I said it was her."

Afterward, Ashwin is overcome by curiosity too. He sits across from them in his uniform, hands folded as he talks about visiting his grandmother in Mumbai when he was a kid and learning to make samosas. One day he hopes to open a restaurant where he can use her recipe.

"That's love," he says. "An old woman making something for one person, and then years later, even after she's gone, feeding all these different people on the other side of the world."

It's more than one word, but Mae doesn't mind.

Not long after that, Ida returns with a middle-aged Asian couple in tow. "These are our neighbors," she says, introducing them to Mae and Hugo. "Not in real life. Just on the train. I told them about your project."

And so they interview the Chens, and then Marcus, their waiter from last night, and then a family of four from Iowa who stop to ask what they're doing. By the time lunch starts and Ashwin needs the booth, Mae feels dizzy from all these stories, all the different lives she's been allowed to glimpse, and she has a list of words to describe love that ranges from *togetherness* to *joy* to *a 1962 Mustang convertible*.

She and Hugo are halfway back to their cabin when they run into Ludovic.

"I heard a rumor that you're making a movie," he says, looking at them expectantly, and so they duck into the open area near the doors, and Ludovic puts on his cap and straightens his tie, and Hugo holds the microphone close so they can hear over the rattling of metal on metal.

Later, after they've done several more interviews and had lunch and returned to their compartment, Hugo sinks down into his seat with a happy sigh. "So is it my turn now?"

Mae is busy fidgeting with the settings on the camera. "For what?"

"For an interview."

"I don't need to interview you. I already know you." It takes her a second to realize exactly what she said. She lifts her eyes to see that he's looking at her with amusement. She doesn't know him; of course she doesn't. She only meant that he isn't a stranger, and even that is only marginally true. She gives her head a little shake. "The point is to interview strangers."

"I thought the point was to interview people on trains," he says with a good-natured smile. He spreads his arms wide. "And here I am. On a train."

Mae gives him a long look, her heartbeat quickening at the thought of sitting him down for an interview, listening closely as he tells her about his dreams and his fears, about what love means to him. She wants to know what he would say. All morning as he's sat beside her, she's wanted to know. But something is holding her back. A week ago, she was with Garrett, and Hugo had a girlfriend so serious that they were planning to take this trip together. A week from now, she'll be in Los Angeles

115

and he'll be back in England, almost six thousand miles apart.

"Maybe after Chicago," she says, putting her camera away.

Hugo

Before long, the city of Chicago rushes up to meet them. Hugo peers out the rain-speckled window at the skyline, the tops of the buildings lost in the clouds. It's so different from home, where everything is built low to the ground, where you can look up without losing your balance.

As they get closer, dozens of rails converge all around them, littered with rusty freight cars that sit ghostlike in the mist. Then the light disappears, and Hugo feels a jolt of excitement as they sweep into the tunnels underneath the sprawling city.

He looks over at Mae, who is still collecting her things, which are scattered everywhere: a tube of lip gloss, a crumpled copy of their tickets, a pair of socks. Hugo can only imagine what her bedroom must look like.

"Got everything?" he asks, arching an eyebrow.

She gives him a look as she tosses a stray cord into her bag. "You know there have been studies that prove the most creative people are the most disorganized?"

"Were you one of the featured subjects?"

As the train slows, they both stand up, but the space between the seats is too narrow and he almost falls backward trying not to bump into her. She reaches out an arm to steady him, her nose practically touching his shirt, and they both laugh. But underneath that, his heart is thumping wildly at the sudden proximity.

The train jerks to a stop, and this time he's the one to catch her. They stare at each other for a second, both flustered, and then she reaches for her rucksack, which is wedged onto a small shelf, and steps out of the compartment.

Across the hall, the cowboy walks out at the same time. He gives them both a nod, then adjusts the brim of his hat before heading off. Mae turns around with a slightly bemused look. "Didn't expect him to be getting off *here*."

"What, there are no cowboys in Chicago?"

"Maybe he came to wrangle some pizza."

"Is that a code word for love?" Hugo asks, waggling his eyebrows suggestively.

Mae laughs. "No, I meant actual Chicago-style pizza. It's a thing."

"Then maybe I'll have to wrangle some myself," he says, and when she gives him an exasperated look, he puts a hand over his chest, trying to keep a straight face. "Pizza. Not love."

Ludovic gives them a hand as they step off the train,

and Hugo feels strangely nostalgic as they say goodbye. It's been only twenty-four hours, but somehow it seems like much more. As they make their way down the platform, his mobile begins to ding. He reaches for it and sees the texts stacking up one after another.

Poppy: So how's Margaret Campbell, the sequel?

Alfie: Yeah, are you two in looooooooove yet?

Isla: You are a five-year-old.

Alfie: I know you are, but what am I?

Oscar: Bloody hell.

George: Seriously, though. How's it going?

Alfie: Yeah, are you in looooooooove yet?

Isla: Don't be silly.

Poppy: He only just split up with Margaret Campbell, the first.

Alfie: Doesn't mean he's not in looooooooove.

Poppy: Doesn't mean he is.

Hugo: Do I need to be here for this?

Alfie: I'm going to take that as a yes.

Hugo: You can take it however you want.

Oscar: Sounds like a yes to me too.

Alfie: The real question is . . . what are the sleeping arrangements??

Hugo looks up as Mae climbs onto the escalator ahead of him. He follows her, standing a few steps below, deep in thought. Halfway up, he clears his throat. "So." When she twists around, he lifts his eyes to meet hers. "I was thinking I'd just . . ."

119

"What?"

"Well, we sort of agreed that . . ." She turns away as they reach the top, emerging into a cavernous marble building, which is noisy and echoing with footsteps. Hugo digs in the pocket of his jeans for a scrap of paper. "I wrote down the name of a hostel that's not too far from your hotel."

"Oh," Mae says, finally understanding. He expected her to be relieved, but instead she looks uncertain. She takes the paper from him and examines it. "I should go with you. I mean, not to stay. Just to make sure you get in and everything."

A few days ago, he would've guessed he'd be claustrophobic by now, eager for some space after being stuck overnight in a shoebox with someone he hardly knows. He figured at least one of them would try to scarper the moment they arrived. But to his surprise, he finds he's not looking forward to parting ways just yet. And neither, it seems, is she.

"We can drop off your stuff," she says, "and then . . ."

She trails off, and he finds himself smiling at the open-endedness of it all. "Brilliant."

As they walk toward the exit, he wonders what it means that he's spent his whole life longing to be alone, only to cling to the very first person he meets when he finally gets the chance for some solitude. Maybe he's not cut out for this after all. Maybe if you're born a pack animal, it's simply not possible to become a lone wolf. Even for a week.

But right now he's not all that bothered by it.

Outside, the clouds are a deep gunmetal gray, and

the sky is starting to spit at them. Mae looks up at him expectantly.

"What?" Hugo asks.

"Do you have an umbrella?"

He shakes his head. "No. Why, do you?"

"No," she says. "But you're English."

"So?"

"So I thought you'd have one."

"Nope. No brolly." He pretends to reach into his rucksack. "But I think maybe I've got my chimney sweep in here somewhere . . ."

She rolls her eyes at him. "I'm pretty sure a chimney sweep is a person, not a tool."

"Well," he says, laughing, "sorry to disappoint, but I don't have any of the above."

They begin to walk faster, blinking away the rain. It's not like back home, where the rain is sideways and pelting; here, it comes straight down like someone has dropped a bucket over the city, and it's not long before they're both completely drenched. As they wait to cross at a stoplight, Mae holds a hand over her head.

"I'm not sure that's really helping," Hugo says over the roar of the rain, which is coming down so hard that it's splashing up all around them.

She looks over at him, water dripping from her eyelashes. "Got any better ideas?"

"Yeah," he says. "Let's peg it."

And so they run, their rucksacks thumping against their backs, their trainers soggy and slipping. By the time they reach the enormous brick hostel, they're both panting hard and laughing a little too. Once inside, they stand beside a rack of brochures about Chicago, their clothes dripping water onto the floor. Mae wrings out her hair as she peers into the lobby, which is full of ratty-looking armchairs occupied by scattered groups of teens and twentysomethings.

"Maybe this won't be so bad."

Hugo shrugs. "As long as they have a towel, I'll be fine."

"I just feel bad that—"

"I'm not fussed about where I sleep. Honestly. All I care about is getting a slice of that Chicago pizza I've heard so much about."

"That we can do."

Something about the *we* makes his heart race.

They push open the door and squelch their way into the lobby in wet shoes. At the front desk is a guy with blue hair and a painful-looking nose ring. He doesn't move his eyes from the computer as they approach.

"Pardon me," Hugo says after an uncomfortable silence. "I'm wondering if you have any beds available for the night?"

"Forty-eight bucks for a dorm," the guy says, sounding terrifically bored. "One thirty-eight for a single."

Hugo drops his rucksack on the floor and stoops beside it to unzip the front pocket, fishing around for his wallet. "Right. I'll take a dorm, then. How many beds in each?"

"Four to sixteen." He finally looks up and registers Mae. "I can try to get you a shared bunk, if you want."

"No, it's just for me," Hugo says quickly. He's still feeling around inside his rucksack, aware of Mae standing above him. He opens the main part of the bag, pulling out a jumper and a couple of pairs of trousers and a book he hasn't started yet, but it's not until he feels his fingers brush the bottom that the worry starts to kick in.

"What are you looking for?" Mae asks, though she must have already guessed.

Hugo gives her a sheepish smile. "Just my wallet. I'm sure it's in here somewhere . . ." He tries the front again and finds his passport, tucked inside the smart brown case, and he tugs it free with no small amount of relief. But the wallet isn't there.

Maybe his mum was right.

Maybe they all were.

Worry starts to turn to panic as he stands up and feels around in the pockets of his jeans and his jacket; then he kneels to search the rucksack again. He knows the wallet isn't there, but he's not sure what else to do in the moment except to keep looking, and so he does, tossing the rest of his clothes onto the dirty floor as the blue-haired receptionist peers at him over the counter.

This goes on until Mae kneels beside him, resting a hand gently on his shoulder, and this tiniest of gestures sends a small shock through him. "Did you take it out on the train at all?" she asks in a low voice, and he realizes for the first time that they have an audience. The people in the lounge have mostly stopped what they're doing to stare at the array of clothes fanned out on the grimy linoleum.

Hugo closes his eyes, trying to remember. And then his stomach lurches. "Bollocks," he says with a groan. "I took out twenty dollars to give Ludovic just before we got off."

"We were supposed to tip him?" Mae asks, going pale.

"It was for both of us. But I must not have . . ." He glances down at the pile of clothes in despair. "I'm such an idiot."

"We'll figure it out," she tells him. "We'll call. Or go back to the station. Maybe they have a lost-and-found."

Hugo feels suddenly exhausted, a spreading weariness that makes his bones ache. Two days. That's all it took for him to prove he's not up to this.

He sits back on the cold, wet floor and looks up at Mae. "I hate to ask," he says miserably, "but do you think I could borrow a few quid—dollars—until this gets sorted?"

Mae looks at Hugo as if weighing something. His mind is whirring through all that will happen if the wallet is well and truly lost: the hassle of canceling credit cards, trying to sort new ones, having to ring his parents and tell them what happened. He's so busy with his thoughts that he's not fully listening when Mae finally says, "No."

"No?" he repeats, confused. "I swear I'd pay you back . . ."

"No, I mean you should just come to the hotel with me. It seems silly for you to stay here, especially now, when we were fine sharing last night." She flushes, realizing they still have an audience, and adds, "We can ask for a cot. It was your room to begin with, and you were just trying to be nice and make sure I felt comfortable, but . . ."

Hugo raises his eyebrows, waiting. He can feel a smile building inside him, but he manages to hold it back.

"I already feel comfortable with you," she says. "So let's just go get some dinner, okay?"

"Okay," he says, letting the smile surface. He gestures at the tangle of clothes on the floor all around them. "As long as it's on you."

Mae

Later, they wander the rain-slicked city, ducking into shops to stay dry. In one of them, which is full of Chicago-themed souvenirs, Hugo tries on a hat shaped like a football.

"Do I look like an American?" he asks with a grin.

"You look," Mae says brightly, "like an idiot."

She picks out a delicate snow globe with a jagged skyline for her dads. The spotty cell reception along the route had made phone calls tricky, so they've been texting her constantly instead:

Dad:	My phone is broken.
Mae:	Sorry. What happened?
Dad:	Wait—never mind! There's been a miracle!
Mae:	Huh?
Dad:	My phone—it's working again!

Mae:	Clearly.
Dad:	I just figured it must be broken, since I hadn't heard from you AT ALL today.
Mae:	Bravo. Well played.
Dad:	Thanks. Was the miracle thing too over the top?
Mae:	Nope. You really sold it.

And:

Pop:	I just emailed you an article about the Pennsylvania Dutch.
Mae:	Great, thanks!
Pop:	Are you still there?
Mae:	Like . . . on the phone?
Pop:	No, in Pennsylvania.
Mae:	We're actually in Ohio now.
Pop:	Okay, then I have another article for you, about the steel industry in Cleveland.
Mae:	Can't wait.

But now that she's in Chicago, Mae knows she owes them a call.

Eventually, she and Hugo get tired of wandering and find a narrow pizza restaurant with steamy windows. Inside, there's a line to be seated, and they wait behind a family of three—a mom, a dad, and a girl of about twelve, all of them black. When they step up to the hostess, who is white, she grabs four menus.

"Actually," the father says, "we're just three."

The hostess glances around him at Hugo, then at Mae, and it takes a long moment for her to register the kind of mistake she's just made. A look of embarrassment passes over her face, and she hastily returns one of the menus.

"Sorry," she says quickly. "Right this way."

The mother gives Hugo a rueful look before following her husband and daughter, and he smiles back at her, but the moment they're gone, it falls away.

"I'm sure she didn't mean anything by it," Mae says, trying to catch his eye. But he won't look at her.

"Yeah," he says, his jaw tight. "I'm sure."

At the table, they both study their menus, but Mae finds she can't concentrate on food, not when Hugo is so clearly out of sorts.

"Hey," she says, her voice gentle. "Does that kind of thing happen a lot?"

He shrugs. "Sometimes."

"I'm sorry," she says, thinking about all the waiters and flight attendants and hotel clerks who have looked from her to Pop to Dad over the years, their foreheads wrinkled like they're trying to work out a particularly hard puzzle. This is different, of course. But she can still recognize the oddly blank expression on his face, a calm surface to hide all that's churning underneath. "I should've been more—"

"Don't worry about it," he says, snapping the menu shut. But when he looks up at Mae, his face softens a little. "It's just . . . I'm used to having people around who get it. You should see Alfie when stuff like that happens. Even Margaret. So without them . . . I don't know. I guess it just made me feel a bit lonely."

Mae's heart twists at this, and she feels such a pang of regret that she wishes she could reach across the table and take his hand. But instead, she just nods. "I get that," she says, her throat a little tight, and they both sit there quietly for a moment, watching each other across the table. Then Hugo's stomach lets out a loud growl.

"And hungry," he says with a sheepish smile. "Apparently."

"Apparently," she says, and they pick up the menus again.

When they get to the hotel later, the storm has picked up, and they stand at the window and watch as scribbles of lightning flash over the lake. Every few minutes, thunder rattles the glass, but neither of them moves, mesmerized by the fireworks.

Mae looks sideways at Hugo, realizing just how aware of him she is: the dimples when he smiles and the shape of his nose and the way his shirt rises slightly as he stretches, revealing a stripe of brown skin above his jeans. They're standing only inches apart, and the space between them feels important right now, like it's the only thing that might keep this whole situation afloat.

"It's like magic, isn't it?" he says, his eyes still on the window.

"The lightning?"

"Just . . . all of it."

Mae isn't entirely sure what he means, but she likes watching his face, the way his eyes flicker in the light, the way every inch of him seems so alive right now.

"We hardly ever get storms like this at home," he says as a flare of lightning splits the darkness wide open. For a second, it looks like the world has been turned inside out, then it rights itself again. "Do you ever feel like what's happening at this moment will never happen again? Like you could never repeat it, no matter how hard you tried?"

Mae smiles, but the question doesn't seem to require a response. There's another crack of thunder, and the space between them mysteriously shrinks until his arm brushes against hers.

Her stomach does a little jig, and the reminders go ticking through her head:

He just broke up with someone, and technically so did she.

They won't see each other again after this week.

He lives on the other side of an ocean.

This whole thing is strictly business.

She has more important things to think about.

(It's just that right now it's hard to remember what they are.)

"So," she says, trying and failing to sound casual, "any word about your wallet?"

Hugo slips his phone from his back pocket, tearing his gaze from the window to look. His shoulders sag. "Nothing."

They went back to the station earlier, but nobody had turned in a missing wallet. Afterward Hugo had emailed his parents to borrow money. "The only good thing," he said grimly, "is that it's late there. So there's very little chance of them ringing back till tomorrow."

Mae thinks again of her own parents and her promise to call them. But she hadn't been counting on sharing a room with Hugo, and she feels a wave of exhaustion at the thought of lying to them. Again. So instead she sends another text, promising to try them in the morning.

It's still early, not even nine-thirty, but as soon as she sits down on the bed, Mae realizes she wants nothing more than to put on her pajamas and curl up under the covers. She's just not exactly sure how to get from here to there. A bellhop has brought up a cot for Hugo, but it's still sitting near the door, folded in half like an oversized taco. Their backpacks are leaning against each other outside the bathroom.

Hugo walks toward the bed, and Mae sits up straighter. He stops on the other side of it, leaning over the ocean of white sheets between them, and smiles at her in a way that only makes her heart beat faster.

"So," he says, "what do you reckon we should do now?"

The question hangs in the air for a few seconds while Mae tries to think of an appropriate response.

"'Cause I was thinking," he continues, "that maybe we get into pajamas and put on a film."

"Yeah?" she says, still unsure about the logistics of all this. But then he walks over to the cot and starts to wheel it into the space between the foot of the bed and the dresser, and Mae—grateful for something tangible to do—hurries over to help him set it up.

When they're done, they take turns changing in the bathroom, and it's less weird than Mae thinks it will be, walking back out into the room in her pajama bottoms and a T-shirt that says *The Future Is Female*. Hugo gives her a friendly smile, then heads in to put on his same gray shirt and rubber-ducky pajamas from last night. He shuts the lights off before crawling onto the cot, and from where she's propped against several pillows in the bed, Mae points the remote at the screen behind him.

"Let's watch something frightening," Hugo says as the thunder crashes again. "It feels like that sort of night, doesn't it?"

"I'm not really a scary-movie kind of person."

"But you're a film buff."

"A film buff who also happens to be a giant chicken."

"Maybe a comedy, then," he says. "Just not anything sad. We haven't known each other long enough for you to see me cry."

He's only joking, of course. But still, Mae tries to remember the last time she cried during a movie. Whenever she watches something with Nana or Priyanka or even her parents, she's the one passing the box of tissues, and she can't help wondering what that says about her.

She flips through the channels, stopping when it lands on an old film.

"*Murder on the Orient Express*?" Hugo says, half laughing. "I thought we already established that nobody was murdering anyone on the train this week."

"That's fine with me, but Sidney Lumet would probably

find your version a little boring."

"Who's Sidney Lumet?"

Mae sits up. "*Network*? *Twelve Angry Men*? *Dog Day Afternoon*?"

"Nope, nope, and nope."

"You haven't seen *any* of them?" she asks, indignant. "What movies *do* you like? I guess I should've probably asked this before I got on a train with you."

"Definitely seems more important than the serial-killer question," he agrees. "I'm almost afraid to tell you this, but I'm not a huge movie person. I don't mind going to the cinema here and there, but I'm never that fussed about what I see. I suppose I prefer to watch TV or read books." There's a short silence, and then he says, "Are you going to throw me out now?"

She laughs. "I was thinking about it."

"For what it's worth, I'd be delighted to watch *your* film."

"Not an option."

"Why not?"

"Because . . ." she says, searching for an answer. "Because now that I know what we're working with here, there are a whole lot of other movies you should see before my rejected audition film." She turns up the volume on the TV. "Starting with *Murder on the Orient Express*."

As they watch, Hugo keeps shifting around on the cot, which creaks and groans beneath his weight. Eventually, he sits up so that his head is blocking the entire screen.

"Uh . . ." Mae says, and he scrunches down again.

"Sorry. It's just . . . I'm too close. It's hard to watch."

She glances over at the sprawling bed and the stack of pillows beside her. "You can sit up here if you want," she says, trying to sound breezy. "Just till the end of the movie."

"Yeah?" he asks, sitting up again.

Mae swallows. "Yeah."

The bed is so big that her half barely dips when he climbs on. There are several pillows between them, but they're still careful to keep to the edges, both with their arms folded across their chests, eyes fixed on the TV— though Mae can no longer concentrate on the mystery unfolding on the screen, not when Hugo is so close.

He glances over at her. "Do you still feel like you're on a train?"

Until that moment, she didn't notice, but now she realizes she can feel the phantom motion beneath her too. She nods.

"I wonder if tomorrow night we'll feel like we're on a hotel bed," he says.

She smiles. "I don't think it works like that."

"Who actually uses this many pillows?" He tosses a few of them off the edge, breaking down the barrier between them. "It's like being stuck inside a marshmallow."

Outside, the rain is still pinging against the window, but Mae is distracted by the newly empty space between them. She starts to run through her list of reminders again: *He just broke up with his girlfriend. They won't see each other after this week. He lives on the other side of an ocean.*

Et cetera, et cetera, et cetera. But this kind of vigilance is exhausting, and already her eyelids are growing heavy in the flickering dark.

Sometime later in the night, she wakes to find their hands clasped between them.

Though it might just as easily have been a dream.

Hugo

Hugo's eyes flash open at the sound of his mobile.

It's only after he's pulled his hand from Mae's to silence the ringing that it registers he was holding her hand at all. He blinks, still bleary eyed, wondering when that happened.

Across the room, the TV is still on, but it now features a man in an apron using a machine to blend vegetables, blaring on about all the many features in a flat American accent. Hugo rubs his eyes, then reaches for his mobile, and when he realizes the call came from his parents, he sighs.

It's a little after two in the morning, which means it's eight o'clock at home. For a second, he misses it fiercely: his brothers and sisters around the kitchen table, his dad frying bacon, and his mum already on her third cup of coffee. Then a heavy dread settles over him at the thought of actually ringing them back. He slips out of bed and into the bathroom, closing the door gently behind him.

"Haven't you ever heard of time zones?" he says when their faces appear on the video chat. They always look slightly befuddled by this mode of communication, moving their heads in birdlike fashion as they both try to center themselves on the small screen.

"We got your message about the wallet," his dad says, "and I have to say, I'm disappointed in you, son."

"Look," Hugo says with a sigh, "it was an accident. I just—"

"Now I owe your mum five quid."

"Frank," his mum says, giving his shoulder a smack.

"And another five to Alfie."

Hugo groans.

"This is why I told you to get a money belt," his mum says, still glaring at his dad in a way that makes it clear she's forgotten Hugo can see her too. She turns back to the screen. "I read an article that says everything is safer that way."

"Right, but I wasn't pickpocketed," he says, though maybe it would've been better to be mugged than to be irresponsible. At least then it wouldn't have been his fault. He sits down on the closed seat of the toilet. "I just forgot it. Stupid, I know."

His mum simply nods, as if she'd been expecting as much. The lack of surprise on her face only makes it worse. "Are you okay, darling?" she asks, and for some reason, this makes him feel like crying.

"I'm fine," he manages to say.

"Do you still have your passport?"

He nods. "It's just my credit cards and the dollars I took out from the bank, and—"

"Are you in the loo?" his dad asks with a frown.

"Yeah."

"Why?"

Because, Hugo thinks, *I was in bed with a girl I only just met, and who I'm starting to suspect I might like, even though I only just broke up with another girl who happens to have the exact same name, and who was supposed to be here with me instead, which makes this all more than a little bit confusing.*

But he doesn't say any of that. Instead, his groggy brain works to catch up with the lies he's already told them, and he says, "Because I couldn't find the light switch in the room."

Behind them, Hugo can see Alfie walk into the kitchen, still wearing pajamas. He grabs an apple from the bowl on the counter and squeezes his face between theirs. "Hugo," he says, leaning forward. "Heard you lost your wallet on the first day."

"Second," Hugo says grimly.

"Well done, mate. Were you drunk?"

"Alfie," says their mum.

Hugo shakes his head. "No."

"Stoned?"

"*Alfred*," their dad says with a look of shock.

138

"No," Hugo says quickly.

"Just being yourself, then?" Alfie says with a good-natured grin, and when Hugo doesn't say anything, only glowers at the screen, he laughs. "Well done, you. We miss having that sort of top-notch attention to detail around here. Hurry back, all right?"

Hugo lifts a hand to wave weakly as his brother disappears again. "Where's everyone else?" he asks his parents, suddenly feeling homesick.

"Oscar is upstairs," his dad says. "Poppy's gone down to Brighton for the day with that McWalter boy, heaven help us. And Isla and George are . . . well . . ."

They exchange a look.

"Over at the university," his mum says.

Hugo frowns. "How come?"

"They wanted to have a look around," she says, "since the housing assignments arrived yesterday."

"They did?"

She twists her mouth up to one side. "Listen, darling . . . they put you together."

"What?" Hugo's brain feels slow and muddled. "Who?"

"All of you. Oscar and Alfie. Isla and Pop. You and George."

"Me and George?" Hugo repeats numbly.

"It could be worse," says his dad. "You could be with Alfie."

"Hey," comes a distant voice from somewhere behind them.

"George had a feeling you wouldn't be too keen on this," his mum says, which makes Hugo's stomach feel like lead.

"The others are going to stay where they are, but he said he's fine to room with someone different if the university will let you switch. He's going to leave it up to you."

Hugo's throat is completely dry. "Okay."

"I'll text you the email for the housing office, in case you want to try," she says. "But make sure you talk to George about it first. I know he's anxious to hear from you."

"Of course," Hugo says, staring at his bleary reflection in the mirror. There's a short silence, and then he says, "I should probably go. It's late here. Or early, I guess."

"Right," she says. "Look, just send us the address of your next hotel and we can ring the bank and have them send new credit cards."

Hugo nods. "Brilliant. Thanks."

"What will you do for money in the meantime?"

"I'll just . . ." he begins, then pauses, choosing his words carefully. "I made a friend on the train. I can probably borrow some money from . . . him."

"So you're having a nice time?"

"I am," Hugo says. He opens his mouth again to describe it to them but realizes he has no idea where to begin. It's only been a couple of days, but already so much has happened. Already he feels like the space between them is made up of more than just miles.

"I'm glad," she says. "Just try to hang on to that passport, okay? We'd still like to have you back here at the end of all this."

Hugo feels something slip in his chest, like the locking of a bolt.

"Yeah, and don't forget we love you the best," his dad says with a grin, which is what he always says to each of them.

"Love you too," Hugo manages.

After they hang up, he sits there beneath the harsh bathroom lights, staring at the blackened screen. He thinks about Isla and George wandering around the campus, peering into the windows of the residence halls where they'll all be rooming together, much the way they do now, as if nothing has changed at all, as if they never even bothered to leave home.

How is it possible to be so disheartened at the thought, yet still feel so alone without all of them? He meant what he said to Mae last night. It wasn't just what happened at the pizza place. It was the sudden realization that after being tethered to his family for so long, he was now adrift. Which is exactly what he'd wanted. He just hadn't expected it to make him feel quite so lonely.

With a sigh, he switches off the bathroom light and steps quietly back into the room, hoping not to wake Mae. He looks from the bed to the cot, surprised by how much he wants to curl up beside her again, to listen to the sound of her breathing, to feel the warmth of her hand in his—

He stops himself there.

Better be the cot, he thinks.

The infomercial for the vegetable chopper is still on, making the room flicker with light. Hugo walks around to Mae's side of the bed and picks up the remote. When the picture snaps off, the room goes dark, a dark so thick that there's nothing to do but stand there, waiting for his eyes to adjust, afraid that if he moves he'll trip over something.

He goes to set the remote back on the table but manages to knock something else off instead. Worried it might be a piece of jewelry, he drops to his knees, feeling around on the carpet without any luck. After a minute, he sits back again, and when he does, it's to find himself eye level with Mae, who is now awake and staring at him with an unreadable expression.

"What are you doing?" she whispers, though it's only the two of them in the room.

"I . . . well, the TV was on, and then I dropped something, so I was trying to—" He starts to stand up but manages to bash his knee against the corner of the table in the process. "Bollocks," he says, hopping around in a circle, and when he stops again, Mae is standing right beside him.

"Are you okay?"

To his surprise, he feels his eyes prick with tears.

What a question, he thinks.

"I'm fine," he says in a voice so heavy that she steps forward and slips her arms around him. Hugo stands very still, wondering if he's dreaming. "What's that for?"

"I don't know," she says, resting her cheek against his chest. "Nothing. Everything."

After a moment, he raises his arms, allowing himself to hug her back. Her head fits just below his chin, and he wonders if she can hear his heart beating like something that's trying to escape. When she starts to step back, it feels to Hugo like a kind of loss. But then he realizes she's looking up at him, almost like she's waiting for something, and he lowers his chin to meet her gaze.

"Hugo?"

"Yeah?"

"You have really lovely eyes."

He laughs, mostly because it's too dark to even see. But then before he can overthink it, he takes a step forward, and he leans down and kisses her.

For a few seconds, they're all searching hands and beating hearts; her lips are soft, and her hands brush the back of his neck, sending a shiver through him. All he wants is to tumble sideways onto the bed with her, to burrow under the covers and stay there forever. But instead they remain where they are, pressing themselves closer and closer together in the dark.

Outside, the storm has stopped. But if you could hear the way Hugo's heart is thundering, you wouldn't be so sure.

Mae

In the morning, Mae is woken by her phone, which is buzzing madly on the bedside table. When she sees that it's a call from home, she goes very still. Then she bites her lip and lifts the phone to her ear.

"Hi," she says, sitting up in the bed. Beside her, Hugo opens his eyes briefly, yawns, and then closes them again.

"Well, hello there, stranger," says Pop, his voice so big and warm and familiar that Mae feels a rush of sadness at being away from her dads. "Thought you'd forgotten about us already."

"Never," she says, her voice full of unexpected emotion. "I was just tired last night."

"I knew you wouldn't sleep on the train," Dad says. "Was it awful? Did you already use up that bottle of hand sanitizer I got you?"

"It was fine," Mae tells them. "And clean enough."

"How were the views?"

"How's the Midwest?"

"How was Pennsylvania?"

"How was Indiana?"

Mae laughs. "It was all great. Probably not as scenic as it'll be out west, but still kind of fun to see."

"How's it going with Piper?"

She glances at Hugo, who rolls over and snuffles a little in his sleep. "Great," she says, her face flushing. It feels wrong to be talking to her parents while she's in bed with a boy, even though it's not exactly like that. Nothing happened last night. Not really.

But then, also: a lot happened.

For Mae, it was never like that before, certainly not with Garrett, and not with the handful of other boys she's kissed. With them, there was always a certain amount of awareness of what was happening, the clinking teeth and roving hands, all the various moving pieces.

But with Hugo, there was no thinking, only feeling. Everything else melted away, and the world went quiet. There was something almost inevitable about it, something automatic, like it was the most obvious thing in the world, to be kissing him like that. And when they finally stopped, taking a giant step back from each other, they were both laughing a little.

"Hi," she said.

He grinned at her through the dark. "Hi."

This whole time, they'd been avoiding the bed because

145

it felt like a question too big to answer. But now it was right there, and they were right here, a feeling of electricity between them so powerful it felt like it could light up the room.

"Now what?" she asked, full of nerves and excitement.

"Now," Hugo said, "we sleep."

They climbed into the bed from opposite sides, and Mae was grateful when he positioned himself at the very edge. She did, too, but the bed was enormous, and soon it started to feel like an ocean between them. After a minute, Hugo stretched a hand out into the middle, casually and quietly, and she smiled and inched hers out to meet it. Then they lay there in silence, their fingers twined, until the space became too much to bear, and Mae scooted over to his side of the bed, throwing an arm across his chest. She felt him let out a happy sigh, and she tucked her face into the hollow of his shoulder, and they fell asleep that way.

Now she watches him as her dads continue to pepper her with questions. "Is she a nightmare? Or is she cool? Does she have any weird habits that you can already tell are gonna drive you nuts this year?"

When Mae doesn't answer right away, Dad lowers his voice.

"Is she in the room with you right now, so you can't tell us?" he asks quietly. "Listen, if she's horrible, just say *grapefruit*."

Mae shakes her head. "Dad."

"Can you tell what we're having for breakfast?" Pop says, laughing. "What should she say if she likes her? *Coffee with soy milk*?"

"Don't be ridiculous," Dad says. "If she's cool, say *cantaloupe*."

"Cantaloupe," Mae says with a note of finality. "So how's Nana?"

Pop laughs. "Back to normal, I guess. We offered to come down again for dinner tonight, but she's apparently playing poker with some friends."

"They'd better be careful," says Mae. "She cleaned out my savings this summer."

"We're going for brunch tomorrow instead."

"Give her a hug for me."

"We will," Pop promises. "And say hi to Cantaloupe for us."

"That's not her name," Dad says, exasperated. "It was a code for . . . never mind. You'd make a terrible spy."

"I'm completely okay with that," Pop says. "Love you, Mae."

"Love you guys too."

She hangs up and glances over at Hugo. Here in the hotel bed, with the light from the window falling across his forehead, Mae is amused by how much this feels like a scene from one of her grandmother's old romances. They've watched a million of them over the years—Nana for the swoony men, Mae for the cinematic history—and she's always found them faintly ridiculous.

"Come on," she'd say when the couple first kissed or when they were brought together by the most unlikely circumstances. "There's just no way."

Nana would usually just turn up the volume. But one

night this spring, soon after finishing a full month of chemo, she hit Pause and turned to Mae with a look of great patience.

"It's not supposed to reflect reality," she said. "Reality is all well and good. But sometimes you just want to pretend the world is a better place than it actually is. That great and wonderful things can happen. That love triumphs over everything."

It isn't until now, though, that Mae fully gets it, the pleasure of letting reality fall away. Whatever is happening with Hugo is just as ridiculous as those movies. Maybe even more so. It's unlikely and temporary and deeply uncharacteristic. But still, she can't shake the feeling that she's fallen straight into one of those stories.

This is what she's thinking as she watches Hugo, who she's assumed is asleep. But then his eyes pop open so suddenly that she yelps. He laughs and grabs her around the waist, pulling her close, making it alarmingly easy to forget everything else.

After a few minutes, she sits up again, and Hugo rolls out of bed, padding over to the window. He pulls back the curtains, and the light comes flooding in.

"Wow," he says as Mae walks up beside him. It's their first real view of the lake, which shimmers beyond the city, disappearing into the horizon. "That's . . . beautiful."

She knows he's talking about the view, but when she turns, he's looking at her in a way that makes her blush. "Let's go explore."

They decide that the first stop should be a diner. "Of

all the things I want to see in this city," Hugo says, "the most important is a stack of waffles the size of the Hancock building."

At the diner, his knees brush against hers underneath the table, and Mae feels the spark of it each time. As she watches him pour an absurd amount of syrup onto his waffles, she realizes how much she wants to tell someone about this. The minute he gets up to use the restroom, she sends a text with a heart eyes emoji to Priyanka, laughing as she imagines her friend's face when she gets it. Mae has never used one of those in her life. She's never even wanted to. Not until this very moment.

She waits for a response, but nothing comes, which means Priyanka must be in class. She opens a new message to Nana instead.

Mae: So I used your line.

Nana: And??

Mae: It worked.

Nana: Always does. So you like him?

Mae: That seems like it would be a spectacularly stupid thing to do.

Nana: Why?

Mae: Because it's only a week.

Nana: That's more time than you think.

Mae: Not really.

Nana: Is he dreamy?

Mae: Nana!

Nana: Just tell me.

149

Mae:	It would not be inaccurate to say that he's dreamy.
Nana:	Listen . . .
Mae:	?
Nana:	Sometimes it's good for you.
Mae:	What?
Nana:	To be spectacularly stupid.

Mae sets her phone down when Hugo slides back into his seat. "Hey," she says. "Can I ask you a question?"

"Sure," he says as he pours more syrup over his waffles.

Now that she's started this, she's not entirely sure how to proceed. "Was Margaret . . ." she says, and he snaps his head up, looking startled. "Were you two . . . ?"

"What?"

"You were in love, right?"

"Yeah," he says, lowering his fork. "We were."

"So what happened?"

He looks uncomfortable. "We just grew apart, I suppose. We'd been together a long time, and something had gotten a bit lost, and . . . Why do you want to talk about Margaret?"

"I'm just curious."

"I'd rather talk about you."

"What do you want to know?"

"Well, I'm curious whether there have been many . . ."
She frowns at him. "What?"

"Waffles," he says, then lets out a slightly nervous laugh. "What do you think? *Blokes*."

"I wouldn't call it *many*," she says. "But there have been a few."

"No boyfriend, though?"

"Not currently."

He raises his eyebrows, waiting for more.

"I was seeing this guy over the summer," she admits, realizing she's hardly thought about Garrett at all since she left. "But it's over. *Really* over."

"Really over, huh?" he says with a grin.

"Do you think I would've kissed you like that if I had a boyfriend?"

"No," he says quickly. "Of course not."

"I wouldn't have," she says, eager for this to be understood. "That was . . ."

"What?" he asks with a smile.

"Not like me."

"Me neither," he says, and when she gives him a skeptical look, he holds up his hands. "Honestly. I'm not some kind of player who meets random girls on trains and then snogs them in hotel rooms. Nothing like this has ever happened to me before. Really."

He's so good-looking that she finds this hard to believe, and he must see it in her face, because he leans forward across the table.

"Okay," he says, "you want to know the truth?"

Mae nods.

"The truth is that Margaret was the first and only girl I've ever kissed."

"Seriously?" she asks, surprised by this.

"Seriously. We met when we were fourteen and basically were together ever since."

"Wow."

He looks down at his plate, scraping at the syrup with his fork. "Yeah."

"Was it really different, then?" Mae asks. "With me?"

"What?" he says, letting out a laugh. "I can't answer that."

"I'm just curious. From a purely scientific perspective."

He shakes his head. "You're mad."

Mae shrugs. "If it helps, it was really different for me."

"It was?" he asks, looking pleased. But then he furrows his brow. "In a good way?"

She nods. "In a very good way."

He grins, and then they both return to their food. But they can't help casting glances at each other every now and then, both of them smiling. Under the table, his knees bump against hers, and she feels the ripple of it travel straight up into her chest, where it bobs around like something lovely and weightless and bright.

After a little while, he nods. "It was different for me too."

Hugo

After brunch, they walk down Michigan Avenue. They've left their bags at the hotel, but Mae still has her trusty camera with her, and whenever they pass something noteworthy—the greenish river or the ornate building made of limestone or a little boy in a pirate's hat—Hugo waits while she pauses to capture some footage.

"B-roll," she says.

He gives her a mystified look. "What's that?"

"Just extra footage to intersperse with the interviews."

He can't help smiling. "I like it when you talk film. You sound very impressive."

"Well, it's not my first rodeo."

"Is that another movie thing?"

"No," she says, laughing. "It just means I've done this before."

"Right. So tell me: How does the B-roll fit into the rodeo?"

Mae shakes her head at him, but he can see that it lights her up, talking about this film.

"Well, I don't want the interviews to feel stagnant," she says. "Part of the story is the train itself: where it's going, where it's come from. So I'm trying get some shots along the way to weave in: people passing by, birds flying overhead, the light changing over the city. Plus, any major landmarks and cool sights and stuff like that."

Hugo steps in front of the camera with a grin. "Do I count?"

"As a landmark?" she says, pointing it away from him. "No."

"How about as a cool sight?" He leans closer to her as people stream around them on the sidewalk. "I don't know if you know this, but I'm very, very cool."

When she laughs, it feels to Hugo like he's won some sort of prize.

"That might be true," she says, "but you still don't make the cut."

"Why not?" he asks as they start to walk again, weaving past some people taking selfies in front of the river. "I'm part of the trip too."

"Yeah, but the film is about the interviews. Not us."

He smiles at the word *us*. "But you're the one doing the traveling. It's your journey."

"It's not," she says, looking over at him sharply. "It's theirs. That's the whole point."

"But surely there must be documentaries that include the filmmaker?"

She frowns at the sidewalk. "Maybe," she says after a moment. "But this isn't one of them."

"Why couldn't it be?"

This time she's the one to stop. Her eyes are shiny, and her hair is tangled from the wind. She seems to be deep in thought, and while he waits, Hugo counts the freckles on her nose.

"Because," she says eventually, and there's an intensity to the words, "I don't know how to be on both sides of the camera."

Hugo almost makes a joke about the simple logistics of this—*You just take two steps to the left!*—but he can see how pained she looks, so he stays quiet. There's more he'd like to know, but he can almost see the window closing, something in her face shifting, and then she turns and begins to walk again. He follows her, both of them silent, until they pass a huge grayish building, where Hugo notices a rock embedded in the side, and he nearly trips over her as he hurries to take a closer look.

"Whoa," he says as she joins him. He points to a dark stone with words carved beneath it. "That's from the Great Wall of China."

Her eyes widen. "Wow."

"And look," Hugo says, getting even more excited. He shuffles to the left, where there's another stone, this one white and uneven. "The Colosseum." His eyes dart up and around to all the many other rocks embedded in the building. "And the Alamo! Saint Peter's! Bloody hell . . . that's from the Berlin Wall."

Mae is trailing after him as he skirts the building, his head tipped back to take it all in. He's aware that he sounds like a lunatic, but he can't bring himself to care. All these places, all these tiny pieces of the world assembled right here in front of him. His mouth has fallen open as he scans through them: bits of the Arc de Triomphe and Westminster Abbey and the Taj Mahal, rocks from Antarctica and Yellowstone and even the moon. The *moon*!

"This is incredible," he says quietly, peering at a stone taken from the Parthenon. He turns to Mae. "How did I not know about this? How is it not the first thing people tell you to do in Chicago?"

She laughs at his enthusiasm. "I don't know. I never heard of it either. But it's pretty cool."

"No, Mae," he says in a stern voice. "The pizza last night was *pretty cool*. So were the waffles this morning. But this? This is something else entirely."

Their train is only a few hours away, and there's so much more of the city to see, but Hugo insists on staying until he's had a chance to look at each and every stone, pacing the perimeter of the building in a daze. When they finally leave, his mind is still busy with it, the idea of all those different places gathered like that, the way the whole world could be contained in a single building.

He feels a little giddy as they make their way farther along Michigan Avenue. It's a beautiful day, the sky shot through with silver, the heat just starting to lift. As Mae darts into a shop, Hugo's mobile begins to buzz in his hand. He waits outside to read his siblings' texts as they arrive one after another:

Alfie: Hey, Hugo. I bet George will bake you fresh scones every morning if you agree to live with him . . .

George: Sod off, Alfie.

Alfie: Just trying to help you out, mate.

Isla: You were the last one to share a room with him, Alf.

Alfie: So?

Oscar: So now he's gone off us.

Alfie: So?

Poppy: Good lord. Connect the dots, man.

Alfie: Hey! I'm a delight.

Isla: Not the first word that comes to mind.

Alfie: Is that because the first word is genius?

Isla: Do you really want me to answer that?

Hugo's stomach twists, the guilt settling over him. He wants to tell them it's not about George. It's not about any of them. But he knows that's not entirely true. How is it possible to miss someone—to miss *five* someones—and still be so outrageously happy to be away from them?

A new message appears, this one separate from the group:

Poppy: Don't worry about George. Really. He'll be fine either way.

Hugo: You think?

Poppy: I realise this isn't always easy, but you should just do
         what you want.

What I want, Hugo thinks, looking up at the clouds.

He stares at the phone for a second before writing: *I
don't want to go back*.

Then he erases the letters one at a time, his heart beating
very fast. He didn't even realize he was thinking that, but
the words feel solid and heavy in his mind.

I don't know what I want, he types instead, but his face
is burning because he's not so sure that's true.

Poppy: Well, don't wait too long to work it out.
Hugo: Thanks, P. You're the best.
Poppy: I don't know about that, but I'm at least better than
         Alfie, right?
Hugo: Top three, for sure.

When Mae comes out of the shop, he gives her a smile
and starts to follow her up the street, but his mind is still
turning over the words in his head: *I don't want to go back*.
He tries his best to stuff the thought down again, but now
that it's out there, sunlit and exposed, it's difficult to tuck
away.

At the end of Michigan Avenue, past the old stone
water tower, there's a thumbnail of beach. Sitting in the
shadow of the towering Hancock building, right at the end
of one of the busiest shopping streets in the world, it's a
strange sort of oasis. They cross the street and walk out

onto the sand, which is soft and glittering—full of people, and crowded with towels—then pick their way to the edge of the green-blue lake. It's rough today, a reminder of last night's storm, and Hugo holds his trainers in one hand as he inches closer to the water. When it rushes over his feet, he shivers.

"It's freezing," he says, delighted, and Mae steps in too. She takes out her camera, turning in a circle to capture the water below and the sky above and then the sun glinting off the buildings behind them. She laughs as a wave splashes her legs, licking at the edges of her dress, and the sound of it makes Hugo feel light. Glancing down, he spots a piece of sea glass half-buried in the wet sand and stoops to pick it up, thinking of the stones on the building, each marking a spot on the globe. He tucks it into his pocket, happy to have captured a sliver of this day, this city, this moment.

After a few minutes, Mae heads back up the beach, and Hugo follows her. They lie on their backs, arms thrown over their eyes, mouths filled with the gritty taste of sand. It's itchy and hot and wonderful, and Hugo thinks he could stay here forever.

"We can't both fall asleep, okay?" he says. "Otherwise we might miss our train."

Mae turns her head to look at him, and he can see the freckles across the bridge of her nose. "We've been up for, like, two hours. You already need a nap?"

"It's sunny," he says. "And I'm still jet lagged."

"You can sleep on the train. Now you have to talk to me."

"Couldn't it also be argued that we could sleep now,

talk later?" he asks, stifling a yawn, but she just crinkles her nose in a way he finds irresistible.

"How did you decide to take a train?" she asks. "And why here?"

"Well, I don't have a license, and Margaret hates to drive, so that ruled out a road trip."

"You don't have a license?"

"There's one car and eight people in my house. Makes it a bit hard to practice. Plus, I've always thought trains were romantic," he says, then immediately feels his face start to burn. "Not like that. I just mean . . . they're sort of nostalgic. You know?"

Mae smiles. "My grandmother says she once left her heart on a train."

"With a boy?" Hugo asks. "Or with her luggage?"

"A boy."

"That's good. Hopefully, mine wasn't in my wallet."

She reaches over and puts a hand on his chest, and he can feel his heartbeat quicken beneath it. "Nope," she says, her face very close to his. "Still there."

"It was her idea," he says after Mae takes her hand away. "Margaret booked the whole thing. At the time, I thought it was because she wanted to spend more time together, and for me to be there when she got to Stanford. But now I'm not so sure. I think maybe she felt guilty."

"For what?"

"Leaving me behind."

They're both quiet, watching a bird circle above. Then Mae turns her head in his direction. "Well," she says, "you're here now."

Hugo reaches into his pocket for the piece of sea glass, pale green and startlingly smooth. He turns it over, watching it glint in the sun, then closes his hand around it.

"I'm here now," he says.

Mae

It feels like it's been years since they were last at Union Station, though it's only been about twenty-four hours. While they wait on the glossy wooden benches, a video call from Nana pops up on Mae's phone. She's already starting to walk away as she answers, intending to find some quieter spot, but when Nana's face appears, the first thing she says is *wait*.

Mae stops in the middle of an aisle, confused. "What?" she asks, looking down at the phone. Nana is sitting on the window seat at her apartment, the black cherry tree behind her already starting to turn yellow, and it's been so long since Mae has seen her there, in her natural habitat, that she can't help feeling a little emotional.

"Go back to wherever you were," Nana says sternly, her face a little too close to the phone. "I want to clap eyes on this fellow of yours."

"No way," Mae says, glancing back at Hugo, who is sitting on the bench where she left him, reading his book of facts about the United States. "I'm not doing that."

"I'll give you twenty bucks."

"Nana."

"Fifty."

"No!"

"I'll let you pick the movies at Thanksgiving."

Mae laughs. "Fine."

When she walks back over, Hugo looks up from his book. "Did you know that Chicago isn't called the Windy City because it's windy?"

"Yes," Mae says, then turns the phone around. "Nana, this is Hugo."

Hugo blinks at the screen, momentarily startled. Then he gives a little wave. "Hello!"

"Well, aren't you handsome," Nana says, getting so close to the screen that her nose disappears, and there's nothing but a pair of watery blue eyes and a wrinkled forehead. "Mae told me as much, but I had to see for myself."

"I did not—" Mae starts to say, then turns to Hugo. "I didn't tell her anything."

Hugo laughs. "It's nice to meet you. I've heard such lovely things about you from your granddaughter."

"Listen, I've known Mae a long time, so I thought you could use a few tips," Nana says. "First of all, she's always got one eye behind that camera of hers, so sometimes you have to take it away so she doesn't trip."

"One time," Mae says. "That happened one time."

"And she's afraid of heights, so don't go joyriding on top of the train or anything."

"Noted," Hugo says, nodding very seriously.

"She hates spiders—"

"Covered that one already."

"And talks a *lot*."

"You guys know I'm still here, right?" Mae says, her eyes traveling up to the board, where the track number for their train has just been posted. "Hey, we gotta go."

"Last thing," Nana says, shifting her gaze to Hugo. "She's one of the best people I know. And she's a real catch. So be good to her, okay?"

Mae closes her eyes for a second, mortified. "Thanks, Nana," she says as she brings the phone up to her face again. "I love you, and I'll call you when we get to Denver."

Nana gives a little wave. "Happy travels!"

After hanging up, Mae turns to Hugo. "Well, that's Nana. She's—"

"Brilliant," he says with a grin. "Let's make sure I'm there when you call her from Denver, so I can hear the rest of her tips."

This train is bigger than the last, with two floors and an observation car at one end. An attendant named Duncan—a short white man with bright red hair—leads them to their compartment, which is about the same as the last, two seats and a fold-down bunk at the top.

But this time, when he leaves them, there's no awkward silence or uncertainty. This time, as soon as he's gone, Hugo takes a step forward and puts a hand on her elbow, and Mae tips her head up to look at him, and they smile at each other like they're the holders of some great secret.

"You still have sand in your hair," she says, reaching up to brush it away, but before she can finish, he's folded her into his arms, and they're kissing again.

Mae has wanted to do this all morning. Sitting across from him at the diner, walking beside him along Michigan Avenue, lying next to him on the beach: it was underneath and around every other thought, a persistent drumbeat beneath every gesture, every word, every look.

She knows this can't last—whatever it is; that a few days from now, they'll be getting off at different stations, going in different directions. But she doesn't care. Because for now, they have this: a happiness so big it doesn't leave room for worries.

When Duncan returns, he has to clear his throat several times before they realize he's standing in the hallway. They break apart so quickly that Hugo nearly falls back against his seat, and Duncan stares hard at his notepad, trying not to laugh.

"Sorry to interrupt, but will you two be joining us for dinner tonight?"

After they've made their reservations, Mae's phone buzzes, and she grabs it before Hugo can see the long row of exclamation points that Priyanka has sent, followed by a second text that says *Call me.*

"I'm gonna make a quick call," she says to Hugo. "So I'll just—"

"No, you stay here," he says. "Meet me in the observation car when you're done."

On the way out, he leans to give her a kiss on the cheek, and then she waits until she hears his footsteps on the metal staircase to call. All Mae says when she picks up is *hi,* but this is enough to make Priyanka immediately start laughing.

"What?" Mae asks, grinning into the phone.

"Nothing. It's just that I can practically hear you smiling. It's so unlike you."

"Hey! I smile."

"Yeah, but hardly ever about a *boy.*"

Mae flops back onto the seat and puts her feet up on Hugo's. "So how's college life?"

"No way. We're talking about you first. Tell me everything."

And so she does. By the time she gets to the part where they kissed last night, Priyanka is laughing again. "Only you would use your grandmother's line to get a guy to kiss you," she says. "Bet you don't think those movies of hers are so unrealistic anymore, huh?"

"This isn't like that," Mae says. "It's just a fling."

"It is *not.*"

"How do you know?"

"Because a fling suggests it doesn't mean anything," Priyanka says. "And I can tell that it does."

"No, a fling is a measurement of time. And this has an expiration date."

Priyanka sighs. "Stop being so . . . you."

166

"What does that mean?" Mae asks, indignant.

"Just that it's okay to give in and enjoy it. You're on a train making out with a guy you barely know. It's romantic."

Mae laughs. "A week ago, you thought he was going to kill me."

"Well, he didn't. And you sound really happy. So don't overthink it. Just—"

The line goes dead, and when Mae lowers her phone, she sees that there's no service anymore. She waits a few minutes, and when it doesn't return, she sends a quick text: *Sorry I lost you. But I'm off to go enjoy it. Aren't you happy I'm taking your advice?*

It bounces back, but there's nothing to be done about that now, so she winds her way through the other sleeper cars, past the dining room, where the tablecloths are already out, and into the observation area. Hugo is in one of the seats facing out toward the huge rounded windows that reach all the way up to the ceiling, and when Mae sits down beside him, he turns to her with a smile.

"How's your friend?"

"Good. We got cut off."

"Hopefully not before you had a chance to tell her all about me," he says with a grin, and she punches his arm.

"Someone's pretty full of himself."

He laughs. "Someone was told this morning that he's a good kisser."

"Someone had better be careful about getting a big head."

"Someone will try his best," Hugo says, propping

his feet up on the ledge and looking out the enormous windows at the houses whipping past. "This'll be brilliant when we're in the mountains, won't it?"

Mae nods and takes her camera out of the bag on her lap, ready to capture the changes in scenery as they head west, first through Iowa and Nebraska, and then on to Denver, which they'll reach tomorrow morning.

"I think I've already spotted some good potential interviews," Hugo says. "As your assistant director, I feel like I should get first crack at choosing one this time."

She laughs. "That's a pretty big promotion for someone who couldn't stop talking through the shots yesterday. What are your salary requirements?"

To her surprise, he leans in to give her a quick kiss, then sits back, looking pleased with himself. "I think we're all sorted now. Unless you'd like to discuss some sort of raise."

She grabs the front of his shirt, pulling him back toward her, and this time she kisses him in earnest. When they sit back again, she's grinning like crazy, and so is he.

"I'd say you're off to a good start," she says. "What else you got?"

Hugo nods at an older black couple sitting a few seats away. They have a tablet propped on a tray beneath the window; it shows a digital map with a blue dot that's following their route. They've also got binoculars, a compass, and two packs of Starburst. "You should ask them. Clearly, this isn't their first rodeo."

The way he says *rodeo* is so charming that Mae feels desperate to kiss him again. It's enough to make her want to write a list of funny American words—*dude* and *zonked* and *cotton candy*—and have him recite them all afternoon. But instead she begins to adjust the settings on her camera. "Good call."

"So what do you do with these, anyway?"

She glances up at him. "What do you mean?"

"Your films. Do you post them somewhere? Have screenings? Send them around to your friends? If my name's going to be in lights, I need to know where I can find it."

"I have a website," she says, still tinkering with the dials. "I put my favorites up there."

"What about the rest?"

She shrugs. "I learn from them and move on."

"So you could spend weeks—"

"Months."

"—on a film and then never show it to anybody?"

"Sure. If I'm not happy with it."

"How often does that happen?"

"Often," she says with an air of resignation. "I have a folder on my computer called *Rejects* that's alarmingly full. Sometimes you get to the end and the magic just isn't there."

"Is that what happened with USC?"

"That was different." Mae looks over at the couple with their maps and gadgets; the man holds out a stick of Starburst, and the woman takes one off the top. "You know when you think you're about to eat a pink Starburst, but you realize too late it's an orange one?"

Hugo smiles. "I like the orange ones."

"Well, you're just weird, then," she says, giving him a playful kick. "But I don't. And I really thought I was sending USC a pink one."

"You have no idea what went wrong?"

There's a part of her that wants to tell Hugo what Garrett said. But every time she thinks about it, she feels such irritation at the critique—*Impersonal! Seriously?*—that she can barely concentrate. She tried to watch the film one more time the night before she left, already composing the text she'd send to Garrett—which involved a certain number of *actuallys*—but in the end, she didn't work up the nerve. Now there was a word attached to the failure, something too specific to ignore, and she wasn't sure she wanted to see it through his eyes. Even so, the rebuttals continue to scroll through her head, stubborn and persistent.

"No idea," she says to Hugo, who doesn't look convinced but also doesn't press the issue.

They're well out of the city now, the houses getting farther apart as the train moves across the state. The windows have a slightly yellow tint, turning everything sepia toned, making it feel like they've fallen into one of Nana's old movies.

Mae looks around the car. There are people playing a board game at one of the tables, a kid teaching his grandfather how to take a selfie, two men drinking beers and talking about this year's wheat crop, a young couple reading their books. All of them on their way somewhere, barreling across the country in this long metal tube.

"I really would love to see it," Hugo says, and she turns back to him, a little dazed.

"What?"

"Your film."

"Oh," she says with a frown. "I don't think so."

"Would you at least tell me what it's about?"

"Hugo . . ."

He doesn't look the least bit put off. "Will I have a guess, then? Is it about a dancing platypus?"

"What?" She lets out a surprised laugh. "No."

"Is it about a porcupine who can't find his way home?"

"Not exactly."

"Is it about the first man to win a bowling tournament with a tennis ball?" he says with a grin. "Or a woman who swallows a piece of gum and discovers a gum tree in her stomach years later? Or a girl who runs away to Antarctica and becomes best friends with a walrus? Or a boy with a scar on his forehead who goes off to a wizarding school?"

Mae is shaking her head. "I'm pretty sure that last one's been done before."

"I've got it," Hugo says, his face brightening. "Is it about *you*?"

"No," she says, and her smile slips. "Not exactly."

He looks at her closely, so closely that she finds herself shifting beneath his gaze. "Well then," he says, "maybe that's the problem."

Hugo

As they near Iowa, the land lengthens out like someone took a rolling pin to it, flat and low and endless. Hugo can't get over all the cornfields, miles and miles of them as far as he can see. They ripple in the wind like they're made of water, full of whirlpools and eddies, and he wishes he could stick a hand out the window and let it pass over the feathery tips.

Mae is at the far end of the car, chatting with a couple about her film, and when Hugo closes his eyes for a second, the thought bubbles up again: *I don't want to go back.*

It fizzes inside him, bright as a sparkler.

A crow flies by out the window, coasting effortlessly at the same speed as the train, and he realizes his mind is already tiptoeing in that direction, spinning over an imaginary globe.

It wouldn't be forever, he thinks, and the arguments begin to line up in his head then, one by one, a blindly hopeful procession.

People take gap years all the time. And he's got money saved, some from summer jobs and some from when the six of them modeled for a local department store as children (a deeply embarrassing chapter of their lives). It's not a lot, but he could do it on the cheap, find discount flights and stay in hostels, live off bowls of peanuts in random pubs if he had to. He's already proved he can get himself from London to Denver, at the very least. (Wallet aside.)

Maybe he could simply defer his scholarship and start uni the following autumn, graduate a year behind the others, give himself a chance to try something new before then, to take what he's felt this week and carry it with him over the course of a whole year.

Because that's the thing: it's only been a few days, but already he feels entirely different. And now that he knows, how can he do anything but keep going?

The idea flutters in his chest like a bird in a cage, and he looks around for Mae, suddenly eager to tell her. At the end of the busy car, she's sitting at a table with a Hasidic couple, her notebook open in front of her as she listens to them, and he smiles to himself, struck once again by her passion. But then he imagines trying to explain this to her without it sounding like he's just going to skive off for a year, and he can feel his excitement start to wilt.

Mae knows exactly what she wants, and that's never been Hugo's strong suit. Now that he's found something, now that he's got a plan—or at least the start of one—he wants to be sure of it before telling her.

They spend the rest of the afternoon doing interviews: an economics professor from Idaho who was recently widowed, a family from Singapore on their first trip to America, a mother and daughter who are making a pilgrimage to Salt Lake City. A few people decline, and one even laughs in their faces. Another—a grizzled white man with a long beard—simply gives them the finger. But most people have stories to tell and are eager to share them.

The couple they saw earlier—Louis and Katherine—turn out to be celebrating their recent retirements, and they're in it for the long haul: Washington, DC, all the way to San Francisco.

"Then what?" Mae asked, and Katherine smiled.

"Exactly."

At the end, Hugo couldn't resist posing one last question. "So what's your favorite color Starburst?"

"I like the red and orange ones," Louis said, "and she likes the pink and yellow ones."

"Which is how you can tell we're perfect for each other," Katherine added.

At dinner, Hugo and Mae are seated across from two white women in their fifties, Karen and Trish, sisters on their way back from visiting their mother in Iowa.

"Does she live on a farm?" Hugo asks, because from what he's seen of the state so far, that seems to be all there is. But they both laugh at this.

"Where are you from, darlin'?" Trish asks. She has

curly blond hair and very red lipstick, and she's wearing a shirt with little sequins on it. Her sister, Karen, is more muted; she has the same color hair, but hers hangs long and straight, and she has glasses and very little makeup on. They both peer at him with open curiosity from across the table.

"England," he says, and to his surprise, they both say "Aww" and scrunch up their noses in a way someone might when they've come face to face with a kitten.

He can feel Mae watching him with amusement, but he doesn't look at her, because if he does, he knows he'll be distracted by how she purses her lips when she's thinking about something, or how the dress she's wearing today—a yellow so sunny that he can't stop looking at it—inches up when she sits down, and how even though she's so much shorter than he is, her legs somehow seem to go on forever in it.

"Have you ever been?" he asks the sisters, who both laugh.

"No, we've never *been*," Karen says, mimicking his accent. "But maybe one day. I'd sure like to see that castle. What's it called? The one where the queen lives."

"Buckingham Palace," Hugo says. "But that's in London. I'm from a place called Surrey, which isn't too far from there."

"So how did you end up on a train in Iowa?"

"How does anyone end up on a train in Iowa?" Mae jokes, and they both turn their attention to her.

"You're not from England," Karen points out.

"No, I'm from New York. But also not the city."

"How did you two meet?"

"It's a long story," Hugo says, reaching for Mae's hand underneath the table. She clasps his back, and he feels an instant warmth spread through him. Outside, the sun has dipped low, casting long shadows on the fields of corn. They pass a herd of cows huddled close, a road with a dusty pickup truck lumbering by, a small town with an American flag waving high above the buildings. It all feels unreal somehow, sliding past like this, as if it's part of a film montage.

Once they've ordered—a steak for him, some sort of chicken dish for her—they hand back their menus. The sisters are on their second glass of wine each, and Trish winks at them from across the table. "If you'd just spent six days with our mother, you'd be drinking too."

Karen lifts her glass. "Amen."

"So what's England like?" Trish asks.

Hugo shrugs. "You know, mostly just tea and crumpets. That sort of thing."

He's only teasing, of course, but they both nod very seriously. "Do you go to college here or there?" asks Trish.

"Neither," he says. "Yet."

There must be something in his voice that warns her off a follow-up question, because she nods and turns to Mae. "How about you?"

"I start at USC next week," she says. "That's where I'm headed now."

"Well, isn't that wonderful," Trish says, then nudges

Karen. "It's wonderful, isn't it?"

Karen nods. "Wonderful. My three are still little, but I'd love it if they got into somewhere like that one day. Or somewhere in England," she says, looking over at Hugo. "Do you miss it?"

He grins at her. "Would it be absolutely horrible if I said no?"

"Trust me," Trish says, "we get it. We just spent a week watching soap operas and learning to crochet. Home can be overrated."

"It's just that I've never really been anywhere else," he says. "And it's nice to be on my own for a bit. But it's only been a few days. I'm sure I'll start missing them all soon."

"You have brothers or sisters?"

Hugo glances sideways at Mae, then says, "Both. There are six of us."

"Older or younger?"

He hesitates, as he always does at this point in the conversation. "The same age, actually. We're sextuplets."

They both stare at him blankly.

"Multiples," he says. "We were all—"

"Yeah, darlin', we know what sextuplets are," Trish says, shaking her head. "It's just . . . wow. There are really six of you? All the same age?"

He nods.

"Are you identical?"

"Some of us," he says. "But I'm the handsome one."

When Mae laughs at this, he feels a rush of pleasure. Behind them, a bald man with a handlebar mustache turns

177

around in his seat. "Did you say you're a sextuplet?"

Hugo nods, realizing how many people are staring at him. The booths are small and pressed close together, a whole dining room shoved into a train car.

"My cousin has triplets," the man says, "and I thought *that* was a lot of work."

A woman a couple of tables over cranes her neck to look at Hugo. "I'm a twin," she says in a low voice, sounding shy about it.

Hugo realizes that half the people on the train are staring at him now. He's used to this sort of thing back home, where the six of them are fairly well known—though even there, it's rare for someone to recognize him when he's not with his siblings. Once when he was in London with Margaret, a group of young girls stopped to ask if he was one of the Surrey Six. They fell into giggles when he said he was, and asked him to autograph two receipts, a phone case, and even someone's forearm. But usually it takes the whole gaggle of them to elicit any sort of attention.

Here in America, it's different. The books aren't published on this side of the ocean, and there aren't many readers of the blog in this country either. Americans have their own sets of famous multiples. So he's chalked up most of the stares he's gotten to the color of his skin or the fact that he's traveling with a white girl. Or maybe, if he's being generous, to his height.

But now, once again, he's no longer just Hugo. He's one-sixth of something bigger.

And even amid the general merriment of this train

car—the curious questions and eager faces—this feels like a kind of loss.

Their waiter arrives, shaking his head as he sets down their plates. "Man, I've got five brothers and sisters, too, but I can't imagine dealing with all of us at the same time. Your mom is a damn hero."

"How many sextuplets are there in the world?" asks Karen as she begins to slice up her chicken. "There can't be that many."

"I'm not really sure," Hugo says around a forkful of lettuce. "I haven't met any others."

"Are you famous, then?"

He shrugs, not wanting to get into it. "Mostly just in our town."

"Is it hard to remember all their names?" Trish wants to know.

"I've got them pretty well down at this stage."

"Do you all get along?" asks the man behind them. "Did you guys fight a lot?"

"Never," Hugo says, and around him, there's a ripple of laughter. "Not once."

"Do you have a favorite?"

"Yeah. Me."

"Do your parents have a favorite?"

"Yeah. Me."

"Are you all going off to college together?" asks Trish, and Hugo feels the air around him deflate again. He blinks, trying to come up with an answer, then takes a bite of his steak and chews it slowly.

Mae watches him for a second, then puts a hand on his knee, which he didn't even realize was bobbing underneath the table. "I think it's still to be decided," she says, and Hugo looks over at her in surprise. It's like she's managed to look straight into his head, and he wonders if maybe she's right. Maybe it's not so decided after all.

Across the table, Trish takes a swig of wine, and Karen's attention moves to the window, and the man behind them turns around again. Slowly the dining car returns to its usual noises as the world outside slips into darkness.

Trish tilts her head at Mae. "So if you live here," she says, her eyes tracking over to Hugo, "and he lives there, how does this work?"

Hugo doesn't even have a chance to revel in the fact that she assumes he and Mae are a couple. The question hits him square in the chest, knocking the breath right out of him.

"Yeah," Karen says, "what happens when you two get off the train?"

For a second, they're both quiet. Then Mae looks at Hugo, and he looks back at her. Beneath the table, her hand slips off his knee.

"That," she says, "is a very good question."

Mae

Mae wakes to stillness. The low rumble of the engine has disappeared, the train no longer moving. There's a faint red light in the hallway, but otherwise the room is so dark that it takes her a few tries to find the curtain. She pushes it back, but all she can see is her own dim reflection.

Above her, Hugo is snoring, and she listens to the sound of it, steady and reassuring. The first night, Mae had tried to stay awake as long as she could, anxious about her own snoring, which Priyanka once compared to the sound of a dying warthog. But somewhere along the way, she drifted off. When she woke a few hours later, she heard the uneven whistle of Hugo's snores above and realized she wasn't the only one.

After that, she stopped worrying so much.

Now she sits up, bent low so she doesn't hit her head,

and slips on her shoes. In the hall, she pauses to look at her phone. It's after three, the deepest part of the night. The curtains are drawn on all the other compartments, doors shut tight and locked. Mae closes theirs gently behind her, then walks toward the bathrooms, where she's surprised to see Duncan standing against one of the main doors. His face is pressed to the window, and he's twirling an unlit cigarette between his fingers. When he turns around, he looks startled to see her.

"Can't sleep?" he asks, leaning a shoulder against the heavy doors. "It's hard to get used to those beds."

"Where are we?"

He sweeps a hand toward the window, the vast blackness beyond it. "Heaven," he says, and when she looks at him blankly, he laughs. "Just kidding. This happened in Iowa a few weeks ago, and the joke worked a lot better there." He raises an eyebrow. "*Field of Dreams*? No? Never mind. We're in Nebraska."

"This isn't a station."

He glances out at the darkness. "No."

"Then why are we stopped?"

"Mechanical issue."

"Is it serious?"

Duncan shrugs. "Don't know yet."

"Can we go outside?"

"Not now. But if it looks like we're gonna be here for a while, they'll probably let us get some air later. We once got stuck for eleven hours, and we ordered pizza right to the tracks. It was awesome."

Mae glances around. It's not exactly that she's claustrophobic. When she was eleven, she saw a story about a director who filmed an entire movie while crouched in the backseat of a car. After that, she took to finding hiding spots, scaring the life out of her dads, who kept discovering her in closets and hampers and wardrobes. She has no problem with small spaces.

This is something different, a slight sense of unreality. Here in the middle of nowhere, stuck on the tracks in this deepest of nights, she can't help feeling unmoored. It's like more than just the train has paused, like time itself has stopped for the moment.

In the fluorescent light of the train, she can see the dark circles under Duncan's eyes, and he puts a hand over his mouth to hide a yawn. She looks at him closely, realizing he can't be much older than she is. "How long are your shifts?"

"Not too bad. I got to sleep a little earlier."

"Are you always on this route?"

"Yup. Chicago to Emeryville. I get off, smell the bay, turn around, and come straight back. Then I sleep for three days and do it all over again."

"You must know it well. This part of the country."

"Only what I can see out the window," he says with a shrug. He gives her a smile that's meant to be charming. "So where's your boyfriend?"

Mae doesn't bother to correct him. She likes the sound of it: *boyfriend*. "He's asleep."

"How long have you been together?"

She doesn't answer him. Instead, she walks to the other set of doors, across the car. Through the grimy window, the sky is thick with stars. There's the sound of clanking outside, metal on metal, and Mae looks over at Duncan.

"That's either a good sign," he says, "or a bad one."

She glances down at her phone, thinking suddenly of home. Her dads are early risers; they're probably at the kitchen table right now, arguing about how many cups of coffee is too many. She starts to thumb over to her list of favorites, when she realizes there's no service.

"This whole route is pretty patchy," Duncan says. "We're in a dead zone now."

"You make it sound like the start of a horror movie."

He laughs at this. "I can never watch those things."

"Me neither." She looks again at the stars out the window. "What happens if we're stuck here for a while?"

"Then we're stuck here for a while. Me and this guy in the dining car, Raymond, we always make bets on delays. The over-under on this one is six hours."

"Are you over or under?"

"Over," he says. "We're already an hour in, and it doesn't seem like we're going anywhere soon."

"Hey, Duncan, can I ask you a question?"

"Sure."

"What's your biggest dream?" She doesn't have her camera with her, but she finds she wants to know anyway.

He doesn't hesitate, not even for a second. It's as if he gets asked this question every single day. "A cabin on a lake. Maybe up in Wisconsin. I'd go ice fishing in the winters and take a boat out in the summers. Maybe get a dog to sit with me on the porch. No work. No schedules. No passengers." He cracks a grin. "No offense."

"None taken."

"Just those stars," he says, jabbing a thumb at the window. "But without the glass."

Mae nods. "That sounds nice."

"Sure does."

She doesn't ask his word for love. He's still looking up at the stars with a thoughtful expression, and that feels to Mae like answer enough.

"Good night, Duncan," she says with a smile, and he gives her a little wave.

"Good night, Margaret Campbell, room twenty-four."

Mae flinches at this, the reminder that's trailed her halfway across the country. She's not Hugo's girlfriend. She doesn't know what she is, but it's not that.

Just enjoy it, Priyanka said, which has never been a problem for Mae. In fact, it's what these types of things have always been: fun and breezy and uncomplicated. There's no reason why this should be any different.

It's not that she doesn't believe in love. But seeing other people's stories unfold always feels like watching a movie she would never have picked out for herself. Somewhere there must be a version that's more like the films in her head, bright and colorful and unique.

"You're a tough nut to crack," Nana once told her, and Priyanka's warning that she's too careful with her heart is still ringing in her ears.

But they're both wrong. Her heart isn't the problem.

It's that she's never met someone she actually hopes will break through.

When she reaches the door to their compartment, she pauses for a moment. Beneath her feet, there's a faint vibration, almost like the purring of cat, but nothing else. After a few seconds, it disappears again, and they're no longer even idling. They're just stuck.

Trains are meant to be in motion. People too. They should be on their way somewhere, slicing through the dark rather than huddling here beneath it.

She slides open the door. Hugo is still asleep, his face mashed into the pillow, his arm hanging over the edge of the bunk. She steps up to the bed and studies him for a second, then—unable to resist—stands on her tiptoes and kisses him on the nose.

His eyelids flutter, and when they open, he looks sleepy and unfocused.

"Hugo?" she whispers.

"Yeah?"

"Doesn't it sort of feel like this is a dream?"

"Yeah," he says, then closes his eyes again. Mae is about to crawl into her own bunk when she hears his voice again. "A good one?"

"Yes," she says, and he shifts over, leaving room for her to climb into the bunk beside him. It's not graceful; she scrabbles to find the step, then bumps her head on the ceiling, and when she tries to shimmy in beside him, her foot gets caught in the safety net. But eventually she burrows her way into the small space, and he slips his arms around her so that she can feel the thud of his heart against her back as she falls asleep.

Hugo

Sometime just before dawn, Hugo wakes with a start. The light behind the curtains is dull, the train jostling beneath them. One arm is draped over Mae's shoulder, his nose buried in her hair. He doesn't remember her climbing into bed with him, but it somehow also feels like she's always been here, curled beside him in this tiniest of spaces.

She's breathing softly, whistling a little each time she inhales, and he disentangles himself carefully, reaching for his mobile, which he tucked beneath his pillow. The glow of the screen brightens the room, and he turns on his side to keep from waking Mae. It's just before 5 a.m., which means it's late morning back home. He finds a text from his dad with a picture of the breakfast table. In it, there are seven plates piled with bacon and eggs and toast, and one empty one in the middle. *Come home soon*, it says. *We miss you.*

Hugo lowers his mobile, filled with a clawing despair.

A quote flashes into his head from a Samuel Beckett play he read in his literature class this year: I can't go on, I'll go on.

The words had chimed at something in him even then, but now they feel like a drumbeat, and he opens his mobile again to write to Alfie, a test balloon that sets his heart beating wildly.

Hugo: What if I didn't come back?

Alfie: Ever??

Hugo: No, I was thinking more like a gap year.

Alfie: I can't tell if you're taking the piss.

Hugo: I'm not.

Alfie: Wow. That would be like the complete opposite of pulling a Hugo.

Hugo: Do you think Mum and Dad would kill me?

Alfie: Yes.

Hugo: But after that, they'd be okay with it?

Alfie: As long as you get your arse to uni at some point.

Hugo: George would never forgive me.

Alfie: You know how he is. He just likes to keep the flock together. But I'm sure he'd come around eventually.

Hugo: Maybe.

Alfie: Yeah, maybe.

Hugo: It's a bit mad, isn't it?

Alfie: I don't know. It kind of makes sense. Your heart was never in it.

Hugo: It's in this.

Alfie: So you'd give up the scholarship?

Hugo: Hopefully just defer it for a year.

Alfie: Better check to make sure we're not a package deal. Five out of six isn't bad, but you know they might not see it that way.

Hugo: I wouldn't go ahead if it messed up anything for the rest of you.

Alfie: But you really want it?

Hugo: I really, really want it.

Alfie: Then I hope they say yes.

Hugo rests the phone on his chest, watching it rise and fall in the gray light. He feels caught somewhere between asleep and awake. Before he can think better of it, he's searching his contacts for a name: Nigel Griffith-Jones, Chair of Council, the University of Surrey.

When Hugo's finished with the email, he thinks of the text from his dad again, the empty plate among all those fuller ones. Then he takes a deep breath and hits Send.

Hours later, when Mae begins to stir, Hugo is still awake. He's staring at the ceiling, feeling slightly frozen, paralyzed by what he's done. She twists to face him, her hair tangled but still smelling like lavender from the hotel shampoo, and rests her hand so casually on his chest that he relaxes again.

"Did I snore?" she asks, yawning.

"Only . . . a lot."

She laughs. "You're not so quiet yourself. How long

have you been up?"

"A while," he says, and there must be something odd in his voice, because she lifts her head to look at him. The edges of the curtains are laced with light, and her eyes still look sleepy and unfocused.

"What were you doing?"

"Some planning. Some worrying. Some thinking."

"About?"

He wonders if she can feel his heart pounding underneath her hand. "About possibly taking a gap year."

She stares at him. "Seriously?"

"Seriously," he says, allowing himself a small smile. "I emailed someone on the university council to see if it's possible to defer the scholarship. I want to be sure before I get my hopes too high."

"Your hopes are already high," she says, looking at him fondly. "Have you told your family yet?"

"Just Alfie. George will hate it. And my parents will think that I can't manage on my own or that I'll just be skiving off. But this wouldn't be a lark. I'd obviously love to see some of the world. But it's so much more than that."

Mae rests her chin on his chest, listening.

"I want more time," he says, and there's a catch in his voice. "It's always been easier for the others somehow. To be themselves *and* part of the group. But being here this week—it's made me realize that I need space to sort that out for myself." He reaches over and tucks her hair behind her ear. "I know you're not a detour person—"

Her forehead crinkles. "What do you mean?"

"Only that you know exactly what you want," he says. "Which is a good thing. But I think maybe this can be too." He traces a finger over the back of her hand, deep in thought. "Did I ever tell you my mum used to call me Paddington? Getting lost was my specialty."

She smiles at him. "Maybe it still is."

"I've spent my whole life trailing after them, and this is the first chance I've had to be on my own, and I suppose I'm just not ready for it to end yet." He laughs. "Does this make any sense, or do I sound like someone having a midlife crisis?"

"It makes total sense."

He nods. "I just hope the university lets me. Alfie thinks they might only be interested in a complete set."

"A complete set of what?"

"Sextuplets," he says, his voice flat. "That's how it always works. For interviews and photos and ads; for anything, really. People always want the whole six-pack."

Mae rolls her eyes. "You're people, not cans of beer. Besides, it's only a year, right? They'll still get all six of you eventually."

"I don't know if they'll see it that way. It would be one thing if I had a good reason . . ."

"You do."

"That I want to skive off for a year and travel the world?"

"It's not skiving," she says. "You just said so yourself. And even if it was, who cares? It's your dream."

"As of five minutes ago."

"No," she says, looking at him seriously. "You've known for a long time that you want something different. It just took you a while to figure out what it was."

"I can't decide if you're the cleverest girl I've ever met or you're just as mad as I am."

Mae's eyes are shiny with laughter. "Why can't it be both?" she says brightly.

Below, there's a chorus of *bing*s from her mobile as they return to an area with reception. "We should get up," she says. "Breakfast probably ends soon."

"Wait, what time is it?" he asks as Mae leans over him to open the curtain, and the light comes streaming in to reveal a flat, dusty landscape. "Did we miss our stop?"

"No, they would've woken us. We were stuck for a while last night. You were half-asleep." She's already wriggling away from him, unhooking the safety net so she can swing her legs free and step next to the lower bunk. When she hits the floor, it's with a loud thud. "There's just no graceful way to do that, huh? Come on. I want pancakes. And bacon."

Hugo closes his eyes for a second, thinking again of the text from his dad with a pang of guilt. When he opens them, Mae is unplugging her mobile from the charger. As she starts to scroll through a long series of texts, her face goes pale, and she grips the edge of his bunk to steady herself.

"What?" Hugo asks, his stomach knotted. Mae is always so unshakable; it's alarming to see her like this.

She looks up as if she's forgotten he's there. "We lost

service again."

"We'll get it back in Denver. Is everything—"

"No," she says, shaking her head. She looks like she might cry. "My nana had a stroke."

Hugo's heart judders at the bluntness of the word. "I'm so sorry," he says, though it sounds woefully insufficient. "Will she be okay?"

"I don't know," Mae says numbly. "I think so. My dads are on their way to the hospital now. The doctor told them it was a small one, so hopefully she'll be fine, but . . ."

"But it's still really frightening," Hugo says, and she nods without looking at him, her head bowed over the screen. He feels frozen with uncertainty, not sure if he should leap down and hug her or stay where he is. This is big, what's just happened, and in the grand scheme of things, they hardly know each other. It's been less than a week. But it doesn't feel that way.

It doesn't feel that way at all.

The train is slowing down now, and an announcement comes over the speaker. "Fort Morgan, Colorado," says the crackling voice. "This is Fort Morgan. We've got fifteen minutes here, which is enough time for a cigarette or some air, but not enough time to leave the platform. So feel free to step off, but keep your ears open for that whistle."

Mae grabs her hoodie from the hook near the door. "I'm just gonna . . ." she says, but she doesn't finish the sentence. Instead, she slides on her flip-flops, unchains the lock, and heads around the corner.

For a few seconds, Hugo stays where he is, feeling like a

balloon with a pinhole, the air seeping out of him so slowly that it's hard to tell if it's even happening.

By the time he scrambles off the bed and tugs on a shirt and a pair of trousers, the train has stopped. He takes a gulp of cool air as he steps down onto the platform. There's nothing much here, just a small depot and a gravel parking lot. A few other people from their car have gotten off, too, some of them smoking, others squinting at the sky in hope that the sun might come out, though a line of clouds is gathering in the distance.

He spots Mae all the way up front near the engine, looking very small and very much alone. As he walks toward her, she lowers her mobile, which was pressed to her ear, and stares at it for a second, as if considering whether to launch it onto the tracks. Then she bends down and puts her hands on her knees instead, trying to collect herself.

"I'm okay," she says as he approaches, her head still lowered.

"You don't have to be."

"Yeah, but I am." She sucks in a breath, then stands up. He can see that her eyes are rimmed with red. "It's just this stupid—where the hell are we, anyway?"

He glances back at the sign on the platform. "Fort Morgan, Colorado."

"I know, I just mean . . . how are there so many places in this country without phone service?" she says, waving her mobile around. "It's nuts."

"Nuts," he agrees, and her face softens.

"I need to call my dads."

He takes a step closer. "Of course."

"You don't have to—look, it's going to be fine. She went through chemo this spring, and I think this can just happen sometimes. But she's survived a lot worse. She'll pull through. She always does. It'll be fine."

Hugo puts a hand on either side of her arms, and she goes very still. "You're allowed to be worried."

"I know that," she snaps, wrenching away, but he doesn't move. He bends so their faces are level and sees that her eyes are filled with tears.

"It's okay to be upset," he says quietly.

She shakes her head, but her lip is quivering. "I'm fine."

"Stop saying that. It's just me. You can talk to me."

"I hardly even know you," she says, looking up at him through blazing eyes, and Hugo steps back, stung. He tries to compose his face in a way that doesn't show this, but he can tell that he's failed. Her shoulders sag.

"I'm sorry," she says quickly. "That's not what—"

"No, you're right." He kicks at a gray stone on the ground, watching it skip over the pavement. The train is loud beside them, a sound like the rush of waves at the beach yesterday. Beyond the tracks are a rusty water tower and a distant construction site, but otherwise the landscape is flat and gray and muted, nothing to see for miles around. All that emptiness stirs something in Hugo, and he lets the thought float up again like a brightly colored balloon: *I don't want to go back.*

"Really," she says, putting a hand on his arm. "I didn't mean that."

"I know," he says, because he does. It's not her. It's just the wall she puts up sometimes. But he's managed to knock enough bricks out by now that he can see through it anyway.

He can see *her*.

"The truth is," she says, not quite able to meet his eyes, "you probably know me better than a lot of people in my life do. Which is a weird thing to say, when it's only been a few days."

"It's not, actually," Hugo says with a smile. "It's not weird at all."

She nods, and so does he, and then the whistle sounds, and the conductor—who has been standing nearby—shouts to the passengers still lingering on the platform: "All aboard!"

Above them, the sun is starting to burn through the clouds. The train is louder now, hissing and popping and giving off a hazy heat as they begin to make their way along the length of it. Halfway down, Hugo bends to pick up the gray stone. He slips it into his pocket. Then Mae reaches for his hand and they walk the rest of the way together.

Mae

Mae nearly walks straight into a metal post as she gets off the train in Denver, but she's saved by Hugo, who uses her backpack to steer her around it. She's busy texting Pop, and then Dad, and then both of them for good measure. She's written to Nana several times, too, though Mae knows her grandmother is probably sleeping.

All she wants is to talk to one of them. Any of them. It's been forty minutes since she got reception back, and after eight phone calls and over a dozen texts, she still hasn't heard a thing, which only deepens the gnawing in her stomach.

"Do you not find it a bit odd," Hugo asks, "that this is called Union Station too?"

She gives him a blank look.

"Same as Chicago. Do you think Denver copied Chicago,

or the other way around? Or maybe there was a bloke named Union who really loved rail stations, and he built—"

"Hugo?"

"Yeah?"

"Would you be offended if I did my own thing this afternoon?"

He tips his head to one side. "Is it because of my theory about Union Station?"

"No," she says, smiling in spite of herself.

"Then I completely understand."

At the hotel, which has a life-sized cow sculpture in the lobby, they check in at the front desk. "It's under Margaret Campbell," Mae says, once again trying not to think too hard about this. It didn't bother her at the beginning. After all, it's her name too. But now, each time they get on the train or give their information at the end of a meal service, she's reminded again that Hugo is supposed to be traveling with his ex, and she wishes it didn't bother her as much as it does.

"Any mail for Hugo Wilkinson?" he asks, looking on hopefully as the clerk checks a stack of envelopes. But there's nothing. "Guess I'm still skint."

Mae pulls out her wallet. "It's okay. You can borrow some more."

"How do you know I'm good for it?"

"I don't," she says with a shrug.

He digs in his pocket and hands her a blue button that matches the ones on his jacket. "Collateral."

"Thank you," she says, accepting it solemnly. "But you

199

do know we could also just use an app, right?"

"Right," he says. "Though it probably wouldn't be anywhere near as safe or reliable as a button."

She nods. "That's true."

They drop their backpacks in the room, then walk back downstairs, past the giant cow sculpture, and out the revolving doors. The sky is a bright, cloudless blue, and Hugo takes a deep breath. "What's that smell?" he asks, and Mae laughs.

"I think it's fresh air."

He takes another whiff, looking satisfied by this, then turns to her. "Look, this is a bit awkward, but I'm going to need some space now."

Mae's heart swells inexplicably, and she smiles at him. "Is that so?"

"It is," he says. "I'm not sure if anyone's told you this before, but you can be bit clingy, and I think—"

"Okay," she says, laughing. "I'm going. You'll be all right?"

He puts a hand on his chest. "Me? I'll be fine. It's you I'm worried about. I give it three minutes before you start missing me desperately."

"Three?"

"Maybe even only two."

"Hey," she says, and his expression becomes more serious. "Thank you."

"Of course," he says. "Just ring if you need anything, yeah?"

"I will."

Once they've parted ways—Mae heading in one random direction, Hugo in another—she tries phoning her dads yet again, but the calls go straight to voice mail. She sends another text to Nana, then waits for a second, hoping for a response. But still nothing.

In the distance, the Rocky Mountains are stacked up against the horizon, white capped and imposing. Mae stares at them for a moment, feeling very small, and then she shoves the phone into the back pocket of her jeans and begins to walk in the other direction.

As she waits for a light to change, she notices how spacious it is here, the streets all wide and breezy beneath the sprawling blue sky. It's so unlike the cramped and busy sidewalks of New York, which is the only city where she's spent any real time.

"You know what I miss most about Manhattan?" Nana once said when she was staying with them, and Dad—who can never resist an opportunity to tease her—was the first to chime in.

"The rats?" he suggested, which made her groan. Unlike Pop, who grew up there, Dad only lived in the city for a few years after college, and he's much happier in the Hudson Valley, where there are more trees than people.

"The way you're never alone," Nana said dreamily.

"Exactly," Dad said with a grin. "Because of all the rats."

Mae knows he doesn't hate it. Not really. It's where he met Pop, where they brought Mae home from the hospital, where his whole life began. He might grumble about the smell of the city and the crowds on the subway and the heat in the summer. But mostly, he's just giving Nana an excuse to defend the place she loves, a small kindness dressed up like something else.

That's what Mae is thinking about now as she walks the streets of Denver, and about a thousand other memories of Nana too. But when she realizes what she's doing, she shakes her head, trying to scatter the thoughts. Because this isn't a memorial. Nana will be fine. She always is.

There's a bookshop called the Tattered Cover on the opposite corner, and she heads toward it, eager for the distraction. Inside, it's warm and inviting, with huge wooden beams and rows upon rows of shelves. Mae takes a deep breath, inhaling that particular perfume of paper and glue. By the time her phone rings, she's on her second loop of the store, deep in the autobiography section. When she sees that it's Pop, she hurries back out onto the street before picking up, her heart in her throat.

"How is she?" she says instead of *hello*. "Where have you been? Is everything okay?"

"It's okay," he says, his voice gruff. "We're at the hospital."

"How's Nana?"

"She's doing fine. It was a mild stroke, but they've run a lot of tests, and the doctors think she'll be totally fine."

"Was it because of the chemo?"

"They're not sure," he says. "She's been through a lot this year. It could've been anything. But we all know a measly stroke is no match for your nana. Neither are the nurses, as it turns out. I'm pretty sure she made at least one of them cry over a poker hand."

Mae loosens her grip on the phone. "Can I talk to her?"

"She's sleeping now, but I'll tell her you called."

"I should be there," she says, which is true, truer than Pop even knows. If she hadn't lied to them, if she hadn't gotten it into her head that she needed an adventure, she'd still be there right now. The knowledge of this is like a weight on her chest, and she takes a jagged breath. "I should be home with all of you."

"It's fine, kid," Pop says. "Really."

But still, she's hit by a wave of guilt so strong her legs feel a little shaky. "I could get on a plane tonight," she says, spinning in a circle, taking in the blur of old buildings and distant mountains. "There must be tons of flights from Denver. I could make it back by—"

"Mae," Pop says, and she stops short. "She told me you'd say that."

"She did?"

"Yeah. I'm supposed to tell you to stop worrying and enjoy the trip."

Mae is quiet for a moment. "Should I? Stop worrying?"

"Honestly? I'm still working on that myself. But if there's one thing I've learned in life, it's to do what Nana says."

"But you'll check in with me, right? And let me know if anything changes? I'm getting on another train in the morning, and I'll be in San Francisco the next afternoon. But I could jump off somewhere along the way if you guys need—"

"Mae, honey, it's okay. We're going to take her back

upstate with us tomorrow, and then she just needs to rest. We've got it covered here. Really."

She bites her lip, but the knot in her chest has started to unwind. "Okay. Well, make sure to tell her I love her. And Dad too."

"I will."

"And you," she says. "Obviously."

He laughs. "I obviously love you too."

Hugo

Hugo sits at the bar of an Irish pub, watching a football match on the fuzzy television that hangs above the shelves of liquor.

"Go on," he says as the Chelsea striker drives the ball up the pitch. It's stolen by one of the Liverpool defenders, and he groans. "Bloody hell."

He nearly texts George, the other big football fan in their house. But then he realizes he still hasn't written back to the group message about housing from last night, and the reminder makes his stomach churn.

When the match is over, he asks the barman for the Wi-Fi password and finds that an email from Nigel Griffith-Jones arrived hours ago, just after they got off the train. Hugo takes a long swig of his drink before opening the message.

Dear Mr. Wilkinson,

Thank you for the note inquiring about your scholarship to the University of Surrey, but I'm afraid we cannot agree to defer it at this time. As I'm sure you know—and will see if you refer to the original agreement with the late Mr. Mitchell Kelly—this offer has always been contingent on having all six of you attend the university together. In accordance with his wishes, we've organised a great deal of publicity surrounding your upcoming matriculation. Because of these special circumstances, I'm sure you can understand why we must insist you all begin in the same academic year.

If there are other factors I should be aware of with regards to this request—any medical or mental health reasons, for example—please do let me know, and we can talk further. Additionally, if you'd like to consider the possibility of all of you starting in the next academic year instead of this one, that's something we can discuss. But as it stands now, I'm afraid that if you were to refuse to comply with the terms of your scholarship, certain contractual provisions mean we'd have to reevaluate the other five as well.

Please feel free to call my office with any questions. Otherwise we're looking forward to having you and the other members of the Surrey Six with us this autumn!

Sincerely,
Nigel Griffith-Jones
Chair of Council
University of Surrey

Disappointment blooms inside Hugo, and for a while he just sits there, his future closing in around him again. For a brief moment, it had been all dusty train stations in far-flung towns, endless blue oceans, and mountain vistas. Now, once again, it's something smaller than that: interviews in which the six of them explain how much they love being at uni together, a tiny room shared with George, dinners at home on the weekends.

It's like a light has been switched off, and where there was just a series of brilliant colors, there's now only black and white.

His first instinct is to text Mae, but she has bigger things to worry about right now. He knows this is no great tragedy, being forced to go home and attend a top-notch university for free. So instead he writes to Alfie: *No go.*

A few minutes later, the reply comes through:

Alfie:	What did they say?
Hugo:	All for one, and one for all.
Alfie:	Sorry, mate. It's rubbish sometimes, being a musketeer.
Hugo:	It could be worse.
Alfie:	How?
Hugo:	We could be septuplets.
Alfie:	Or octuplets.
Hugo:	Did you tell any of the others?
Alfie:	No.
Hugo:	Don't, then.
Alfie:	It won't be so bad, you know.

Hugo:	I know.
Alfie:	You can travel next summer. Or after we graduate.
	The world isn't going anywhere.
Hugo:	I'll see you in a couple of days, okay?
Alfie:	See you soon.

He opens a new message, then heaves a sigh before writing to George:

Hugo:	I call top bunk.
George:	Really? You're in?
Hugo:	I'm in.
George:	Brilliant! It'll be fun. Trust me.
Hugo:	Can't wait.

He pauses for a moment before sending this last text, wondering if he should add an exclamation mark instead. But in the end, he can't bring himself to do it.

Afterward, he goes for a walk, trying to unscramble all the thoughts that are whirling around in his head. He makes his way down to the river, past the station where they'll be catching the train tomorrow morning, and the baseball stadium, which sits hushed and quiet beneath the late-afternoon sun.

The streets are lined with old warehouse buildings, and when he passes a western shop, he can't resist stopping in to try on a cowboy hat. "I don't think it suits me," he says to the saleswoman, squinting at the too-tall hat, which makes him look like a cartoon character.

She scrutinizes him in the mirror. "Maybe you just need some boots too."

He laughs at this, but it reminds him that he still has no money, so he stands outside on the street and texts his mum, who writes back immediately.

Hugo: The credit card didn't show up in Denver.

Mum: Maybe it's holding out for the beach.

Hugo: Very funny. Would you see if they'll send one to my hotel in San Francisco?

Mum: Will do. Are you getting on okay? Do you miss us? Do you still have all your other belongings?

Hugo: Yes, yes, and yes.

Mum: You're loving it, aren't you?

Hugo: I really am.

He wants to say more. Wants to tell her about his note to the chair and the disappointing response. But it doesn't matter anymore; it's already over, and telling her what he's been thinking—how reluctant he is to return home—would only make her worry about him.

Instead, he sends one quick text to his dad: *I miss you too. But not as much as I miss Mum's cooking.* Then he pulls up a map, trying to decide where to go next. But in the end, he's too distracted for sightseeing, so he heads back to the hotel instead.

As he makes his way through the lobby, he spots Mae in one of the overstuffed armchairs, headphones in and computer balanced on her knees. For a second, he just watches her, the way she bends over the screen with a look of intense concentration, and he feels a surge of affection so strong that he isn't sure whether he should be running to her or running away.

As he approaches, he's startled to see that her eyes are filled with tears.

"Are you all right?" he asks with alarm. "Is your grandmother . . . ?"

"No, she's okay. Or she's going to be."

Hugo exhales, relieved. "Good. That's . . . great."

"I know," she says, breathing out too. "I haven't talked to her yet, but she's going home with my dads tonight, and it sounds like she'll be fine."

"So why the tears?"

"Oh, I was just . . ." Mae laughs a little helplessly as she pulls out her headphones, then spins the computer so he can see the paused video. "I was listening to Ida."

"Ah," he says, sitting down on the chair across from her. "That'll do it."

There's a harpist playing in the corner of the lounge, and the last notes of a song vibrate out across the room. The small audience claps appreciatively, and Hugo joins in. When he turns back to Mae, she's smiling at him.

"What?"

She looks sheepish. "I sort of missed you."

"I sort of missed you too," he says, his heart wobbling in his chest. He looks down at his hands. "I heard back from the university."

"And?" she asks, but there's something muted about

it, and he realizes she already knows. She probably knew from the moment he walked up.

He shakes his head. "They said no."

"That's it?" she says, already looking slightly fearsome. "Just no?"

"They want all six of us for publicity purposes," he says. "Which doesn't surprise me, if I'm being honest. I just didn't realize it was officially part of the deal, and I guess I was hoping they might—"

"That's absurd. They're not buying hot dog buns. You're six different people with six different personalities." She pauses, narrowing her eyes. "The problem is they've got themselves a good story now. And if you don't want to be part of it, you've got to tell them a better one."

"How do you mean?"

"What did you say in your email?"

Hugo shrugs. "I asked if it would be possible to defer the scholarship."

"That's it?"

"More or less."

"Good grief," Mae says, rolling her eyes. "Next time please do not send a potentially life-changing email in the middle of the night without consulting me, okay?"

In spite of himself, Hugo laughs. "Okay."

"Look, this is what I do," she says. "I tell stories. And stories are magic. Trust me on this. You can't just tell them you want to skip out for a year. You need to explain why you want to go. Paint them a picture. Tell them all the things you want to do. Tell them how much it's killing you to just blindly follow the same path as all your siblings. Tell them you need a year to figure out who you are, and then you'll come back a better, more focused person, and it'll be a win for everyone."

For some reason, he's finding this all fairly amusing, and though he knows she's serious, he can't seem to wipe the grin from his face.

"Hugo," she says, leaning forward and putting a hand on each of his knees, "I'm not kidding. If you don't believe this, why should they?"

"All right." He holds up his hands. "All right. I'll give it a go."

Mae looks enormously satisfied. She stands up and thrusts her laptop at him. "Good. I'm gonna go up and take a shower. You stay here and get to work."

And then she's gone. Hugo stares at the computer, wondering if she's right. The email from the university seemed fairly final, but it couldn't hurt to try explaining himself a bit better. He closes the window with the clip of Ida's interview, his head already buzzing with his arguments. But just as he's about to open a blank document, he notices a folder called *Rejects*.

He freezes, remembering their conversation the other day. It's almost certainly in there, the film she submitted to USC, the one she never wants to talk about. And now that it's only a couple of clicks away, Hugo is burning to see it.

He lets the mouse hover over it a second, his curiosity overwhelming.

But at the last minute, he sits back again. It would be

too big a betrayal of trust.

Instead he opens a new document, staring at the white screen for a few seconds.

He thinks: *Why I can't go home just yet.*

He thinks: *Please just let me do this.*

He thinks: *Maybe a few seconds wouldn't hurt.*

And then he clicks over to the *Rejects* folder and opens it.

There are easily two dozen files there, all with cryptic names like *That One Tuesday* or *Typical Weekend* or *Snow Day*. There's one called *For Dad* and another *For Pop*. One called *Groceries* and another called *You Are Here*. He wants to watch them all, wants to dive straight into her head. But then he spots the one called *USC* and goes straight to that.

When he opens it, the window is black, with a small title card that says *mae day productions*. He takes his earbuds out of his pocket and slips them in, glancing around the lobby to make sure nobody is watching. Then he presses Play.

There's a shot of clouds and some music, and then the camera pans down from above in an impressive sweeping shot and zooms in on a girl about their age walking toward a small yellow house.

Hugo thinks: *I should stop watching.*

But he doesn't.

She starts to reach for the doorknob, then changes her mind and sits down on the porch steps as two male voices drift out the window, arguing about whose turn it is to fold the laundry. The camera pulls in close to her face as she listens.

The camera work is impressive, and the shots all look stylized in a way that's truly distinctive, bright and glossy and uniquely heightened. But he can't help noticing there's something a bit hollow about it, too, something a little detached.

Though maybe that's how it's supposed to feel. Hugo honestly isn't sure.

Someone walks up behind him, and he slams the computer shut so fast it almost goes sliding off his lap. When he turns to look, it's just a middle-aged woman with a glass of wine. She gives him a funny look as she squeezes past his chair, walking over to a group of couples assembled near the harpist. His heart is pounding as he opens the computer again, exits the window, and closes the folder, covering his tracks.

He looks once more at the blank document and decides he'll work on the letter later.

As he steps out of the elevator on the eighth floor, Hugo tries to compose his face in a way that doesn't make him look as guilty as he feels. But his hands are sweaty, and his stomach is doing flips, and he thinks maybe he should tell her before he gives himself away.

When he walks in the door, she leans out of the bathroom and smiles at him. She's in her pajamas, and her hair is wet, and the whole room feels steamy.

"Did you do it?" she asks, and he looks at her, startled, before realizing she's talking about the letter.

"I started," he says. "But I'll finish tomorrow."

She sets down her hairbrush and appears in the doorway

again. "So that means you think it's a good idea?"

"I do," he says, and her face brightens. She walks over to him smelling like soap and something else, something clean and lemony, and he's about to confess it all, feeling powerless in the face of so much citrus. But then she circles her arms around his waist and stands on her toes and kisses him, and just like that, he forgets about everything else.

Mae

The next morning, Hugo is still acting weird.

Their train is delayed, so they've parked themselves on a couch at the station, which is clean and bright and filled with comfortable chairs and beautiful lamps and low wooden tables, making it feel more like a living room than anything else.

Mae's got her computer out, taking notes as she flips through the various interviews they've recorded so far. Hugo is sitting beside her, knee jangling. Outside, they can see the trains coming and going, and people keep streaming into the station, their voices bouncing around the cavernous space.

"I'm gonna get a coffee," she says. "Want one?"

Hugo shoots to his feet with a suddenness that startles her. "I'll get it," he says, then promptly trips over the table in front of them, his long legs tangled. He barely manages to right himself before crashing into her laptop.

"You okay?" she asks, but he goes hurrying off without looking at her. She watches, amused, as he disappears into one of the shops, then reappears a moment later and hurries back over. Before he can ask, she says, "A vanilla skim latte, please."

He nods sheepishly and wheels around again.

But it only takes him a couple minutes to return.

"I don't have any money," he says, and Mae hands over her credit card.

"Buy yourself something nice," she jokes, but he doesn't even manage a smile.

She frowns at the back of his gray sweatshirt as he heads into the shop again, wondering what's wrong. Nothing really happened last night—they watched a terrible TV movie and then fell asleep—but maybe that was it? Maybe he was hoping for more. After all, he had a girlfriend for almost four years, which is practically a lifetime. It's entirely possible that he expected to do more than just cuddle when sharing a bed with a girl. He didn't *seem* upset, though. Maybe a little distracted. But then, they both had things on their minds. Besides, he was the one to fall asleep first, snoring so loudly that Mae had to keep turning up the volume before eventually giving up and switching off the lights.

When he comes back, he's holding two paper coffee cups, the words *You Go* written across the side of one of them, which makes her laugh. He hands over hers, then sinks onto the couch, his eyes on the clock as he swigs from the cup.

"You okay, *You Go*?" she asks with a grin, but he only nods.

With a shrug, she reaches for her phone and finds a text from Priyanka, who has been checking in about Nana: *Any updates?* Just as she's about to write back, another message pops up, and her heart lifts at the sight.

Nana: So you're not the only one who had a big adventure.

Mae: Hi! How are you feeling??

Nana: I'm fine. Heading back home with your worrywart parents today. I tell you what, though . . . I'm going to miss these doctors. They won't stop flirting with me.

Mae: Sounds about right.

Nana: How's the train?

Mae: Just about to get back on.

Nana: And how's the boy?

Mae: Very cute.

Nana: And how's my favorite granddaughter?

Mae: She misses you. A lot.

Nana: I miss her too.

Afterward, Mae feels calmer, the muscles in her shoulders finally relaxing. It doesn't matter that she already heard from her dads; she needed to hear from Nana herself. And now that she has, the world feels right side up again.

She sips her latte while scrolling through video files on her computer, trying to figure out what the shape of this film will be. The interviews are coming along well—they're moving and emotional and so very real—but she isn't sure yet how to string them together in a way that will make the film feel like a cohesive piece, rather than a collection of random parts.

She doesn't realize Hugo is watching over her shoulder until he sneezes, and then she whirls around, startled by how close he is, his face just inches from hers. She can see the astonishing length of his eyelashes and a little bit of stubble near his jawline, which he must've missed while shaving. She has a sudden urge to touch it.

"Could I ask you a question?" he says, and she nods, curious. His eyes are golden brown in the column of daylight from the giant windows above them, and there's a groove in his forehead as he frowns at the computer screen. Looking at him, she feels such a strong swell of—what? Fondness? Attraction?

Maybe it's just that she's starting to miss him already.

"What will you do," he says, "if they say no?"

She knows right away what he means. "I'll keep trying," she says matter-of-factly. "I already have an appointment with the dean of admissions about transferring."

"You do?"

"Yup. Four o'clock on the first day of classes. And if that doesn't work, I'll go back again the next day. And the next. And if they still won't let me try again, I'll make another film, and then another, until there's one so good they have to listen."

The look on Hugo's face is one of admiration. "I wish I

loved something the way you love filmmaking."

"You want to travel."

"I want to escape. That's not the same."

Mae shrugs. "It looks the same in the end."

On the board above the doors, the time for their train changes: another delay. Hugo takes a long sip of his coffee, then leans his head back on the leather couch with a sigh. "I couldn't write the letter."

"Well, luckily, we've got thirty-four more hours on a train, so . . ."

He shakes his head. "I couldn't sleep last night, so I tried to start it again, and I just—it all felt so flimsy. No matter what I said, it made me sound like a twit who can't be bothered to go to uni even when it's being offered up on a platter. I sounded like the worst possible version of myself, and honestly, I'm not even sure—"

"It's just a hangover," she says, and his eyes widen.

"I'm not—" he sputters. "I didn't—"

"No," she says with a smile. "I just mean . . . when I come up with a great idea for a film, it's like being drunk. You know that giddy feeling you get when you're psyched about something? It's exciting because it's all potential. But then you wake up the next morning and reality has sunk in. You start to wonder if the idea was really as good as you thought, and you suddenly see all the holes in the plan, and that high from the night before starts to crash. That's the hangover."

"Fine," he says. "Maybe I'm a little hungover, then."

A woman walking past with two small children shoots

them a stern look before hurrying the kids along, and Mae and Hugo both laugh.

"All I'm saying," she says, "is that only the best ideas usually survive the hangover. And I think yours is one of them. Don't give it up without a fight just because you're scared."

"I'm not—"

"You are. And that's okay. It's scary to think about doing something totally different. Especially something like this. To go off on your own for a year, leave your family behind, take such a big chance—I think it's really brave. But it's not gonna just happen. If it's what you want, you have to make your own magic. Lay it all on the line."

He tips his head to one side, his expression hard to read. "I will if you will."

"What do you mean?" she asks, blinking at him. The way he's looking at her so intently makes her heart pick up speed.

"Lay it all on the line."

"I don't—"

"You should be in it."

"What?"

"Your film," he says. "When you talk like that . . . well, you're a bit inspiring. And that's what you need here. It shouldn't just be about other people's stories; it should—"

"We're not talking about me," she says, suddenly flustered. "And it doesn't matter what you think it should or shouldn't be. It's not your film. It's mine."

"I know that. All I'm saying is that you're brilliant at

what you do, and you're also just brilliant in general. And I think if the film were a bit more personal—"

Mae stiffens, the word sending a ripple of doubt through her. She narrows her eyes at him. "What?"

"Just that maybe if it were more personal, it would resonate more."

This knocks the wind right out of her. She stares at him for a second, trying not to let that show. "It's literally a collection of personal stories," she says, her mouth chalky. "Most of them about love."

"Right," he says. "Right. But it's not exactly personal to *you*, is it? Of course, the substance is a bit different this time, but if you were to frame it with your own—"

"*This time?*" she says, and he freezes. Then his face goes slack, and a look of panic registers in his eyes, and Mae understands all at once what happened.

She glances at her computer, then back at Hugo, her mouth open.

"You watched it."

He swallows hard. The guilt is all over his face; he doesn't even try to hide it. "I'm so sorry. I just—"

Mae stands abruptly, her coffee sloshing in the cup. "I *told* you," she says, her voice hard. "I told you I didn't want to show you."

"I know, it's just—"

"And you went ahead and did it anyway?" Her face goes hot as she thinks about him watching the film, not sure if she's more angry or embarrassed. Either way, it feels like the ground has disappeared beneath her feet. "I actually can't believe you did that."

Hugo scrambles off the couch, looking rattled. "I'm sorry," he says, a little breathlessly. "I just—"

"What?" she snaps, then says it again: "*What?*"

"I really wanted to see it."

She stares at him, stopped short by the unexpected honesty. "Why? Why do you care so much?"

"Because I wanted to know more about you," he says, his voice rising so that two businessmen on the couch behind them half turn, flapping their newspapers. He takes a breath to steady himself before speaking again. "And I thought this might be a big piece of the puzzle, but then it turned out it wasn't exactly—"

"What?" she asks, glaring at him.

"Nothing."

"*Hugo.*"

He shifts from one foot to the other, eyes on the floor. "I don't know. It wasn't a puzzle piece after all."

"What does that mean?" she asks in a cold voice. But something inside her is collapsing because she knows somehow what he's going to say next, has been waiting for it since the moment this conversation started.

"Just that . . . it's brilliant. But I suppose I thought there'd be more of you in it." He lifts his eyes to look at her. "I figured it would be more personal somehow."

Mae sits back down on the couch, trying not to look like she's just been punched in the stomach. But that's how it feels. It's so much worse coming from him, which makes no sense because he doesn't even know what he's said. Not

223

really. Garrett was being a critic, but Hugo—he was simply looking for Mae in her film.

And that's why it hurts so much. Because he didn't find her.

It feels like her heart—her careful, insufficient heart—has been trampled on, and when he sits down at the other end of the couch, she looks over at him wearily.

"I'm sorry," he says again, his eyes searching her face. "Don't listen to me. I'm not even a film person. And besides, I only watched, like, twenty percent of it."

"Great," Mae says. "Then I'm only twenty percent mad at you right now."

He looks hopeful. "Really?"

"No!"

"I didn't think it would be such a big deal."

She laughs, a brittle sound. "Well, it is. It might not have felt personal to you, but it's *very* personal to me. I thought I was telling a story that meant something. I thought I was putting my whole heart in there, and it's pretty awful to find out that's not enough."

"Mae—"

"Don't," she says, shaking her head. "You know what the worst part is? You went behind my back. I mean, how would you feel if I looked through your phone without asking?"

"Here," he says, digging it out of his pocket and thrusting it at her. "You can. You should. It's only fair."

Mae manages to catch the phone right before it slips to the floor. "I obviously wouldn't do that. I just can't believe you *would*."

224

"I'm sorry," he says miserably. "I'm an idiot. I know that. But I'd hate if this meant . . ."

"What?"

"It's just . . . I like you," he says, a note of desperation in his voice. "A lot. And this was so bloody stupid of me. But I'd be gutted if it changed anything between us."

His phone, which is still in Mae's hand, chirps once, then twice.

"I don't know what this is to you," he continues, his eyes locked on Mae's. "But I want you to know that it means something to me. And that the last thing I'd want is for you to lose trust in me. Because I think maybe—" His eyes flick to his phone as it beeps again. "I know it seems mad, but I think maybe . . ."

"What?" she asks again, more impatiently this time.

He lifts his shoulders. "I think maybe I'm falling for you."

Mae takes a sharp breath, her heart bobbling. She stares at him, too surprised to answer. Distantly, she hears an announcement that their train will begin boarding shortly, but it's not until his phone makes another noise that she tears her eyes away, turning it over in her hand.

"Mae," Hugo says, but she's no longer listening.

She's too busy reading the name at the top of the screen. It takes a moment for it to register, and when it does, she hands him the phone.

"It's Margaret," she says, standing up to gather her things. "She wants to see you tomorrow."

Hugo

Hugo's head is a jumble as they board the train. Mae is the one who hands over their tickets to be scanned, who steers them to their compartment, who rearranges the bags in the luggage rack like puzzle pieces so that theirs will fit. He trails after her numbly, shell-shocked from the argument they'd just had and his confession at the end of it.

Mae won't even look at him, and he doesn't blame her.

He glances down at his phone, which is still clutched in his hand, and wonders how Margaret picked the exact worst moment to text. Does she have some sort of sixth sense, or is it just the universe conspiring against him?

He doesn't need to open the messages to remind him what they say. They're already burned into his brain:

Would love to see you when you get to SF.

I can meet you anywhere.

We need to talk.

I miss you.

Now he manages a smile as the attendant—a woman named Azar—squeezes past him and heads back down the hall to get other passengers settled. From the doorway to their compartment, he watches Mae dig through her bag. She's wearing ripped jeans and a navy-and-white-striped shirt, her hair pulled up in a messy bun, and she hasn't said anything in what feels like a long time. The actual space between them might be small, but to Hugo it feels like a million miles.

The conductor's voice comes over the loudspeaker: "If you've just joined us in Denver, welcome. This is the California Zephyr, making stops en route to Emeryville. Breakfast is currently being served in the dining car, and the next stop will be Winter Park, Colorado, in a little over two hours. Enjoy the ride, folks."

Mae grabs her camera bag. "I think I'm gonna go up and do some interviews."

Hugo understands that he's not invited, but he feels a rise of panic at the thought of her leaving when there's still so much that needs to be said. She slings her bag over her shoulder and then looks at him expectantly, waiting for him to move away from the door.

"I'm sorry," he says again. The train is moving now, the sunlight streaming in through the window. "I shouldn't have watched the film. And as far as the other thing goes—"

"Hugo."

"Will you please let me—"

"Can we do this later?"

"I just want to make sure you know that—"

"Please," she says, and something about the way she says it makes him nod and take a step back from the door, his whole body humming with regret.

"Yeah," he says. "All right."

Her arm brushes against his as she whisks past him, and he wants to reach for her hand and try one more time. But instead, his heart sunk low, he simply turns to watch her head down the short hallway and up the narrow staircase.

When she's gone, he slumps into one of the seats in their room and watches the landscape change as the train starts to climb into the Rocky Mountains. They pass rivers and ranches and fields of cattle, sheer rock faces, and streams dotted with fly fishermen, all of it slightly unreal, like something out of an old Western. Every so often, the brief darkness of a tunnel closes in around them, and it feels for a few seconds like there will never be light again.

In thirty-four hours, they'll be in Emeryville, California, which is just across the bay from San Francisco. He was meant to arrive with Margaret, of course, then spend a couple of nights in a hotel near Fisherman's Wharf before driving down to Stanford. When they broke up, he assumed she'd head straight to Palo Alto, and it occurs to him now that maybe the whole reason she's in San Francisco is to see him.

We need to talk.

I miss you.

Without really thinking, he opens his phone and finds the last picture he and Margaret took together. They'd gone to Brighton for the day, and she'd insisted they take a selfie near the water. But as they did, a seagull flew so close to their heads that they both shouted and jumped away. Only its tail feathers made it into the corner of the photo; the rest was the two of them with their mouths open, half laughing and half screaming, Margaret's blond hair streaming behind her as she started to escape toward the edge of the frame.

"Birdbrain," she said, shaking her fist in mock anger.

Later she made him give her a ride on his back because the wedge sandals she'd insisted on wearing were hurting her feet. Then she complained about the food at the café where they had lunch, and had a strop when he wouldn't leave the arcade until he beat his Skee-Ball record. They were both tense as they walked back to the train, annoyed with each other in the way they always seemed to be lately after spending a certain amount of time together. But then another seagull flew past, this one high above them, and Margaret frowned and muttered, "Birdbrain," and that made them both dissolve into laughter all over again.

He pulls up her text messages.

Okay, he types, then slowly erases it.

To his surprise, a video call from Alfie pops up on the screen, and when he picks up, Hugo is even more astonished to see all five of his siblings jockeying for position in the frame.

"Hey, mate," Alfie says, his face looming larger than all the others. "Just figured we'd ring you up to see how you're getting on."

Maybe it's his fight with Mae, or maybe it's just that he's never been away from them for this long before, but the sight of their faces is overwhelming. To Hugo's horror, he feels his eyes fill with tears.

"Don't go falling apart on us now," George says with a grin. "I thought you were meant to be this big world traveler."

Isla, who is standing over George's shoulder, beams into the camera. "He misses us."

"Right, but who do you miss the *most*?" Alfie asks. "Like . . . we want rankings."

"I miss all of you," Hugo says, and he means it.

Poppy elbows Alfie aside, her braids swinging as she moves closer to the screen. "Is the other Margaret Campbell there?"

"Yeah, let us see," Oscar says, craning his neck.

George peers over his shoulder. "We'd love to say hello."

"She's just over in another car right now," he says, trying to keep his voice light, but they know him too well for this, and he can see their faces shift.

"Why?" Isla asks cautiously. "What happened?"

"Nothing. It's fine. Or it will be."

Poppy's face shifts, and she looks at him more seriously. "You like her, huh?"

Hugo's instinct is to laugh or make a joke, but he feels too worn down to pretend right now. "Yeah," he says. "I do."

"Knew it," says Alfie.

"I know it's a bit weird for you because of Margaret," Hugo says, still talking mostly to Poppy, "and I didn't exactly plan this. But I just—"

"Hugo," Poppy says, tipping her head to one side the way she always does when she's considering something. "If you like her, I'm sure she's great."

He lets out a breath. "She is. And I do."

"Okay then," she says, all business now. "Whatever you did, just apologize."

Isla nods. "But not in that blustery, flustery way you usually do. Say exactly what you did wrong and be heartfelt about it."

"And tell her how you feel about her too," says Oscar, out of nowhere. They all turn to him in surprise, but he just grins. "What? I think it's important to be honest."

"What if it doesn't work?" Hugo asks, and there's a catch in his voice.

"It will," says Poppy, and though she can't possibly know that, there's something so reassuring about it that he simply nods.

"Right," he says. "Thanks."

"Let us know how it goes," Isla tells him, and the others bob their heads. All except Alfie, who clears his throat exaggeratedly.

"You know," he says, "this wasn't actually meant to be

231

a group therapy session. We were ringing to let you know we made an appointment with the university tomorrow."

Hugo frowns. "Why?"

"To tell them that it's one for all, and all for one," George says, and when Hugo just stares at him, uncomprehending, he shrugs. "If they won't let you take a gap year, then none of us will go."

"What?" Hugo says, too stunned to think of anything else. He adjusts his grip on the phone and turns his focus on Alfie, who looks rather pleased with himself. "I thought I told you not to say anything."

"I thought you knew I had a big mouth," Alfie says with a shrug. "Besides, it was George's idea."

George smiles ruefully. "Listen, if this family were a cake—"

"Seriously?" Poppy says, rolling her eyes.

"Do I get to be the sugar in this metaphor?" asks Alfie.

"Well, now I'm feeling a bit peckish," says Oscar.

"All I'm saying," George continues, "is that I like it when we're all together. But I also want you to be happy. And I can see that you are. So we want to help."

Hugo blinks a few times, dangerously close to tears. "That's ..." He shakes his head. "That's incredibly generous. But I can't let you do it."

"It's okay," Oscar says. "We'll only be bluffing."

"Yeah, if they say no, we'll back off," Isla tells him. "It's not like we have any other options at this point, and the rest of us still want to go. But we figured a show of solidarity might help with your situation."

Hugo shakes his head. "What if they call your bluff?"

"We'll sort it out," says Alfie. "It's worth a shot, though, yeah?"

Hugo tries to picture it, the five of them trooping into the university council's office, laying out their demands, arguing on his behalf. They're all looking at him with different expressions—Poppy is determined, and George is protective; Isla is concerned, and Oscar is interested, which for Oscar is a massive compliment. Alfie, of course, is just puffed up with pride at the good deed he's currently doing. Hugo has always been able to read them better than anyone, and with each of them, he knows this is a show of love. But he also knows he can't let them do it.

"You're all amazing," he says, his voice filled with sincerity. The truth is, he feels a bit undone by all this. "And it means the world to me. But it's not your job to sort this out."

"It's no trouble," Isla says. "Honestly."

Poppy nods. "We just want you to be happy."

"I will be," Hugo says. "I don't mind coming home. Not really. I'll travel next summer instead. Or on holidays. It'll be fine."

"That's rubbish," Alfie says. "You want to go. I know you do. So why not let us try?"

"No," Hugo says a bit more firmly. "Just—please don't do anything. I love you guys for offering, but it's fine."

Isla looks at him skeptically. "I think that must be a record for the most times anyone has ever said *fine* in a conversation."

The connection wavers, their faces going frozen on the

screen. Then, just as quickly, they're back.

"Hugo?" Poppy says. "I think we're losing you."

He manages a grin. "Never."

"I think she meant the connection, mate," Alfie says, and both Poppy and George reach over to punch him.

"I know," Hugo says as the image flickers again. "Look, I should go. The service is a bit dodgy between stops. But thank you again. Really. You're the best."

"Who, me?" Alfie says.

Hugo laughs. "All of you. I'll see you in a few days."

"It won't be so bad, Hugo," says Poppy, but before he has a chance to find out which part she's talking about— the apology to Mae or the end of the trip, the return home or the start of uni—the video cuts out.

There's a speck of dirt on the window, and Hugo watches it move up and down as they pass fields of horses and cattle, sheep and goats. At a crossing, a rancher leans out of his pickup truck to watch them rumble by, and beyond him a field of wildflowers ripples in the wind.

After a few minutes, he slips his phone into his pocket and stands up.

Mae is in the observation car, sitting alone at one of the tables. Her head is bent over her camera as he slides into the booth across from her.

"That's Mr. Bernstein's seat."

"Who?"

"Mr. Bernstein," she says. "We're in the middle of an interview. He was just telling me about proposing to his wife before he went off to Vietnam."

"For the war?"

"No, for vacation." She looks up at him. "I'm kidding."

"Listen," he says, "I'm sorry about before."

She gives him a steady look. "Which part?"

"All of it," he says.

"You don't have to be sorry about Margaret, you know," she says, fiddling with the lens of her camera. "You have every right to see her. There's a lot of history there, and—"

"I know," he says. "But I *am* sorry about the film. I shouldn't have watched it. Full stop. I betrayed your trust, which was an awful thing to do. And I'm also sorry about—"

"Hugo."

"Look, I know I probably shouldn't have said it like that. But I want you to know it wasn't a mistake. That's how I feel. I like you, Mae. A lot. This week has been incredible because of you, and I swear—" He stops abruptly, looking up at the old man in too-high trousers who is suddenly hovering over him.

"You must be the assistant director," Mr. Bernstein says, shaking his hand. "Are you going to ask some questions too?"

Hugo finds himself nodding.

Mr. Bernstein looks pleased. "Well, what would you like to know?"

"I'd like to know," Hugo says, then turns back to Mae, "if you feel the same way."

"About what?" Mr. Bernstein asks, clearly confused.

But they both ignore this. Mae is staring at Hugo, whose

heart has lodged itself somewhere in the vicinity of his throat. He digs his fingernails into his palm as he waits for her to say something. But her expression is impossible to read.

A year seems to go by.

Then another.

Oh god, Hugo thinks. *What have I done?*

Mr. Bernstein is still watching them, and Hugo can feel his face heating up. Beneath them the train sways as they move deeper into the red, jagged mountains, which rise on either side of them like the landscape of some strange and distant dream.

And maybe that's all this is, anyway: a dream.

Maybe arriving will be no different from waking up.

With each second that passes, he becomes more and more certain this was a terrible mistake, a colossal disaster, an absolute bollocks of an idea.

But then her foot finds his beneath the table, and when he looks up at her, she's smiling.

His heart loosens itself again, a cork coming free from a bottle, and he's so overcome with relief that it's all he can do to stay upright. He raises his eyebrows at her, and she nods, a movement so slight that it would be hard to catch if you weren't looking for it.

Hugo grins back at her from across the table.

"So are we doing this or what?" Mr. Bernstein says, looking from one to the other, and Mae laughs, still looking right at Hugo.

"I guess we're doing this," she says.

Mae

"Your turn," she says when they get back to their compartment after dinner. They're in Utah now, and the sky is soft and pale, the mountains turning to silhouettes all around them. Hugo's forehead is pressed to the window, where below them a narrow river runs placidly alongside the tracks.

He turns around in surprise. "Really?"

"Really."

"But I thought you didn't want me to be part of it."

She studies him for a moment, the brown eyes and the dark hair, the way his mouth is twisted so that only one dimple shows. The collar of his shirt is messed up, and for some reason this makes her heart swell. She leans across to fix it, their faces close, her fingers brushing his neck, and then—unable to help herself—she gives him a quick kiss before sitting back again.

"I changed my mind," she tells him.

His mouth twists in the other direction. "But why?"

"I don't know. I guess I want to hear your answers."

This isn't exactly true, but it's not exactly untrue either. And it makes him smile. "Well, Mr. Bernstein will be a tough act to follow," he says. "Same with that teacher—June? She nearly had me in tears."

"Nearly?" Mae asks, and Hugo reaches out to grab her around the waist, laughing as he pulls her down onto the seat with him. She's balanced awkwardly, half on his lap and half wedged beside him, but it doesn't matter because he's already kissing her, this time with a kind of desperate intensity. When—after a few minutes—they break apart, both breathing heavily, he leans forward and kisses her one last time on the tip of her nose.

"So," he says, shifting over so she can sit beside him, the two of them shoulder to shoulder on a seat meant for one. "Twenty-one hours to San Francisco."

Mae feels the air go whistling right out of her. Suddenly that doesn't seem like very much at all. "And then another sixteen till I leave for LA," she says.

"And then another twenty-four till I go back to England."

She puts her head on his shoulder, and he rests his chin on the top of her head. "It's not enough."

"No," he says, his voice heavy, "it isn't."

She looks past him to where the last few wispy clouds are laced with gold. Utah and then Nevada and then California. She's hardly thought about the fact that she'll be starting college next week, that all she has to do is cross a few more states and head south along the coast and then she's there, in the place where she'll be spending the next four years.

"Your world is going to get so big," Nana told her before she left, and Mae marvels at how much it already has, with Hugo here beside her and the enormous western sky rolled out ahead of them. They spent the whole day doing interviews, and now her head is filled with stories, all of them buzzing madly. She can't wait to piece them together, all these lives that have intersected as they wind their way across the country for different reasons.

She was lying about Hugo, though.

It's not that she's changed her mind about interviewing him. She still doesn't think he belongs in the film. It's something else. Something more important than that.

It came to her earlier, when he was sitting on the other side of the table in the café car, his face nervous as he waited for the answer to a question he hadn't even really been able to formulate. Mae realized that no matter what happens over the course of these next twenty-one hours on a train and then sixteen hours in San Francisco, they'll have to say goodbye at the end of it.

And she's going to miss him.

It doesn't seem like a big enough word, but it's all there is: she'll miss him. Already, and improbably, it feels like a hole has started to open in her chest. So she decided she wants to take something with her. If she can't keep all of him, she at least wants to try capturing a tiny piece.

"How does this work, then?" Hugo asks, noticing her eyes are on the camera, which is sitting on the shelf beside the opposite seat. "Do I get the same questions as everyone else? Or do I get special ones because I'm so—"

"Annoying?" she asks with a grin.

He bumps his shoulder against hers. "I was going to say charming. But sure."

"You get the same ones as everyone else."

"You know," he says, "if I were interviewing you—"

"Which you're not."

"—I'd never ask you the standard questions."

"What would you ask?"

He thinks about this. "I'd ask you the best advice your nana ever gave you."

"She said I should try to meet a cute boy on the train," she says, and Hugo lets out a laugh.

"Did she really?" he asks, incredulous.

Mae nods.

"Well, she sounds extremely clever. I'd definitely want to hear more about her. And your parents too."

"What about them?"

"What they're like, how they met, what it was like growing up with two dads."

She's about to say what she always says to this question: *It was lucky. The luckiest thing in the world. Because my dads are the greatest.*

In the hallway, a door opens and voices call out to each other. But in here it's quiet, just the sound of their breathing and the roar of the train underneath it all. They could be anywhere and nowhere, but they've somehow found themselves here, and she's suddenly grateful for it, all of it, for the extra ticket and the way it brought them together despite everything, the bigness of the world and the unlikeliness of a moment like this.

Hugo is watching her with a look of such warmth that she's reminded of Priyanka's words. *It's like the sun*, she'd said, *in that it makes everything brighter and happier.*

Mae knows her line too: *You can get burnt by it.*

But right now it doesn't feel that way to her. Not at all.

She gives Hugo a rueful smile. "It was hard sometimes."

"I'm sure."

"Not because of them. They're the best. But it's a small town, and I was the only kid with gay parents." She shrugs. "People can be jerks, you know?"

"I do, actually," Hugo says, his face serious. "Though you seem pretty well equipped to handle that sort of thing."

"Maybe," she says. "But it can still sting. I remember one time my dad came to pick me up at school, and the new secretary wouldn't let me leave with him because we don't have the same last name. It was awful. It didn't matter that it's my middle name, or that we look exactly alike, or that he'd picked me up a million times before. She wouldn't budge, so we just had to sit there in her office, both of us stewing, until Pop came to get us." She shakes her head. "Another time, I was at the playground with Pop and some kid came up and said he'd heard he wasn't my 'real' dad. As if biology is the only thing that counts."

"What did you do?" Hugo asks, his eyes big.

241

"I punched him in the stomach," she says with a grin. "I was only six. But still. Not always as calm, cool, and collected as I probably should've been."

"It can be hard to ignore that stuff."

She nods. "Did you guys get teased a lot at school?"

"Not so much there. It helped that there were six of us. But you should see the comments section on my mum's blog." He whistles and shakes his head. "If you've ever wondered where the racist, sexist, antigrammar crowd likes to spend their time, look no further."

"That's horrible," Mae says, alarmed, but he only shrugs.

"Mum's not too fussed about them anymore, and neither are we. Not that I wouldn't mind punching some of them in the stomach. But it's easier to ignore than in real life."

"Yeah, but they're still out there."

"They're still out there," he agrees, burying his nose in her shoulder. She takes one of his hands and begins to trace the lines of his palm, and she feels a rush of pleasure when he flips it over, capturing her hand inside his own.

"What about the blog?" she asks. "Do you read it?"

He laughs. "Not if I can help it."

"I liked the one about how you and Alfie—"

"What," he says with a groan, "you read it?"

"I mean, I wouldn't say I'm a regular or anything, but I had to do my homework on you."

He shakes his head, but one of his dimples has appeared, so she can tell he's amused. "Which one was it? Alfie and I got up to a lot of trouble when we were little."

"The story about you guys running away to London."

"Right," Hugo says, folding his arms across his chest. "That was Alfie's idea."

She was expecting him to laugh, but instead he looks somber.

"What?" she says, and he sighs.

"They rang me earlier, when you were doing interviews. Alfie told the others about the email from the university, and they were all planning to go plead my case tomorrow. Even George."

"Wow," she says, smiling at this. "That's really cool of them."

"I told them not to do it."

She nods. "I figured."

"I don't want them to risk their own scholarships," he says, rubbing his eyes. "And honestly, I can't have them fight my battles. Not anymore."

"I agree," Mae says, looking at him carefully. "That's why I think you should fight your own."

"A letter won't do anything," he says in a tone impatient enough to signal he doesn't want to argue with her. "I know you think this is a hangover, but it's not. The truth is, I was drunk before. And now I've sobered up."

"Right, but—"

"It wouldn't have worked." He stands abruptly, leaving Mae alone in the seat. "I haven't talked to my parents or done any research or even checked my bank account. And now the council thinks I don't want to be there, and I'm worried Alfie and the others will still go and talk to them and screw up their own scholarships, and the whole thing is just—"

"Hugo."

He presses his lips together, his eyes darting. "It was a stupid idea."

"Sometimes those can be good for you," Mae says, smiling as she thinks of Nana. But Hugo's mouth is still a straight line. "So, what . . . you're just gonna go home at the end of this?"

"Yes," he says, sitting down again in the opposite chair. "I'm just going home at the end of this."

They stare at each other, neither quite satisfied. A tense silence hangs between them until, finally, Hugo points to the camera.

"We've lost the plot a bit with this interview, haven't we?" he asks, his voice full of effort. When she doesn't say anything, he leans forward, drumming his hands on the little table. "Shall I ask you about something less controversial?"

"Like what?"

"I don't know," he says, cracking a grin. "Ex-boyfriends?"

Mae gives him a look.

"As assistant director, my job is to get the most thorough interview possible."

"Wasn't I supposed to be interviewing *you*?"

"Are you really not going to tell me?"

"Honestly," she says, "there's not much to tell. I was dating someone over the summer, but it wasn't anything serious. It wasn't anything like—"

She stops, embarrassed. But Hugo's face lights up so quickly and so brightly that she can't help smiling too.

"There were a few others before that," she continues, still distracted by the high beam of his gaze. "But none of them meant anything. I guess maybe they did at the time, but not anymore. They were just fun."

He raises his eyebrows. "And this?"

"This is no fun at all," she says. It's intended as a joke, but Hugo gives her a pained look, and it takes a few seconds for the meaning to settle over Mae too.

This is no fun at all, she realizes, because it's about to come to an end.

Hugo

It was too dark to film the interview last night. By the time they'd finished talking, the sun had slipped behind the mountains completely, turning the square of window a deep purple.

"If I had even one proper light with me," Mae muttered as she tried to find a good angle with the camera. But after a while, she gave up, and they spent the last hours before total darkness—as the train crawled through the barren Utah landscape—lying together in the bottom bunk and watching an Italian film called *Cinema Paradiso* on Mae's phone.

"Is it sad or happy?" he asked as they settled in.

"Both," she said, and she was right.

During the kissing montage, Hugo looked over to see that she was crying. "Are you okay?" he whispered, and she nodded.

"This is my grandmother's favorite part."

"Mine too," he said, pulling her closer, and they fell asleep like that.

But now it's morning, which means it's time. They've already had breakfast, and their beds have been folded back into seats—the last time their compartment will perform this sort of magic trick—and they're somewhere near the top of Nevada now. Everything out the window is a bright dusty-orange, a color Hugo has never seen before, with the occasional ridged mountain rising out of the dirt. The sun is still climbing, and the light—according to Mae—is now perfect.

"Just a minute," she says, and Hugo sits back, content to watch her work, thinking about what a lovely thing this is, to be interviewed by her. And how there will now be other, less joyful interviews ahead of him, where he'll sit down with reporters ranging from the student newspaper to the *Sunday Times* and give them the uncomplicated version of himself, the one who is simply grateful for the scholarship and thrilled to be with his siblings and excited about all that's ahead.

It won't be a lie, because he feels all those things.

But it won't exactly be the truth either.

When Mae is finally ready—the camera stabilized on a makeshift tripod constructed out of a pair of trainers and a hairbrush—she sits forward and looks him right in the eye. "So."

"So," he says, "you probably want to know how someone could possibly be this good-looking."

She laughs. "Not exactly."

"How someone could be this charming, then?"

"I want to know what your biggest dream is," she says, glancing down at the camera, and Hugo uses the moment to gather himself.

"Right," he says. "Well, you already sort of know."

Mae looks at him like he's thick. "Yeah, but now there's a camera."

"Yes. Right. Okay." He swallows hard and eyes the lens. "Well, I never really had one before. Everything was laid out for me a certain way, and it never occurred to me that things could be different. But then I got on this train and everything changed." He glances out the window at the sunbaked dirt. "It's like I'd been living on a map my whole life and have only now realized the world is actually a globe. And even though I have to go back, I know that now. And I can't unknow it."

Mae flicks her eyes up to meet his, but she doesn't say anything.

"I'm starting to realize that a lot of people don't put much stock in dreams. They think of them like these faraway planets they never really expect to reach. I was only supposed to step out of my life for a week, but that's another thing nobody tells you: that once you get there, it's never enough. There are always more planets to see." He smiles and gives his head a little shake. "This makes it sound like my dream is to be an astronaut, doesn't it?"

She smiles at him. "I hope you get to see them one day."

"Me too," Hugo says.

"So what's your biggest fear?" she asks, and he feels his heart jerk as if someone has tugged it with a rope.

He has many fears. Too many to count.

But right now—right in this moment—the biggest one is saying goodbye to her.

Instead, he says, "Sharks."

Mae rolls her eyes at him. "Come on. How many sharks have you ever come across in England? Give me something real."

He thinks about this, his heart still jittery.

"I worry that I'm not enough on my own," he says eventually. "I love being a sextuplet—I do. It can be nice being part of a pack, always having someone around, knowing we're there for each other no matter what, sharing a lifetime of experiences. It's unusual, I think. To be known that well. And it can be really lovely. But I don't want to just be one-sixth of something my whole life either. That's why this week has meant so much. And why I wish it didn't have to end."

He closes his mouth, not sure what else to say. It's strange, talking to Mae and the camera at once; he doesn't know where the interview stops and the conversation between them begins, which parts are public and which are private.

But she just nods and moves on to the next question: "What do you love most about the world?"

"I love . . ." he says, feeling dangerously close to adding the word *you*. He's distracted by the warmth of her eyes and the way she's looking at him, by the still-rising sun out the window, by the impossibility of being here—in Nevada, of all places—with this girl he's known for such a short time but whom he can't bear to think of losing.

"I love . . ." he begins again, then raps his knuckles against the window. "This."

"The train?"

"Yes," Hugo says. "And the window. And the view. It's mind boggling, isn't it? To be so far away from your real life. To see so many entirely new things." He shakes his head in wonder. "I love my parents, even when I don't. And I love my brothers and sisters, even when it feels like there are too many of them. I love my friends from school and my ex-girlfriend and my teachers, even the ones who used to tell me off for daydreaming. I love my room at home, even when Alfie comes back from rugby and his feet smell like shite. I love my mum's books, even though they're mortifying. I love this trip, and the way it came together, and that I get to be here with you. I love what it's made me realize about myself. And what it's sparked in me. But mostly I love this."

Mae follows his eyes to the window again; then she switches off the camera. "Listen, you have to write that letter, okay?"

"I already told you—"

"It doesn't matter. You need to tell them all that."

They've left the desert behind now, and the train has slowed as it climbs up into the mountains. Soon there are thick forests of pine trees and, in the distance, patches of clinging snow. An announcement comes over the speaker:

they've crossed into California.

Which means they're almost there.

"You didn't ask me the last question," Hugo says, and Mae smiles at him, but she doesn't turn the camera back on.

"I figured you were just going to say 'pizza.'"

"Who in the world would compare love to a pizza?" he asks, expecting her to laugh.

But instead she looks at him seriously. "Someone who doesn't know very much about it."

In the hallway, the family staying in the compartment next door trundles past, the voices of the younger kids bouncing around the train. When they're gone, Hugo leans forward, resting his elbows on the wobbly table between them.

"In fact," he says, grinning at her, "I *was* going to say 'pizza.'"

She tosses a pen at him, and he ducks. "You were not."

"I was," he says, though this isn't quite true. The question has been on his mind all week, through every interview and the hours spent with Mae in between, but he hasn't been able to come up with something that captures it. The truth is, love isn't just one word. At least not to him. It's different things for different people.

With Margaret, love was like a blanket, mostly warm and comforting, but occasionally itchy and, toward the end, a bit frayed too.

His parents don't have a word at all. Instead, when he thinks of them, what he pictures is the doorframe in the kitchen where they mark off their heights each year. It's so crowded with scratches and initials that most visitors assume it was something that the children scribbled on when they were younger. To Hugo, though, it measures something more than simply their heights.

For Alfie, the word is *friend*, which is somehow bigger than any of the others that might fit too: *brother*, *sibling*, *family*. Isla is *comfort*, and George is *steadiness*, the twin guardians of their little pack. For Poppy, who is always the brightest, it's *laughter*. And Oscar would hate having a word. He'd much prefer some line of code that nobody else can understand.

The six of them taken together would have to be a different word entirely, of course, and there have certainly been enough used to describe them over the years. But they don't always have to be taken together. Hugo understands that now more than ever.

He doesn't have a word for Mae yet. Her very nearness makes it impossible to think of any words at all sometimes. Right now she's more of a feeling, but even that is impossible to describe.

"Pizza," he says again. "Definitely pizza."

She shakes her head in mock exasperation. "Okay, fine. Then why?"

"Because," he says with a shrug, "it's warm and gooey."

This makes her laugh. "Right. Can't argue with that. What else?"

"And it's always delicious."

"And?"

"There are loads of choices. Everyone can have their own version of it."

"And?"

He pauses for a moment, thinking. "And I always thought it was amazing," he says, laughter bubbling up inside him for no reason other than that he's happy right now, so happy it feels too big to contain. "But if I'm being honest, I didn't know how amazing it could be until this week."

A few seconds later, there's a knock, and when Azar pokes her head in to ask about lunch reservations, they're both still sitting like that, beaming at each other, lost in a universe all their own. It almost feels to Hugo like he's been underwater, and when he turns to the door, everything seems dreamy and slow.

"Last meal," says Azar, which makes Hugo laugh.

"Will there be pizza?"

"Not in the dining car," she says. "But I think they have those frozen ones at the snack bar. They're probably not too bad."

"No such thing as a bad pizza," Hugo says. "What do you say?"

Mae is grinning at him, which is a relief. Because right now Hugo has no interest in the dining car. He doesn't want to make small talk with strangers or interview anyone else. He doesn't want to chat about the weather or listen to people's plans for their time in the Bay Area.

He just wants to sit with Mae, alone in their own corner of the train.

"Pizza it is," she says, her eyes glittering.

They eat out of little cardboard trays in front of the huge sloping windows of the observation car. At one end, there's a historian giving a lecture about the Donner party, and at the other, a group of women are in stitches over something, their scattered bursts of laughter giving the whole car a cheery feel.

"So," Mae says when she's finished with her pizza. Her trainers are propped on the ledge beneath the window, her knees drawn up nearly to her chest. Below them, the green-tipped mountains have tumbled away, and the canyon makes it feel like they too could topple off the edge at any minute. It should be frightening, but it's not.

It's electrifying, being on the edge of all that stillness.

"So," he says.

"Are you going to see her?"

Hugo doesn't pretend not to know whom she's talking about. "I think so," he says without looking over. "I think maybe we still have things to say to each other."

"That makes sense," Mae says, and there's no malice in her voice. No hint of annoyance or jealousy. "I think you should."

They reach out at the same time, their hands brushing against each other in the gap between the seats, fumbling for a second before they manage to grab hold.

"Hey, how'd they decide which surname you got?" Hugo asks. "Your dads."

Mae looks at him in surprise. "They flipped a coin. They weren't into the whole hyphenated thing for some reason. Why?"

"Because I was just thinking," he says, "that if the coin had landed the other way, we never would've met."

She smiles and squeezes his hand a little tighter. "I guess that's true."

"Anyway," he says, his eyes returning to the window.

"Anyway."

"Only a couple more hours now."

"And then sixteen in San Francisco. What should we do?"

"Well, I've heard there's this bridge . . ."

This makes her laugh. "And our hotel is right by Fisherman's Wharf. So we have to go there."

"Oh yeah. Let's definitely go say hello to the sea lions."

"And eat some seafood too."

He wrinkles his nose. "But not with the sea lions."

"No, I think a restaurant."

"And then what?" he asks, because they're in a tunnel now, and everything is dark, and it seems like the right time to finally ask the question.

"And then I go to LA," she says, her voice sounding very small. "And you go . . ."

"Home," he says softly, and the word seems to hang between them for a moment, a gut punch, a reminder, a ticking clock. All at once the light comes rushing back, and he looks down at their knotted hands. "And this?"

She bites her lip, searching for an answer. "Honestly," she says after a few beats, "I don't know."

The pine trees out the window are a blur of green, the

world rushing by too fast. "I don't either," Hugo admits, and they're both quiet for a long time after that.

"Cookies," Mae says eventually. "I think we need cookies, don't you?"

Hugo watches her head down the stairs that lead to the café before he returns his gaze to the window, unsettled. They're not far from Emeryville now, and then there's the bus ride into San Francisco, and then what? He decides he'll meet up with Margaret tomorrow, once Mae is on her way down the coast. He doesn't want to waste any of the time they have left, doesn't want the two things to be muddled at all. He and Mae will eat clam chowder by the bay and walk the hills and see the sights. And then they'll spend one last night together before saying goodbye.

Her phone begins to buzz from the ledge, and Hugo reaches for it so it doesn't topple off. It's a call from home, and he stares at the screen until it goes dark again. But a second later, there's another call. And then another. And one more.

He holds the phone in his hand, his nerves vibrating just as fast.

A minute later, a text from Mae's dad pops onto the screen:

Call us as soon as you can. xx

Hugo's heart falls, because nobody rings that many times if everything is okay. For a brief, insane moment, he wishes he didn't have to tell Mae. He wishes he could hide the phone, throw it off the side of the train, let it get buried at the bottom of this mountain. He wishes he could protect her from whatever this news turns out to be.

Which sounds noble, even though it's actually selfish.

Because mostly he knows that the minute she talks to her dads, something new will be set in motion, and he'll be that much closer to losing her.

He stares at the phone in his hand, his mind desperate and scrabbling. Should he put it back on the ledge and pretend he never saw the message? Should he just hand it to her when she returns and let her read the text herself? He looks around the busy train car at the other passengers, all of them talking and laughing and pointing out the window, and his stomach lurches at what's about to happen.

And then, before he has more time to think about how ill equipped he is to handle this, she's back.

"Here," she says, tossing him a box of chocolate chip cookies, which he barely manages to catch. As he does, the phone falls out of his hand and onto the floor.

Mae looks at it, then back at him, and her smile slips.

Hugo realizes then that it doesn't matter how she finds out.

It's clear she already knows.

Mae

Mae's head is swimming as she steps off the train for the last time.

Her phone is clutched in her hand, the news still rattling around inside her: that Nana had another stroke this morning, this one much worse. And that she's gone.

It seems impossible, but it's true. Her brain knows this. It's just that her heart hasn't quite caught up yet.

Already, she's spoken to her dads four times and booked a flight that will leave SFO in exactly three hours. She's checked how long it will take to get to the airport from the train station, and she's even remembered to give Hugo enough money to last him until his new credit card shows up.

But she hasn't cried yet.

She's determined not to cry.

It's not such a hard trick, in the end. All she's had to do is avoid thinking about what's happened. Instead she's tucked it into a corner of her mind and gently shut the door. Later she'll open it. Later she'll think about this absence that she's always known would come at some point, the loss so big it might swallow her whole.

But not now. Not yet.

First, there is a step down from the train. One, and then another. Then there is the platform, and the weight of her backpack, and the door to the station. There is the back of Hugo's head as she follows him, a sight now so familiar it makes her chest ache.

One thing at a time.

This station isn't grand, like the others they've been to, just a squat gray building that could as easily be a post office or a DMV. Mae follows Hugo's backpack as he picks his way around the rows of metal benches. He hasn't said much in the last hour; mostly he's just been there, a solid presence beside her as she made arrangements and sorted out information. He'd known instinctively to hold her hand while she booked a flight and to give her space when she spoke to her dads, and underneath the fog of grief and shock and confusion, she's grateful for that.

He pauses at the glass doors in the front of the building to make sure she's still with him, then walks back out into the daylight. There's a charter bus idling on the street, and a few cars waiting for people in the circular drive, but otherwise it's quiet. Four o'clock on a Tuesday in the middle of August, and the world feels slow and sleepy.

Hugo sets his bag down beside a wooden bench, and Mae leans hers against it. But neither of them sits. Instead, they just stand there awkwardly, an unfamiliar space between them.

"Have you called for a car yet?"

She shakes her head. "I'll do it now," she says, but she's hit by a wave of panic when she pulls out her phone. Because the minute she makes her request, there will be a clock to all this. A countdown. And Mae doesn't feel ready for it.

Hugo looks relieved when she lowers the phone again.

"I hate this," she says, and for the first time in hours, they both smile.

"Me too."

"It's . . . rubbish," she says, which makes Hugo laugh.

"Well said."

She tips her head back. "None of this feels real. I wish we had more time."

"I'm okay with it, actually," Hugo says, but his eyes are shining. "I could use a bit of space."

Mae laughs and steps into his arms. She presses her face against the soft cotton of his shirt, breathing him in. *Don't cry*, she thinks again, because if she does, she knows it might be a very long time before she stops.

"Would you like me to come with you?" Hugo asks, and she leans back to look at him in surprise. "I could, you know. It's on the way home."

For a second, she considers saying yes. She imagines falling asleep on his shoulder on the plane, introducing him to her dads, holding his hand at the funeral. There's a whole long, dreary trip ahead of her, and the idea of taking along a bit of sunshine is more than a little tempting.

But she knows this is something she has to do alone.

"Hugo," she says, putting a hand on his chest, "that's probably the nicest offer ever."

"But?"

"But you only have a couple more days before you have to go back. You should enjoy them."

He presses his lips together so that his dimples appear, and it cracks Mae's heart. "How will I enjoy them without you?" he says, then hurries on before she can argue. "I could change my ticket."

She smiles at him. "You don't even have a credit card."

"We'll sort it out," he says, though they both know it won't happen. They're just talking to talk now, knowing that when this conversation is over, so is everything else.

"I would've liked to see that bridge with you," she says, twisting a piece of his shirt in her hand; before she can say more, he bends to kiss her, and it's a good one, long and deep and sad and true. It's an apology and a promise and a wish.

"I wanted to do that the moment I saw you in Penn Station," Hugo says, and she rolls her eyes at him.

"You did not."

"I did," he says. "Thank goodness you didn't have bunions."

Mae smiles. They're still holding on to each other, and though she's aware of how dramatic it must seem to the other people waiting for their rides—though she can practically see the movie version playing out in her head, sappy music and all—she decides she doesn't care. She's not ready to let go of him yet.

It reminds her of what Ida said, about how young people think they're the first to do everything: to fall in love and have their hearts broken. To feel loss and pain. She gets it now. Because it seems impossible that anyone has ever felt what Mae is feeling at this moment, a mix of emotions so specific it's like she's invented it, like *they've* invented it, the two of them standing here together at the end of a long journey, trying to figure out a way to say goodbye.

"Thank you for taking me," she says, her voice thick. "This has felt like more than a week in the best possible way."

"Thank you for coming," he says. "I quite literally couldn't have done it without you."

A taxi pulls up the circular drive, and a man with a briefcase gets out. Hugo and Mae exchange a look, and then he lets go of her to lift an arm, and the driver nods as he steps out of the car. "Need help with the bags?"

"Just this one," Mae says, and when he grabs her backpack, Hugo's—which had been propped against it—tips over onto its side. They watch as the driver carries hers to the taxi and drops it into the trunk; then they turn back to each other.

Hugo is looking down at her with those bottomless eyes of his, his mouth set in a grim line. "It's not like we'll *never* see each other again," he says, searching her face. "Right?"

"Right," Mae says, though it feels like too great a promise to make when the world is so big and the future so uncertain. "And until then we'll keep in touch."

"And you'll send me the film when it's done."

"Only if you send me a draft of your letter."

He laughs. "You're a bit annoying, you know that?"

"I do," she says with a grin, and then he bends down and their lips meet and she closes her eyes and disappears into him for the last time. The driver honks the horn—two short bursts of noise—but they're slow to break apart, and when they do, it feels to Mae like she's left some essential piece of herself behind.

Don't cry, she thinks again. *Not yet*.

Hugo puts a hand on her cheek. "Good luck at home. I'll be thinking about you."

"I . . ." Mae begins, and then stops abruptly, caught off guard by the words that have lined themselves up in her head: *love you*. She didn't know she'd been thinking them, didn't even know she'd been feeling them. But suddenly here they are, big and scary and important. She bites them back and instead says, "I'll miss you."

"You have no idea," Hugo says, then pulls her into one last hug.

Afterward she sits in the back of the cab, her eyes burning, her hand curled around the blue button Hugo gave her in Denver. They pass over the Bay Bridge, the glittering water and crowded hills of San Francisco appearing all at once, and she wants nothing more than to curl up and cry, but she doesn't. Not yet.

It's nearly dark by the time she gets on the plane, a red-eye back to New York City. She falls asleep almost immediately, wrung out by the day behind her, and wakes hours later to see the sun rising over Manhattan, the rivers on either side of the island set aflame. It was only a week ago that she was here to meet Hugo, and she can't help thinking how strange it is to travel so long and so far—to crawl across an entire country—only to return again in a single night.

Her dads are waiting at the baggage claim. When she spots them, Mae's heart gives a little hiccup. They both look uncharacteristically rumpled; there's a hint of a beard along Pop's jawline, and Dad's eyes are red and bleary. Maybe it's that they had to wake up in the middle of the night to pick her up at this hour, or maybe it's that they haven't slept at all, or maybe it's just the grief, which is still so jagged and raw. It doesn't matter. They're here now, and so is she, and when she gets to the bottom of the escalator, she launches herself into their arms like she's returning from some great voyage.

"I can't believe I didn't get to say goodbye," she says into Dad's familiar tweed jacket, and they both pull her in tighter. "I wish . . ."

She can't finish the sentence; there's too much she wishes.

"She asked me to give this to you," Pop says, leaning back to reach into his pocket. He pulls out a small piece of cardboard: an old train ticket from New York City to New Orleans.

It's then that she finally begins to cry.

Hugo

Hugo sits in the back of a taxi, his hand clasped around a bluish stone he picked up outside the station. He unzips the front of his rucksack and slips it inside one of the pockets, where it's safe beside the others he's collected along the way. It's not quite as impressive as the building in Chicago, but it's something. And anyway, they mean a lot more.

As the car crosses into the city, he can't shake the feeling that something is wrong. It's not just that he misses Mae, though he does. Already he misses her more than makes sense. But there's something else, the answer just out of reach, a prickly feeling in the back of his skull.

It comes to him as he's checking into the hotel, which is miraculously willing to change the name on the reservation. As the clerk looks to see if his credit card has arrived, Hugo drums his fingers on the desk, and he realizes all at once that he should've offered to go to the airport with her. He rocks back on his heels and groans, because what kind of idiot suggests going all the way to New York for a funeral before thinking about the *airport*? That would've made far more sense. But now she's there and he's here, and that's that.

"For you, sir," the clerk says, returning with a thin white envelope that has the logo of his credit card company in the corner, and Hugo breathes out a sigh of relief. Finally. "Can I get you anything else?"

"Just a key, thanks."

The whole place has a nautical theme, the walls covered in paintings of buoys and seagulls, presumably because of the hotel's proximity to Fisherman's Wharf. There's even a captain's wheel hung over the bed, which is draped with a blanket that says *S.O.S.* in huge block letters. Hugo drops his rucksack on top of it, then heads out again, too anxious to sit still.

Outside, the air is thick with salt, and he walks straight down to the water, which is dotted with ships. Beyond them, he can see the rocky silhouette of Alcatraz, and in the distance, the faint outline of the Golden Gate Bridge. He should be excited right now; he's always wanted to see this place. But instead there's a sour feeling in his stomach because he was supposed to be here with Mae, and everything feels a little bit dimmer in her absence.

It's not until he's started to walk down to the pier with the sea lions that he realizes he was actually supposed to be here with Margaret.

He stops to text her back.

Hugo: Coffee tomorrow morning?

Margaret: Brill. I'll look up some places and let you know?

Hugo: Sounds good.

Nearby two seagulls are squaring off over a crust of bread, and all that squawking reminds Hugo that he needs to text his mum too:

Got the credit card. Thank you for sorting it out.

Love, Paddington

He looks out over the bay again, realizing he's made it almost all the way across America without any money, which is either hugely impressive or entirely idiotic. His parents would probably choose the latter, and he wonders if maybe they only sent him off and wished him well because they knew all along that he'd come back to them like a boomerang.

He once read a story about a zebra that escaped from a zoo. For a few hours, it had a grand old time, zigzagging down the motorway and dodging the police. But eventually it was captured again, and that was of course considered a happy ending. Because there's no way it would've survived on its own.

Besides, everyone knows zebras are pack animals at heart.

He decides to skip the sea lions.

Instead he walks until the bridge comes into sight—a brilliant shade of red, like something out of a postcard—

and then he keeps going until he reaches a small beach that overlooks it. He sits on the cold sand and watches the colors fade, moving from gold to pink to purple and finally to gray. When the sun has slipped away entirely, he gets up and walks back to the hotel in the growing dark, tired and lonely and ready to fall sleep in a bed shaped like a boat.

Somewhere in the middle of the night, he wakes up, the imaginary movement of the train beneath him. He reaches for his phone, hoping for a message from Mae, but there's nothing. Instead, there's a text from Alfie.

Alfie: I've been elected to find out how it went with Margaret Campbell, Part Two.

Hugo: She left today.

Alfie: Wow. You must've really bungled that apology.

Hugo: No, her grandmother passed away.

Alfie: Oh—sorry to hear it.

Hugo: Yeah.

Alfie: So what now?

Hugo: Nothing. She's gone.

Alfie: Right, but you like her, yeah?

Hugo: Yes. A lot.

Alfie: Then that can't just be it . . .

Hugo: I think it is. She's gone and I'll be home in a couple of days.

Alfie: Hard luck, mate. I'm really sorry.

Hugo: Thanks. Me too.

Alfie: Did she feel the same way at least? Did anything end up happening?

Hugo pauses, staring at the glowing screen of his phone. After a moment, he writes, *Long story*.

But what he's really thinking is *Everything*.

Everything happened.

Mae

They stop at a diner on the way home from the airport, where they all order blueberry pancakes—Nana's favorite.

"The doctors said she probably didn't feel anything," Pop says. "She was taking a nap, and she just didn't wake up."

His eyes are damp, but there are no tears. He's usually the crier of the family, but Mae can tell he's completely tapped out. He gives her a weak smile, then returns to his pancakes, and Dad picks up the thread. This is what she loves best about them, the way they carry each other, silently and automatically, when the other needs it.

"But I think she knew somehow," he says, putting a hand over Pop's, who clasps it back. They exchange a look. "After the first stroke, the way she was talking, it was almost like . . ."

"Like she was saying goodbye," Pop says.

Mae puts down her fork. "I wish you'd told me," she says, her throat tight. "If I'd known, I would've been here."

What she doesn't say is this: that she *should've* been there.

That the only reason she wasn't, the reason she was thousands of miles away at the time, was because she lied to them.

"She knew that too," Dad says. "And that's not what she wanted. You two had already said your goodbyes."

"Right, but not for—"

"Mae," Pop says, looking at her over the bottle of syrup and the napkin dispenser and the mugs of coffee leaving rings on the table. His voice is strangely calm. "That's the thing. You almost never know when you're saying goodbye to someone forever."

Mae nods, lost for words.

"It's okay," he says gently. "She knew what was in your heart."

On the drive home, they listen to the movie score from *Titanic*, which was Nana's favorite. The rest of them always complained when she put it on, but she was unabashedly, stubbornly in love with it. "You cretins wouldn't know great art if it bit you in the behind," she'd say, to which Pop would roll his eyes and remind her that he runs an art gallery and Dad is an art history professor. Still, she wouldn't budge.

Now Mae listens to the swells of music and feels the emotion in every single note. *Maybe Nana was right*, she thinks, and suspects it won't be the last time.

At home she walks from room to room, running a hand over various items: Nana's chair at the kitchen table; her favorite coat, which is still hanging near the back door; the green mug she always used for her afternoon tea. In the guest bedroom, where Nana lived for the better part of the past year, Mae lingers near the door. She doesn't realize anyone is behind her until Dad clears his throat.

"I loved her," he says. "I really did. But oof—that perfume."

Mae laughs; she can smell it too. It's not the scent itself, which is lavender with a hint of something else, minty and herbal; it's how much she used to wear, the cloud of it that would trail her around the house.

"Best smell in the world," Mae says, breathing in deeply.

Later, after they've all had a nap, they sit around the kitchen table, painfully aware of the empty chair, and go through what else needs to be done for the funeral tomorrow. Pop reads through the final list of appetizers for the reception, and when he's done, Dad grins at Mae.

"Better than train food, huh?"

"Actually, it wasn't so bad," she tells him. "They had a pretty good menu. And we got some good stuff when we were off the train too. The best was the deep-dish pizza in Chicago—we absolutely demolished it."

She blinks a few times, overcome by the memory of that rainy night. Each time she thinks of Hugo, her heart feels like it's being wrung out, and she's so distracted that she almost misses the next question.

"So you got along well?" Pop asks, and when Mae gives him a blank look, he adds, "You and Piper?"

"Oh," she says. "Yeah." It's the kind of drawn out *yeah* that makes it clear she doesn't know where she's going next with this. Her mind begins to toggle through all the many things she could tell them about her future roommate: *We're best friends already* or *She was a total nightmare* or *It'll be better when we're in a dorm room and have a bit more space.*

But in the end, she can't bring herself to lie.

Maybe it's because they're planning a funeral right now, or because she missed them more than she thought she would. Maybe it's the guilt of not having been here, or maybe it's because of Hugo, whose absence she feels like a phantom limb. But whatever the reason, she finds herself saying, "Actually, there's something I have to tell you."

They listen as the whole story comes spilling out— the post that Priyanka had sent her and the search for a Margaret Campbell; the video she sent to Hugo and the moment she met him at Penn Station—and when she gets to the part where they boarded the train, Dad is so red faced and Pop is so white faced that she stops. "Are you guys okay?"

They stare at her.

"I'm sorry I didn't tell you. If I'd known this would happen, I never would've—"

A muscle in Dad's jaw is beginning to twitch. "What were the sleeping arrangements?"

"What were the, uh . . ."

"The sleeping arrangements."

"Well, we didn't really have a choice on the train. But they were bunk beds, so . . ."

"And what about *off* the train?"

Mae squirms in her seat. "It sounds worse than it is."

"Try us," Pop says flatly.

"Hugo was going to give me the hotel rooms, but then he lost his wallet in Chicago, and we'd already shared the smaller room on the train, so it didn't seem like such a big deal to—"

"To what?"

"We got a cot," Mae explains, deciding it's better to leave out any logistics beyond that. "It wasn't a big deal. Honestly."

"So let me get this straight. You lied to us, went off on a cross-country train trip with a boy you'd never met before, and then shared a hotel room with him in a strange city?" Dad says in a strangled voice. "Sure. Yeah. No big deal at all."

Pop folds and then unfolds his hands. "Were you, uh . . ." he says, braving a glance at Mae, then quickly lowering his eyes again. "You were . . . safe, right?"

She groans. "Nothing happened. Not like that."

"Not like *that*?" Dad says, his eyebrows shooting up again. "So does that mean . . . something did happen?"

"Look, it was just . . . I didn't think you guys would say yes if you knew." She ignores the matching expressions on their faces, which tell her she's absolutely right, and keeps going. "But I needed to go. You were the ones who said I

274

had some living to do, and it seemed like fate for this to just fall into my lap. It was never about him. The idea was to figure out my next film, and we were supposed to just give each other plenty of space. But then . . . I don't know. Something happened. We really liked each other."

The worry has eased from Pop's face, and he's watching her now with a bemused smile. But Dad still looks slightly murderous. "I swear, if he touched a hair on your head . . ."

"He did," Mae says, trying not to laugh. "But really, it's okay. He's a nice guy. You'd like him. And anyway, it's over now."

"Good," Dad says. "Because if I ever see this scoundrel—"

Pop is full-on laughing now. "Okay, maybe we can take the whole overprotective father act down a notch here."

"It's not an act," Dad says, scowling. "She just spent a week on a train with some random kid. Oh god, he *is* a kid, right? How old is this guy?"

"Eighteen," Mae says. "Same as me."

Dad grunts. "Still."

"Okay," says Pop. "I think that concludes the lecture portion of our program." He waves a hand at the papers spread out on the table before them: information for the funeral service, a bill from the undertaker, printouts of various prayers and hymns. "As we've all been reminded, life is short. Mae, we would've preferred if you hadn't lied to us. But you're probably right that we would've said no. What's done is done. I'm glad you had a good time. And that you met a boy you like, though as your dad, I confess I'm also happy that part of the adventure is over."

"Thanks," Mae says, smiling at him gratefully. "I really am sorry. Though I kind of thought you'd have found out by now . . ."

"How?" Dad asks, still shaking his head in an indignant way.

"Because I told Nana."

"The one time she manages to keep a secret," Pop says, but he says it fondly.

Dad sighs. "At least tell me you got some inspiration out of all this."

"I did," she says. "I think I might've even gotten a film out of it."

"And?" Pop asks.

"And it might even end up being good." She shrugs. "But what do I know?"

"A lot," Dad says with an intensity that surprises her. "Don't forget that, okay?"

She smiles at him. "Okay."

"So," he says, "think you could give your old men a sneak peek?"

Mae is unaccountably nervous as she pulls her computer out of her bag. She sets it on the table between them, and they scoot their chairs closer. "It's not even remotely close to being finished," she explains as she opens the file. "I still don't have the shape of it yet. This is literally just a bunch of interviews, but it'll give you an idea of what I'm hoping to do."

This isn't the first time she's shown them something at this stage. They've always been her test audience, eager to help and quick to praise. But this time she's too anxious to look at them. Instead she cups her chin in her hands and stares hard at the screen, watching the reel of old friends who go by—Ida and Roy, Ashwin and Ludovic, Katherine and Louis—like she's right back on that train again.

"My biggest dream?" says a young woman named Imani, whom they interviewed outside the bathrooms late one night in the middle of Nebraska. "I already have it."

"What is it?" Mae asked, and the woman's smile broadened.

"Love."

Maybe it's being in the house with her dads, right across from the empty chair where her grandmother used to sit. Or maybe it's that Mae misses Hugo, the pain growing worse with each interview she watches, remembering the way he sat beside her, his eyes bright as he listened to all those stories. She's watched these a dozen times, maybe more, but this time something is different. This time she understands—all at once—what the film is about.

As it turns out, it's not a story about love.

It's a love story.

Her mind is so busy spinning as she thinks through what this means that by the time Hugo appears on-screen, she's almost forgotten he's part of it. She hasn't watched his interview since she filmed it, hasn't let herself, because she knows it will hurt too much.

And she's right. The minute she hears his voice, she feels her heart wrench.

"But then I got on this train," he says with that familiar

smile of his, "and everything changed."

"Ooh, a Brit," Dad says, then looks over at Mae, who is watching the screen with a frozen expression. "Wait, is that him?"

She nods feebly, and they both reach for the volume button at the same time. "Turn it up," Pop says, leaning forward to watch. Every so often, they exchange a look over the top of her head, but Mae's eyes are on Hugo. Behind him the desert whips by, the metallic sound of the rails providing a familiar soundtrack. Mae never realized it was possible to feel homesick for a train. Or, for that matter, a person.

When the interview is over and the screen has gone black, Dad turns to her. "He's in love with you," he says, looking at her in surprise.

"What?" she says, shutting the computer. "No."

"He is," Pop says with a grin. "It's obvious."

Dad is still staring. "And you're in love with him too."

"I'm not."

"You are." He shakes his head. "I can't believe it."

"What?"

"You ran away and fell in love with a boy on a train," he says, his voice full of wonder. Then he laughs. "Nana would be so proud."

Hugo

Hugo wakes early, the light dull around the edges of the curtains. To his disappointment, there are still no texts from Mae. But he has one from Margaret suggesting a coffee shop just around the corner, and he marvels at the coincidence until he remembers that she knows exactly where he's staying because she was meant to be staying here too.

As he walks to meet her, he's oddly jittery. It somehow feels both like a first date and like he's cheating on someone, and by the time he reaches the coffee shop—a small storefront with a few wicker tables out front on a quiet street—Hugo is wishing he were anywhere else. Briefly he considers doing a U-turn and skipping this altogether. But then he sees Margaret waving to him from the window, and he shoves his hands into his pockets, takes a deep breath, and walks inside.

"It suits you," Margaret says, giving him a kiss on the cheek. She's wearing a dress he's always loved—a pale blue that matches her eyes—and her perfume is so familiar that it gives him a jolt.

"What does?"

She winks at him. "Travel."

Hugo runs a hand over his hair, unsure whether she's teasing him. "Who would've thought sleeping on a train would be so comfortable?" he says. Then his face starts to burn because of course he'd been sleeping there with Mae, and of course she doesn't know that, and this whole thing feels like a terrible mix-up and there's no one to blame but himself.

"Better you than me," Margaret says. "I looked up the compartments, and I reckon I would've felt like a hen in a chicken coop in those beds."

"I suspect there's a joke in there about pecking me to death," Hugo says.

She laughs. "No pecking before coffee."

Once they've ordered, they carry their mugs to one of the tables outside. It's still early, and the street is mostly empty, just a few people out running or walking their dogs.

"When did you get here?" Hugo asks, warming his hands on the mug.

"A couple of days ago. Turns out it's pretty quick by plane."

"I've heard that."

"So how was it?"

"Honestly?" Hugo says. "You would've hated it."

"But you loved it. I can tell." She blows on her mug, scattering the steam, and Hugo flicks his eyes away. It feels so intimate, watching her lips form a perfect *o* like that, a reminder of how many times he's kissed them. There's a part of him that still wants to, though whether out of love or sadness, longing or nostalgia, it's hard to be sure. She takes a sip, then looks up at him. "What about her?"

"Who?" he asks, then immediately hates himself for it. Margaret was part of his life for a long time; she knows when he's hedging. Besides, they're broken up now. It's not against the rules to have feelings for someone else. So why does it feel that way?

She gives him a disappointed look. "Hugo."

"Yeah, okay. Was it Poppy or Isla?"

"Neither. It was Alfie. I ran into him at Tesco before I left."

"Should've guessed," Hugo says with a sigh. "He's always had the biggest mouth. I suppose I should just be grateful he's managed not to let it slip to Mum and Dad."

"They don't still think that I'm—?" she asks, looking uncomfortable.

"No," Hugo says quickly. "It's just—you know how they are. They weren't too keen on this trip in the first place. And once I realized about the ticket—"

"What about it?"

"The package was booked under your name, and they wouldn't let me change it. So I needed someone else to come or I wouldn't have been able to go at all."

"Wait," she says, and her face darkens. "Does that mean you had some girl pretend to be me?"

"No, of course not."

"So what, then?"

Hugo swallows hard, realizing how bad this will sound. But he doesn't have a choice. "I, uh . . . I found another Margaret Campbell."

"You *what*?"

"I really wanted to go," he says helplessly. "And they wouldn't change it. So I didn't really have a choice, did I? Alfie and George helped me write up—hold on." He stops short. "Did you think I just invited along some random girl a couple of weeks after we broke up?"

She's looking at him like he's a complete idiot. "Well, *didn't* you?"

"No—not like that. I needed someone with the same name. It was just for the tickets and the hotel reservations and all that. I picked someone who wasn't—I found this eighty-four-year-old from Florida called Margaret Campbell."

Her eyes widen. "You're in love with an eighty-four-year-old?"

"No," Hugo says so loudly that the two women at a nearby table turn around. He lowers his voice. "*No*. She got bunions."

Margaret looks like she's not sure whether to laugh or cry. "So you found a younger version?"

"Yes. No. Not like that. It was just about the name," he says again. "It wasn't supposed to be—" He pauses, frowning at her. "Wait. Who said anything about love?"

"Alfie."

"I'm not in love with her."

"Alfie said, and I quote, 'Can you believe our man Hugo is gallivanting around America with some new bird he's in love with?'"

Hugo puts his face in his hands and groans. "I'm so sorry. You know he's a complete git. He was probably just trying to make you jealous."

"Well," Margaret says, giving him a level look, "it worked."

He blinks at her, taken aback, though he knows he shouldn't be. This, of course, is where they were headed all along. The problem is that he still doesn't know how to feel about it.

Margaret starts to reach for his hand across the table, then changes her mind and rests it on the handle of her mug instead. "Look, I have no idea who this girl is. Do I think it's a bit odd that you've gotten involved with someone who has my same name? Yes. Very. But that's neither here nor there right now. The point is that I've been thinking about us a lot these last few weeks. And when I heard you were taking a gap year—"

"I'm not."

She frowns. "But Alfie said—"

"Alfie says a lot of things," he tells her with a smile.

"Well, when I heard that, I thought maybe you were coming out here for more than just a few days. I thought you were coming to stay." She shakes her head. "It's silly,

I know. We're broken up, and you were with another girl anyway, but I just—I suppose I just wondered if there might be a second chance for us."

"Margaret."

"We let things slip. I know that. But you're the only one I've ever loved, Hugo. And maybe it's because of all these big changes, or maybe it was just knowing you were so far away this week, but I missed you."

Once again she moves as if to take his hand, then realizes what she's doing and stops. But this time, Hugo meets her halfway. He doesn't know what he's thinking. The truth is, he's not, really. It's more habit than anything else. For so long, she was home to him. And now he doesn't know what she is.

"There's no gap year," he says gently. "I'm heading home tomorrow, so nothing has really changed."

This isn't true. At least not for Hugo. Everything has changed. Just not in the way that Margaret was hoping. But he doesn't tell her that.

"What happened to make you go back?"

Hugo twists his coffee mug in circles on the table. "It was too complicated with the scholarship."

"Ah," she says, understanding immediately. "They want all six of you. That's rubbish, Hugo. I'm sorry."

"It's probably for the best," he says, and then he looks up at her with a sheepish grin. "I lost my wallet somewhere around Chicago."

She laughs. "Of course you did. But you would've been fine. You're not as hopeless as you think you are. It's just that you've never had to manage by yourself before."

"That's not—"

"You have a dad who's used to shepherding seven-year-olds, and a mum who literally records every move you make, and five brothers and sisters to follow around. And you had me. You've never really had to look after yourself before. But that doesn't mean you couldn't do it."

He smiles at her. "Thanks."

"Honestly, I'm impressed you were even thinking about it. I never would've expected you to—"

"What?"

"Go after what you want," she says, looking almost apologetic, and Hugo stares down at his mug with a pang of guilt. Because he hasn't done that. Not really. "What changed?"

Mae, he thinks, though he doesn't say it. But they know each other too well for this, and he can see the flicker of hurt in her eyes.

"Ah," she says. "Right."

"I'm really sorry, Margaret."

There are twin spots of pink on her cheeks, which is what happens when she's trying not to cry. But she lifts her chin anyway. "It's okay. I'm glad you're happy."

"I don't know if I am," he says. "But I'm working on it."

"Well, you seem different now," she says. "It's like some sort of spark has been lit." He can tell how much it pains her to say this, how much it costs her. She pushes back her chair and stands up. "Don't let it go out, okay?"

He stands, too, then walks around the table to give her

a hug. They stay like that for ages, her nose pressed into his shoulder, his chin against the top of her head. His heart aches, not because he loves her—he hasn't for a long time now—but because he loved her once, and that's something that never completely leaves you.

"Let's not be dramatic about this," she says eventually, stepping back and wiping at her eyes. "We already split up once. No need for a second round."

Hugo laughs. "Okay."

"So what happens next?"

"With us?"

"With you," she says. "What will you do now?"

"Now?" Hugo says with a smile. "I've got a letter to write."

Mae

When she wakes the next morning, Mae forgets where she is for a second. There have been so many new rooms, so many different views over the last week. But now she's home in her own bed, the familiar sound of the nearby train whistle coming through the window.

She reaches for her phone, her heart falling when she sees there's still nothing from Hugo. It can only mean he's with Margaret, and that shouldn't bother her. After all, they've already said their goodbyes and gone their separate ways. But still, there's a pit in her stomach as she stares at the screen.

How's SF? she types out, then immediately erases it.

She tries again: *I miss you.*

But she deletes that too. It doesn't seem like enough.

What she really wants to say is: *You have no idea how much.*

And what she really wants to know is: *Do you miss me too?*

There's a knock on her bedroom door, and Mae sits up, expecting to see one of her dads, but instead it's Priyanka who pokes her head in. Mae stares at her for a second, then immediately bursts into tears.

"Whoa, you okay?" Priyanka says, hurrying over to sit on the edge of the bed.

Mae launches herself at her friend, folding Priyanka into the world's tightest hug. "What are you doing here?" she asks, sitting back again and wiping away the tears with her sleeve. "You're supposed to be at school."

"Nah," she says. "Pretty sure I'm supposed to be here."

She kicks off her shoes and crawls into bed, too, and they lie on their sides facing each other, the way they used to do during sleepovers when they were little. Mae thought she was done crying, but a rogue tear slides down her nose. "Can you believe she's gone?"

"I can't," Priyanka says solemnly. "It hasn't fully sunk in yet."

"Not for me either."

"There was nobody like her."

Mae's throat goes tight and she swallows hard, suddenly anxious to talk about anything else. "It feels like magic that you're here. How are you? How's school? How's Alex?" But before Priyanka has a chance to answer, Mae lets out a strangled laugh. "Alex!"

"What?" Priyanka asks, giving her a funny look.

"It's just . . . I'm only now realizing how *brave* you guys are."

"What are you talking about?"

"I mean, you're in love with each other, which is crazy enough," says Mae, a little wild eyed. "But on top of that, you're taking this huge leap by staying together in spite of all the time and distance between you. It's totally bonkers when you think about it. But also really, really brave."

"What happened to you on that train?" Priyanka says, laughing. "I sent you off insisting that love was like a pizza."

"That's the thing," Mae says with a grin. "It turns out it *is*."

Priyanka shakes her head in wonder. "What a difference a week makes."

Afterward—once they've caught up more about Hugo and Alex and school and the train, once they've told a few stories about Nana that made them both cry, and made plans to catch up more tomorrow night—Priyanka heads home to get ready for the funeral.

Alone again, Mae walks over to her closet, riffling through until she finds a simple black dress, the only one she owns. When she pulls it out, she sees that there's a piece of blue paper pinned to the tag, and even before she reaches for it, she knows somehow that it's a note from her grandmother.

For a moment, she just stands there, hugging the dress. There are dust motes floating in the light from the window, and the house is quiet all around her, and she closes her eyes. Then she sits down on her bed to read the note.

Dear Mae,

I'm sorry we didn't get to say goodbye. I know you're
probably angry with me. But you know how when
you're sick or scared, people always tell you to think of
something happy? Well, I was thinking of you. Out there
on your big adventure.

I hope you loved it. I hope you saw a lot. And I hope
you fell for the cute boy on the train. You have one of the
brightest hearts I've ever had the privilege of knowing.
Now go out there and let it shine.

Be good. Be brave. Be yourself.

I love you,
Nana

P.S. Don't let your pop eat too much bacon. And make
sure your dad gets those silly tweed jackets taken out a
little. He can't button them, and we all know he's never
going to lose those last few pounds. And make sure
they both come visit you in California. They could use an
adventure too. (Who couldn't?)

P.P.S. Wouldn't it be just like me to write this note and
then *not* die after all? If I forget about it and you find this
when you're home for Thanksgiving and it turns out I'm
still kicking, please disregard all of the above and redeem
this note for a hug instead.

Mae is still crying when she walks over to the desk to get her camera. And when she turns it on and sets it carefully on a stack of books. She's still crying when she sits down on the edge of the bed, the black dress—which she'll need to wear to the funeral in a few short hours—scrunched in her lap like a blanket. It's only when she begins to speak that the tears finally stop. Her eyes are probably red and her voice is a little shaky, but she doesn't care. It's not about how she looks. It's about the words.

"Once upon a time," she says, looking straight into the camera, "my grandmother fell in love on a train." She hesitates, taking a sharp breath. "Fifty years later, so did I."

Hugo

Hugo is sitting at the bar of a Mexican restaurant, polishing off a basket of tortilla chips, when he gets the email.

He sent the letter off the night before. It had taken him all day to write, which should probably be embarrassing. But it isn't. In fact, he's never been prouder of anything. He left it all on the table, and that was the only thing he could do.

Afterward, he thought about sending it to Mae, but he didn't. What he told himself was that she had more important things on her mind. Which is why he shouldn't bother her. And why she hadn't been in touch. But the truth was that the past week felt to him like a dream, and Hugo still wasn't sure he'd woken up yet.

His worry was that maybe she had.

Instead, he sent it only to Alfie, with a note that said,

If this doesn't work, I'm with you guys. But I had to try one more time.

Now, as he sees the name Nigel Griffith-Jones pop up on his phone, he fumbles it, knocking his glass over in the process so that the fizzy drink goes spilling all over the bar.

"Sorry," he says to the bartender, who shakes his head as he reaches for a rag. "I'm so . . ."

But he doesn't finish the sentence. He's too busy reading the email, his eyes skipping over the words.

Dear Mr. Wilkinson,

Thank you for your follow-up letter. While we were looking forward to having all six of you with us for the start of our autumn term—have in fact been looking forward to it for quite some time now—we appreciate the case that you've made. We recognize that university might not be the right path for everyone and that—as you pointed out in your letter—you are, of course, six different people and not a single unit.

As such, we'd like to offer a compromise. We're willing to defer the scholarship as long as you're willing to join us for a few days to take part in the publicity we've arranged for the start of term. The idea would be for you to talk about your upcoming gap year and how you'll be joining us next autumn instead. We feel certain the late Mr. Kelly would approve, so if that sounds acceptable, then we'll see you next month. And we'll be excited to hear more about your travels when you join us the following year!

Sincerely,

Nigel Griffith-Jones

Chair of Council

University of Surrey

Hugo throws his arms up and lets out a whoop, knocking over the basket of chips. The bartender groans.

"Sorry," Hugo says again, jumping off his stool to start sweeping them up. But he's barely paying attention. His mind is going in a million different directions. He should tell his brothers and sisters. He should start narrowing down where he'll go. He should tell his parents. He should book a flight. He should tell Mae.

More than anything, he wants to tell Mae.

A little boy has wandered over from a nearby table, and he stares at Hugo as he picks up the chips. Hugo looks up at him with a grin, practically bursting.

"Guess what?" he says. "I'm going to travel the world."

"Well, I'm going to eat a taco," the boy says, then runs back over to his table.

Hugo lifts a chip in his direction. "Cheers to that."

As he stands up again—feeling light-headed and a little dizzy—his eyes land on a map of California on the wall near the cash register. There's a blue star toward the bottom, the words printed neatly beside it: *Los Angeles*.

And just like that, he realizes he already knows what his first stop will be.

Mae

Later, once all the guests are gone, the three of them collapse onto the couch amid a sea of empty wineglasses and dirty plates.

"Well," says Pop, putting an arm around Dad, who leans against him, "I guess that's it, then."

Dad sighs. "She would've hated those crab puffs."

"Yeah, but she would've loved the petits fours."

"And your eulogy."

"Yours too," Pop says, giving him a kiss. "Though she would've killed you for telling that story about the donkey."

"It's a great story," Mae says, and they both look over as if they'd forgotten she was there.

"Didn't we already send you off to college?" Dad asks with a grin.

Mae laughs. "Yeah, but it didn't take."

Her phone buzzes in her hand, and when she sees that it's an email from Hugo, she sits up, feeling the steady drumbeat of her heart pick up speed.

Dad raises his eyebrows. "Is that him?"

"About time," Pop says. "What'd he say?"

"Yeah, what's going on?"

Mae looks up, still smiling an alarmingly stupid smile, to find them both watching her expectantly. "I'm, uh . . . gonna go upstairs for a bit."

"Say cheerio for us," Dad teases, waving as she hurries out of the room. But Mae barely notices. She's already opening Hugo's email.

All it says is this: *How can I ever thank you?*

Below that, he's forwarded a note from someone at the University of Surrey, and her heart lifts as she reads it.

He actually did it.

She laughs, filled with a sudden joy, because she knows how much he wanted this, how much it means to him. And she wishes more than anything that they were together. (Though hasn't she been wishing that all day?)

She moves on to the letter he sent, the one she'd pushed him to write, feeling giddy that it worked. Near the end, he wrote:

Someone recently told me that if you want something badly enough, you have to make your own magic. You have to lay it all on the line. And most of all, you have to be brave. When you grow up as one of six, it can be hard to say what you want. But that person was right. Which

is why, no matter what ends up happening, I had to write
this letter. Because some things are worth fighting for—
and this is one of them.

It's not exactly a love letter, but it still makes her cry.

When she's done reading, she reaches for her computer
and pulls up the rough cut of her film, including the part
she recorded this morning. And then, before she can think
better of it, she sends it off to him, because it seems that
the very least she can do is try taking her own advice.

The note she includes is short, just a simple answer to
his simple question: *You already have.*

Hugo

Hugo is still awake—his head far too crowded for sleep—when the video arrives. He reads her message with a grin, then opens it up, expecting to see Ida and Ludovic and Katherine and everyone else they'd interviewed last week. Expecting the sort of straightforward documentary he thought they'd been shooting all that time.

But instead, it starts with Mae.

He sits up in bed, clutching the glowing screen a bit tighter.

She actually did it, he thinks, shaking his head in wonder.

Then he hears her say it: "Fifty years later, so did I."

He hits Pause, wondering if he could have imagined this. He rewinds to watch that part again. "Once upon a time, my grandmother fell in love on a train," she says, her eyes so sad he wishes he could be there with her right now. (Though hasn't he been wishing that all day?) She looks straight into the camera when she says it: "Fifty years later, so did I."

Hugo lowers the phone and stares wide-eyed into the darkness of the hotel room, trying to absorb this. He waits for it to happen: that scuttling feeling in his chest that occurred the first time Margaret said a set of similar words, like an animal trying to hide in plain sight.

But it doesn't.

To his surprise, he finds himself laughing instead. Not because it's funny. And not because it's absurd, though it is. It's completely and utterly absurd. They've known each other only a week. But no: he's laughing—he realizes—because he's happy.

And because he loves her too.

It's a joy that moves through him like helium, filling every corner of his body until it feels as if he could float away. He sits very still for a few seconds, thunderstruck, and then remembers that he needs to watch the rest of the film.

Nothing about it is what he imagined it would be, yet every inch of it feels exactly right. The interviews aren't shown as a whole; they're cut into smaller soundbites, and it jumps around so that it feels like all these various people—himself included—are having one big conversation about what it means to be a person in the world. And even more than that, what it means to love.

It's brilliant. It's moving. It's funny and unique and inspiring.

It is, in the end, just like Mae.

When it's over, there are tears in his eyes. He wipes at them, thinking that if he hadn't already bought a train ticket, he'd surely be buying one now.

But since he did, he just sits there in the darkness and starts the film again.

Mae

Out the window of the plane, the clouds are piled up like bath bubbles, and the middle of the country is spread out below in checkered squares of green and gold.

Mae doesn't notice any of it, though; her eyes are closed, her mind elsewhere.

She's thinking about Nana, and how happy she'd be right now to know that Mae is off to college, something that got a bit lost in everything else this week.

She's thinking about saying goodbye to her dads again ("Take two," said Pop as he hugged her), and also Priyanka, who had pulled up in the driveway early this morning ("One last time") before getting on the road.

She's thinking about the text she sent Garrett (*Okay, okay—it's possible you were right*) and the way the film turned out, the quiet pride she felt when she watched the final cut. In her pocket, there's a flash drive that she'll give to the dean of admissions after she lands this afternoon, and it feels strange to carry it around like that, like a portable heart.

Mostly, though, she's thinking about Hugo and the fact that he still hasn't responded, which must mean he hated the film or was scared off by what she said.

Either way, it can't be good.

Maybe they were just never meant to have a happy ending. Maybe it's not that kind of movie.

She's determined not to let this stop her. If the meeting with the dean doesn't go well, she'll be back again first thing tomorrow. And if that doesn't work, she'll try again the next day. And the next.

She'll keep trying. But she's also not worried anymore. It used to be that the thought of spending the next two years taking classes in literature and religion and science felt like missing out. She'd be stuck learning about ancient Greece or the geopolitical situation in Tibet or the poetry of W. B. Yeats while, across campus, the film students would be pulling ahead of her.

But now she's not so sure.

Maybe Hugo has the right idea after all. Maybe it's not the worst thing to take a few detours along the way. She loves the film she made this week, loves it as much as anything she's ever done, and it never would've existed if she hadn't gotten on that train.

No matter what happens next, she'll always be glad she did.

Hugo

The ocean appears all at once, a blue so bright it looks fake. Hugo has seen so many incredible sights this past week, so many mountains and rivers and fields, that it seems unlikely there's any room left for him to be this moved. But it turns out there is.

Even in his dreams, the Pacific Ocean was never quite this color.

The dusty hillsides and rows of fruit trees have given way to sand dunes, the water flashing into view every now and then until, at last, they're clear of anything but the shore. He wishes he could open a window and breathe it in, wishes he could run down to the surf and let the water rush over his toes, wishes the person beside him wasn't a grim-faced executive with a laptop who keeps swearing every time he loses service.

He wishes it were Mae.

They come to a stop along the coast, and the conductor announces they have to wait here for another train to pass. The executive gets up and carries his laptop into the observation car, and Hugo yawns and shifts in his seat. This is the first time the trip has felt long, which is a bit silly, since it's only twelve hours, and they've done much more than that in a day. But there are still seven hours to go, and he can't help feeling restless.

It's like the laws of physics are different now. Twelve hours with Mae is somehow shorter than twelve hours without her. Especially when that time is spent on the way to find her.

He supposes he should have some sort of plan for when he gets there, though he doesn't know a single thing about Los Angeles aside from what he's seen in films. But plenty of them are about showing up with nothing but a suitcase and a dream, so he figures at least he's not the first idiot to try it.

All he knows is that Mae has a meeting with the dean of admissions at four o'clock on the first day of classes.

Which is today.

The train begins to move again, haltingly this time, and Hugo leans to look out over the cliffs. His phone jitters on the tray in front of him, a message from Alfie that says *Miracles do happen*. There's a link attached, and when he opens it, Hugo finds himself looking at his mum's blog, something that he usually tries to avoid.

Across the top, there's the old sketch of the six of them,

Hugo bringing up the rear. But he doesn't mind it so much anymore. Not now that he's found himself so far from the group. In fact, it makes him smile, seeing these younger versions of the six of them.

He skips down to the most recent post, which is dated from this morning:

Those of you who have been following this blog for a long time know that we used to compare Hugo—our sixth out of six—to Paddington Bear.

It started because of a coat he had, the kind with little toggles on it, and when he wore it with wellies, he looked just like the bear. But as the years went on and it became clear that Hugo needed a bit more looking after than some of the others—he was always getting lost or losing things, always lagging behind and daydreaming—the joke became even more apt.

This past week, Hugo has been traveling across America by train. It's the farthest anyone in our family has ever wandered, and now, it seems, he might be about to venture even farther.

We never expected all six of our children to walk the same path. They're too unique for that, and it will be a privilege to watch them decide what to do with their lives. (Except maybe Alfie, in which case it will be a nail-biter.) But we also never imagined one of them would branch off quite so soon. Maybe we should've known. And maybe we should've guessed which one it would be.

There will always be a part of me that wants to send him

off with a tag that says *Please look after this bear.* But the truth is, he doesn't need it. Not anymore. Hugo might be hopeless when it comes to keeping track of his wallet or his mobile or his keys. But those things don't really matter in the end. What he's managed to keep track of is much more important. He knows who he is and what he wants out of life.

Hugo was the last to arrive, and now he'll be the first to go.

We couldn't be prouder.

Hugo's eyes drift up to the top of the screen as the train starts to move again. There's been no reception for most of the trip, but now a few bars appear, and it feels to him like a sign. He looks at the time; it's nine-thirty at home, which means his parents are probably side by side on the sofa, each of them reading a book, as they do every night before bed.

When they answer his video call, they both look surprised to be hearing from him.

"Hugo?" his dad says, his face too close to the screen. "Where are you?"

"I'm in California."

His mum takes the phone. "Hugo, darling? We know all about what's going on. Alfie showed us your letter to the university, and it was just so lovely, and I wanted to say—"

"Mum, it's okay. I know."

"I realize we're not always the best listeners, but I wish you could've said all that to us. We all read it together, me and your father and Poppy and George and Isla and—"

"Mum."

"No, listen. We didn't understand before. But we can tell how happy you've been this week, and if this is what you want, then you should know we're all behind you. They're going to miss you next year, you know, even if they won't exactly say it. And so will we. But if this is what you need to do—"

"Mum?"

She stops. "Yes?"

"Alfie sent me your blog post."

"He did?"

"He did. Thank you. It meant a lot."

"We should've listened to you more," she says. "I'm sorry."

Hugo bites his lip. "I'm sorry too."

"About what?"

"There's something I didn't tell you . . ."

His dad smiles. "About the girl?"

"You know?" Hugo asks, astonished.

"Alfie again," Dad says. "He's always had a bit of a big mouth, hasn't he?"

Hugo laughs. "You're not cross with me?"

"Consider us even," Mum says ruefully. "Where is she now?"

"I'm on my way to see her."

"I thought you were with her."

"I was, but . . . it's a long story." He pauses. "I'll tell you when I get home."

Their faces brighten straightaway.

"It'll be nice to have you back," his mum says. "Even if just for a bit."

Dad smiles, too, a smile that's just for Hugo. "Yes," he says. "We'll be sure to have a plate waiting for you."

The train rounds a bend, and the craggy coast comes into view again. The waves are tipped in white as they rush to meet the sand, and closer to the tracks, the scrubby grass ripples in the wind. It all looks so surreal, so wild and beautiful, that Hugo forgets about his parents for a second. When he hears them say his name, he turns his mobile around.

"Look," he says, moving it so they can see the view.

His mum inhales sharply. "Wow."

"I know."

"It's just so blue," she says as Hugo presses the phone to the window. And for a long time, they stay there like that, the three of them watching together.

Mae

The moment she steps out of the airport shuttle, Mae instantly feels happier. There's something about the air here, which smells faintly of flowers. The sky is a blinding, cloudless blue, and the palm trees rustle as the breezes sweep through them.

She's standing across the street from the admissions office because her flight was late and her meeting starts soon and there's no time to stop at the dorm first. Her boxes arrived there days ago, and she's already heard from Piper—future roommate and imaginary travel buddy—that the room is tiny but nice. She can't wait to see it.

Her backpack—which has been such good company this week—is slumped on the sidewalk next to her, and, looking down, she feels a surge of fondness for it.

It makes her think of home.

It makes her think of her travels.

It makes her think of the future.

But mostly it makes her think of Hugo, which is ridiculous because it was only a week, and now that week is over. She's the one dragging it with her into this new chapter like it meant more than it did.

She gives the backpack a little kick, and it topples over. Then, with a sigh, she stoops to grab it. But before she can, someone bends to help her.

To her astonishment, she looks up to see Hugo.

Her first instinct is to laugh because it's so impossible. But then she sees the way he's grinning at her, and she wonders if maybe it's not.

Maybe it was always going to happen this way.

"I was literally just thinking about how annoying you are," she says, and he looks amused.

"Me?"

"Yes, you. I don't hear anything at all, and then you just show up out of nowhere right as I arrive—wait, how did you even know I'd be here?"

"You told me," he says. "Besides, who else would have a meeting with the dean on the very first day of classes?"

She's still staring like she's not totally certain it's him. "I can't believe you're here. I thought you'd be halfway around the world by now."

"Well, I've got to go back in a few weeks to do some interviews . . ."

"And then?"

"Exactly," he says, beaming at her. "I couldn't have

done it without you."

"No, that letter was all you. And it was amazing. But, hey," she says, smacking him on the arm so that he laughs and ducks away, "why didn't you write back about the film?"

"Because," he says, "I thought it would be better to tell you in person."

She frowns. "Tell me what?"

"How much I loved it."

"You did?" she asks, brightening. They're both smiling so hard that they're on the verge of laughter. "Really?"

"Yes. But it doesn't matter what I think." His eyes are shining, and it makes Mae feel dizzy to look at him, makes her wonder if this is actually real. "It only matters that *you* loved it. And I can tell you did."

"How?"

"I can just tell when you love something," he says, and then she takes a step closer, and his arms are around her and their lips meet, and right then it doesn't matter if this is a hello or a goodbye, if they're making a memory or a promise, because they're here together, and that's enough for now.

"What?" he says when she pauses to look up at him.

She smiles. "I can tell with you too."

ACKNOWLEDGMENTS

Any field notes on gratitude have to start with my agent, Jennifer Joel, who has been such an amazing advocate and incredible friend over the years. I'm also enormously grateful to my editor, Kate Sullivan, for being so enthusiastic about this book from the start, and for making it better every step of the way.

I feel very lucky to be published by Delacorte Press, and I'm especially fortunate to work with Beverly Horowitz and Barbara Marcus, who are both so wonderful. I'm also very thankful to everyone there who had a role in turning this messy pile of words into a hard rectangular object: Alexandra Hightower, Judith Haut, Jillian Vandall, Barbara Bakowski, Colleen Fellingham, Tamar Schwartz, Alison Impey, Liz Casal Goodhue, Adrienne Waintraub, Kristin Schulz, Dominique Cimina, Kate Keating, and Cayla Rasi, among others.

As always, I'm grateful to everyone at ICM, especially Binky Urban, Josie Freedman, John DeLaney, Heather Bushong, and Nicolas Vivas. And to Stephanie Thwaites, Roxane Edouard, Georgina Simmonds, and Isobel Gahan at Curtis Brown. In the UK, it's been a joy to work with Rachel Petty, Sarah Hughes, George Lester, Venetia Gosling, and Kat McKenna at Macmillan.

A great big thank-you to those friends who read early drafts or acted as sounding boards or just generally offered a whole lot of wisdom and support throughout this process: Jenny Han, Kelly Mitchell, Sarah Mlynowski, Jenni Henaux, Lauren Graham, Morgan Matson, and Anna Carey.

And lastly, to Dad, Mom, Kelly, Errol, Andrew, and Jack: the best bunch of train enthusiasts I know.

ABOUT THE AUTHOR

Jennifer E. Smith is the author of eight novels for young adults, including *Windfall* and *The Statistical Probability of Love at First Sight*. She earned a master's degree in creative writing from the University of St. Andrews in Scotland, and her work has been translated into thirty-three languages. She lives in New York City. Follow her on Twitter at @JenESmith or visit her at jenniferesmith.com.